MW01059994

The Bellman's Secret

Dear Joy,
Welcome back to The Maycliff!
Hope you enjoy your stay.
Such a pleasure to meet you.
Warmly, Heidi

The Bellman's Secret

a novel by

HEIDI BARNES

A GENUINE VIREO BOOK | RARE BIRD BOOKS

LOS ANGELES, CALIF.

This is a Genuine Vireo Book

A Vireo Book | Rare Bird Books
453 South Spring Street, Suite 302
Los Angeles, CA 90013
rarebirdbooks.com

Copyright © 2019 by Heidi Barnes

FIRST TRADE PAPERBACK ORIGINAL EDITION

All rights reserved, including the right to reproduce this book or
portions thereof in any form whatsoever, including but not limited to
print, audio, and electronic.

For more information, address:
A Vireo Book | Rare Bird Books Subsidiary Rights Department,
453 South Spring Street, Suite 302,
Los Angeles, CA 90013.

Set in Minion

Printed in the United States

10 9 8 7 6 5 4 3 2 1

Publisher's Cataloging-in-Publication Data
Names: Barnes, Heidi, author.
Title: The Bellman's secret / Heidi Barnes.
Series: The Bellman Series.
Description: First Trade Paperback Edition | A Genuine Vireo Book |
New York, NY; Los Angeles, CA: Rare Bird Books, 2019.
Identifiers: ISBN 9781947856790
Subjects: LCSH Hotels, motels, etc.—Fiction. | Maine—Fiction. |
Man-woman relationships—Fiction. | Bildungsromans. |
BISAC FICTION / General
Classification: LCC PS3602.A7756375 B45 2018 | DDC 813.6—dc23

Dedicated to my amazing children—Nick, Austin, and Catherine—who are the epitome of integrity, wit, compassion, and love. They are my inspiration and the three greatest gifts of my life.

CHAPTER ONE

Home. Not my family's house I fled in my hick town or even my own apartment, but the place I felt most comfortable. The exclusive Maycliff Inn on the rocky coast of Maine. This was my first day back of my second stint as bellman at the stunning waterfront manor in Bar Harbor. Known for its history of summer inhabitants like the Rockefellers, Vanderbilts, and Pulitzers, the island was the elite's playground. I missed the saltwater fragrancing the crisp May air and the sunlight beaming through the lace curtains. Even the incessant sound of seagulls gliding overhead, the sapphire sky, their backdrop.

It didn't matter I was immediately put on menial jobs, like shampooing the carpets, as I was doing, because last summer changed my life. I arrived at the inn in raw form and left seasoned—in work, friendships, and living alone. I even met the love of my life, Mindy. She'd be joining me soon. I was thrilled to be back.

Transfixed by the machine's rhythmic hum, my thoughts traveled to Mindy during our last summer here at the inn. I relished in our first kiss, the one she stole from me at this very spot and I bathed in anticipation of what this summer might bring. Tediously, I pushed and pulled, unaware if the Hoover spat sudsy water on the dirty carpet. This place felt a little eerie when it stood empty and I was on my own. The vacuum's methodical buzz abruptly turned turbulent and started to clatter. A familiar voice rose above its clamor. Tingles swept down my neck as Mary called out my name. I stood motionless, not breathing in the thick air. My body chilled, as an energetic presence absorbed it. The beloved nanny of The Maycliff before it was an inn, Mary, had been found dead at the bottom of the stairs to the maid's quarters. Her tortured soul lingered throughout the inn, some felt. But most were unaware. Was Mary back? Or had she never left?

A sharp tap on my shoulder shot me off my feet, flinging my arms back and catching something to accompany my rapid descent. I smacked into the saturated ground, entangled with an old man, as I bore witness to Mrs. Lyncoff's china vase falling from the credenza. I couldn't save it. Its twin stood wobbling. Mrs. Lyncoff's bulging eyes engulfed my every vein, as she strenuously raised the feeble man back to his feet. I hopped up to help, but she pushed me away and brushed him off.

I handed the man his cane. He winked.

While Mrs. Lyncoff fussed over him, she asked me to ready his room, then come back and clean up the horrific mess. Her head shook.

I didn't know why she was letting this stranger stay at the inn before we opened. It seemed a nuisance to me. But as usual, I got my ass in gear and did what I was told. I made up his room with clean sheets, towels, soap, scrubbed the toilet and tub. First a bellman, now a maid. I should have read that fine print in the employee handbook last year.

Mrs. Lyncoff escorted the gentleman to his room, beside his listless steps. Her arm looped around his, while I swept up the shards of her favorite vase and pushed its twin farther back from the edge.

***

My winter in Boston proved a great experience, new and interesting. But the bellman position differed from that of The Maycliff. Being a hotel and bigger, it was more structured. There were boundaries you couldn't pass and my only job was to carry bags. I lucked out The Maycliff's general manager, Mrs. Lyncoff, had arranged the job for me with her friend in Boston, at the end of last season. But Boston felt big to me— the city, the hotel. I really only wanted to go there to follow Mindy, who was enrolled in Boston University's hospitality program. But as the school year was ending, she decided to return to The Maycliff to wait tables again. We tried to get together in Boston as much as possible but were both so busy. Long hours for me at work, and her at school. But we had a great last night together in Boston, talking tirelessly about everything. One more week of studies before she'd join me in Bar Harbor. I couldn't wait. I'd been a year out of high school, class of '87, and accomplished a lot already. I'd set out to really make something of myself.

The white mansion was offset with black shutters and a big circular drive. Although magnificent in size, it felt boutique with a mere thirty-six guest rooms. The main areas consisted of an elegant dining room adorned with darkened scenic paintings, a bar and lounge surrounded by old English hunting pictures affixed to its pine walls, and a formal parlor embellished with a gold harp and grand Steinway. The inn dressed itself with antique furniture and fireplaces throughout, under its towering ceilings. Its large back terrace stretched the length of the house and overlooked a rolling lawn and Frenchman Bay. Mrs. Lyncoff stressed I was always welcome back. She allowed me to stay in the majestic inn's maid's quarters, as before. Mindy would be renting in town again—that big, old haunted house with her friends. I don't know how she slept at night.

Mrs. Lyncoff allowed us fewer days than last year to open the inn, so she could save on overhead. I had to move twice as fast. She scouted me out, holding the dreaded chore list of hers. I asked her who would replace my good buddy, Steve, and when they'd arrive. But the only info she gave was the new bellman would start in the morning.

Two guys bent over, installing a water fountain in the middle of the circular drive. I wondered why Mrs. Lyncoff would want that structure on the grass. I thought it was better open, to kick a ball around or something. But I guess it would look all right, fancy things up.

Following a grueling afternoon of chopping wood and setting fireplaces, my stiff shoulders and back ached inside out. I climbed upstairs, firmly asleep as my head touched the pillow.

A restful night brought a striking day. Sun beamed down on the fresh sweater weather. The motor's velocity sped up the private road, as the Yamaha peeled across the manicured lawn caressing a tree and distributing tread marks and exhaust, then slowed as it rounded the drive and approached the front door. Its charged engine quiet. A guy hopped off, removing his helmet to his hip, shaking his coffee-colored mane. He broke through the screen door, dimpling its mesh.

"Hey," he slapped his hand to mine. "Riker," he said. "Here for the bellman's job. Who do I see?"

Just then, Mrs. Lyncoff walked in and took over. It was my turn to show this guy around, just as Steve had toured me last year.

My eyes kept focused on the black shark entrenched on Riker's bulging upper arm in clear view of his pale tank top. He didn't appear to listen to what I said as we circled the inn.

And every third word was a curse beginning with an "F." But that wasn't my problem. We finished the tour outside the staff entrance, by the woodpile and garage. He grabbed a smoke from his pocket and caught me off guard when he asked about Steve. Mrs. Lyncoff must have mentioned Steve's suicide to him. I just let him know Steve was a great guy, and the bellman job had big shoes to fill. Riker didn't respond, just gloated he'd graduated high school a couple of years ago. I found that hard to believe because he looked much older. He went on to say his old lady just dumped him, so he was a free man. Best thing that could have happened.

"I have a girlfriend, Mindy. She'll be here soon, in a few days. She waitresses at the inn."

"You been dating long?"

"Since the end of last summer," I said. "And it's going great."

"I don't think you can trust any girls. They all have secrets. Do you know any of hers? Sometimes that's a way to tap into them, if you can find out what they're hiding deep down."

I thought for a moment. "Yeah, I do," I said hesitantly.

"Well? What makes her tick?"

He stared me down as I mulled over the question. The delivery area where we stood closed in on me.

"Ah, you don't know," he said.

He gave me a bit of advice, to dump her now. "They're all bad news. The better you treat her, the worse things will get," he went on to say. I didn't like that counsel, so I changed the subject. He bore a strong Bronx accent. Mostly what I heard was what he didn't say because he didn't have to: "Don't mess with me."

After the tour, Mrs. Lyncoff told us to start our errands list. I put Riker on kitchen duty, cleaning all the dishes and glassware, while I brought the flower vases and liquor up from the basement. It's not that I wasn't frightened of the dungeon anymore, but a little adrenaline was much more exciting than the monotonous task of washing plates. And anyway, it was an initiation for Riker. Everyone had to do it once.

Trudging up the stairs with the last of the vodka and Scotch, the elderly guest stood facing the old worn, stone statuette of a lady perched on a fragile marble table, hands clasped behind his back, seemingly aloof. So I slipped quietly by on my way to the bar. I unloaded all the boxes of liquor and began to set up, placing the hard liquor on the shelves as I had remembered them. It felt pretty cool standing there. If only I could bartend this year— would be a nice change and more respectable position. In the middle of set up, the old man hobbled in, perusing the room. Seemed oblivious to my being there.

"Hello, sir."

He didn't answer, but I'm not sure he heard me. In awkward silence, he wandered across the hall to the dining room. It's as if he reminisced. I wondered if he'd worked at The Maycliff before. But he was pretty old to have done so.

I realized I hadn't checked on Riker for a couple hours. I found him buried in a cupboard. Good to know he was a hard worker. He conked his head on top of the shelf when I called his name. Apparently, Mrs. Lyncoff had already checked on him and told him to pick up speed. It felt good being boss. No longer the newcomer. I held a position of authority.

I caught eyes peering in to the peek-a-boo window set inside the swinging kitchen door. That creeped me out until I realized who it was: the old man. Just curious, I guess. Mrs. Lyncoff suddenly swept through the door, opening the way for him. He just looked in for a moment and excused himself to his room. Mrs. Lyncoff followed behind.

I felt a sudden tight squeeze around my chest from behind. "Stan, you're back. We heard you were returning," Tracy squealed.

She stepped in front to give me a whopping kiss on the cheek. Then pulled me in for a noogie before slipping back. "Put up your dukes," she said as she raised her fists. "You ready for me? I hope you've done some training."

"Well, I can see you're as feisty as ever," I said.

"I've been warming up all winter for you. Come on, turkey. Let's have at it." Her fists still going. "Okay, you little wuss, I'll let you go this time." She dropped her hands and grabbed mine. "Let's go. The girls have been waiting to see you. They're in the linen closet. How was Boston?"

I gave her a brief on the job and the city, as she curled her arm around mine tightly.

The girls sat dragging on cigarettes, blowing into the nearby linen, jabbering about their winter off on unemployment. A few more puffs and the sisters–Sue, Sarah, Sam, and their mother, Betsy—smothered me consecutively with hugs. Between that and the smoke, I thought I would suffocate.

"We brought you a gift," Tracy slyly grinned.

I reluctantly opened the package and removed the tissue, to find a skin-colored inflatable. "A pool toy?"

"No, silly. A pool-boy toy," Tracy said. "It's a blow-up girlfriend, for those lonely summer nights." The girls cackled in unison, as I observed my feet. Thankfully, my pager saved me.

Mrs. Lyncoff asked me to man the front desk, since the front desk clerks hadn't arrived yet. Hopefully, Mrs. Lyncoff had hired new staff. The old ones, Chuckie and Joan, were sketchy.

The phone lines rang incessantly. Of course, the first call I answered had to be a travel agent. Last year I'd been caught off guard by an obnoxious travel agent who fired questions at me I didn't know the answer to, because Joan hadn't trained me properly. This time I knew the drill. We offered ten percent commission off-season, but not during peak. Unfortunately, the agent was interested in August, the busiest month, so she didn't book. Too bad for her clients. She said they really wanted to stay at The Maycliff. If only they knew their travel agent blew it, because she wouldn't get commission. No "thank you" or "goodbye," just click. The lines started to rev up. I put people on hold, telling them I'd get right back to them. But soon all three lines were full, red lights flashing. Which one should I pick? I randomly chose and answered a quick question, then pushed the red hold button again, rotating through the lines. A balancing act. I saw one flashing light go out then another until I was left with one call.

This potential guest requested a lot of information. I explained we were the most exclusive and highest-rated inn around—the only five-star, five-diamond property in the whole of Maine. We were located right on the water. It's very quiet and elegant. We're away from the hustle and bustle yet walking distance to town. There are fireplaces and vaulted ceilings throughout and it's decorated with antiques. We also had an excellent restaurant open daily. Our chef was superb. Then I breathed. He seemed excited, said it sounded fabulous. I asked him if I could make a reservation for him and he eagerly accepted. I booked him for July. It was filling up fast, so he was lucky to get a room. I felt pretty good. It was the first reservation I'd ever made.

Another call was for a meeting. "Yes, sir. You said Teamsters Local 10, fifteen rooms for October?"

The man agreed.

"Hmm...let me just see if Norma is in. She handles conferences." I rang her line, not knowing if she was here yet, but no answer.

I took down his name and number and assured him I'd pass it on to Norma as soon as possible. Aren't they mafia related, the Teamsters? He seemed so nice. But I didn't want to mess with him—give him wrong information or make promises I couldn't keep and end up in a body bag.

After a couple hours, when the phones started to dull, Mrs. Lyncoff relieved me of the desk and requested I check on Riker. The only thing I found were deliveries plonked atop the serving station. One box read, "BEETS." I thought that kind of odd. Don't remember beets ever being served last year. I called Riker's name, but no answer. I wandered through the bakery and down the hall, peering into the laundry room. I eyed a pile of blankets on the floor, with a mass of dusty hair protruding from one end. I crept over and hesitantly looked down at the face. It was Riker. I focused intently to see if he was still breathing but couldn't tell if his chest moved.

"Hey, Riker."

Nothing.

I nudged him with my foot. "Riker, hey," I shouted.

He came to. "Oh man, my back. I had to lie down."

"Yeah, it's not fun. Looks like you're almost done though."

"Oh, I'm done all right. Heading out."

"Let's finish it together. Will be quicker," I suggested.

"No way, man. I'm spent." He threw the blankets off and out he strutted through the service door, screen slamming behind.

I retraced my steps to the kitchen, shoulders slumped. I knew I had to finish the job or it was my butt on the line. How the hell did I get stuck with this? That new guy had an attitude.

I'd better get a grip on him fast or Mrs. Lyncoff would blame me for his incompetence. I was the head bellman, here to train him. I heard the engine rev, getting louder as he floored his bike around the circle and up the long drive. Then silence.

I picked up a dish and held it out, facing me. My reflection appeared meek. Who was this guy staring back at me?

The days passed slowly in anticipation of Mindy's arrival. I showered early, using two coats of shampoo and finishing with an equivalent of dippity-do and an extra shot of deodorant. When my teeth gleamed, I chugged and swished some minty wash. Grabbed an iron out of the maid's closet and pressed my blue Izod and jeans. I passed by the front door all morning, peering outside often. Pacing in between chores. Perspiration trickled down my back.

She slammed the front door of her friend's car. My chest started to thump. Her face beamed with excitement, as she walked in the inn. I had held out for a long-awaited hug and anxiously strutted toward her. Like a flash, she looked past me. Her smile could have taken on Manhattan.

"Riker!" she shouted with glee.

Her face lit up, as she hurried to him and wrapped her arms around his neck, then surrendered a kiss on the lips. My gut sunk.

"What are you doing? You didn't tell me you were working here?"

"I thought I'd surprise you," Riker said.

I wanted to vanish.

"Well, you sure did. This is great," she said. "You must have met Stan?"

"Yep."

She strolled over and gave me a peck, then stood between Riker and me. The pitch in her voice still raised and her arms flailed, Mindy explained she and Riker were roommates last year. They lived in the big house with another guy and a couple of her girlfriends. And they'd be doing the same this year. I had thought it was only girls. Riker became distracted as Mrs. Lyncoff passed, so I asked Mindy to dinner that evening. But she said she needed to get moved in and organized. We'd do it another time.

Mindy's attention focused back on Riker. "Now we'll see each other all the time," she squealed.

My left eye started to twitch.

CHAPTER TWO

Five nights raced by to opening day, the twelfth season the inn had been in business. Chuckie stood proud as he'd tended the front desk since its beginning. Thankfully, Joan moved to night audit. Maybe Mrs. Lyncoff didn't like those two working together, with their occasional indiscretions. She probably drew the line when she found out they were having sex in unmade rooms at break-time. My god, if he could get some, I should be well on my way this summer. Really lucky. Nevertheless, they acted no different than last year: Chuckie still a jackass and Joan, a donkey. At least she reminded me of one. Both embraced me awkwardly when I saw them.

Riker arrived at the inn with Mrs. Butterfield, who'd been a patron of the inn since its birth. He picked up her and her dog, Pickering, up at the airport, a flight in from New York. They checked in early, as their room sat ready. Mrs. Butterfield's polished British words commanded her traditional welcome tea and biscuits. I thought Riker should handle this. So I showed him what to do and scooted. I pointed out what a nice dog Mrs. Butterfield had. He loved to be petted. Privately, I hoped the varmint took a bite out of him, like he did me last year.

"Stanley," Chuckie shouted. "Go put the vacancy sign up. And stand by the road and look for a green bus. Flag 'em down. The tour group coming in today just called. They're lost."

Tour group? "Who's coming?"

"Psychics and Mediums."

That's kind of weird. And if they were psychics, wouldn't their abilities enable them to find the place? Wonder if they could predict Chuckie getting fired? I could but hope.

Riker leapt down the stairs holding Pickering in his arms. What the hell?

"You were right, Stan. He is a nice dog." Chuckie shot me a discerning look, questioning why I would tell Riker such a thing.

"Here, hold him a minute." I reached out to grab the mutt when he snapped sharply, followed by a low-pitched growl. I escaped him piercing me this time, though.

"Man, you have bad Karma," Riker said. He handed the dog to Chuckie while he grabbed a croissant from the kitchen and stuffed it in his mouth. Then he and Pickering ventured out for a walk.

How come that dog was okay with him? That guy looked like a hoodlum.

"Stanley," Chuckie pointed. "The sign."

"No worries, I'm on it." I was glad to get out of there.

The workers on the fountain just finished filling it with water and headed to their trucks. The strange man who'd checked in early, stood beside it, staring into it. Its trickling had a soothing e̶ffect. He reached in his pocket and pulled out a shiny penny. His hands looked purple and cold. He grasped it in thought before tossing. The first one to make a wish. That was foolish. Those stupid wishes never come true.

Twenty minutes by the roadside, I watched cars zoom by in both directions. It seemed pretty busy for May. I motioned

19

to the green bus heading into town. They followed down the long, winding drive, while I ran beside. I expected to see strange looking women in witch hats. But out of the bus marched a diverse group—men and women, fat and skinny, short and tall, odd-looking and not. I guessed them to be frauds. I didn't really believe in that stuff.

Riker had returned from his walk and stood guard at my post, waiting for luggage calls. He and Chuckie engaged in conversation sharing a laugh. They appeared quite chummy for having just met. Chuckie managed a fast, group check-in with the leader, and dispersed the keys promptly. The bags were tagged with room numbers, so Chuckie sent everyone on their own with keys, while Riker and I brought the luggage to their rooms, one by one. He seemed to deliver more bags than me. Did he think this was a race?

The screen door propped open. A slight guy swayed his way through. He gently touched Chuckie's hand, "James. A pleasure." He crumpled his head to one side. "Where's the bar?"

"Over there," Chuckie pointed. "But nobody's manning it yet."

"Oh no, honey. That's me." He pointed toward his own chest. "I'm manning it."

As he strolled away, hips shifting, Chuckie rolled his eyes and Riker shook his head.

I stepped outside for fresh air. As Norma headed in she dragged me with her. She arrived to meet the lady in charge of the tour group she'd arranged, Petra. Petra floated down the stairs wearing a feathered vintage hat and carrying her crystal ball, I supposed she thought magical. At least it looked the part. She offered Norma a reading, which she declined. Instead, Norma sacrificed me as bait.

Petra took me into the lounge and sat me down. She looked deep into her mystical ball, waving her hands in circular motions above.

"I see you come from a complicated family," she started. I shrugged. "Do you have a girlfriend?"

"Well, yes."

"Hmm," she murmured.

Hmm?

She grabbed my hand and flipped my palm up, following the lines with her finger.

She looked intently. "I see a black shadow hovering over your future." She paused for some time, the lines creasing deeper into her forehead as her focus intensified. She breathed heavily before looking up. "Any missteps on your end can cause this inn to downfall. You have challenges ahead, both personally and professionally."

Huh? This doesn't sound good. She focused back on the ball.

"Be careful and choose the right path. And you should live a long, healthy life."

Should? I stepped away, shoulders limp, thanking the strange lady for her time. Now I felt worse than ever. I kept thinking about Mindy. I couldn't believe that psychic. Black shadow. What did she know? She couldn't even find the inn.

Chuckie grabbed me to deliver lunch to the strange man staying at the inn. He rested in the cocktail lounge, a comfortable setting amongst built-in bookshelves filled with old classics. I was told the top shelf of books, too high to reach, were fakes glued together, a hidden cabinet I was dying to peak behind. They looked so real. Mrs. Lyncoff referred to the old man as Mister Mac. We only served picnic lunches, as most people ventured out for the day, unless we had a conference in or special arrangement, like weddings or cruise ship luncheons in the fall.

I grabbed one of the prepared lunches out of the fridge and reached for a tray, when I noticed smoke seeping from the oven. I carefully opened its door, spewing out more fumes. I turned off the gas and waved a cloth furiously to air out the kitchen. I didn't want the fire alarm triggered like last year. Mrs. Lyncoff would have my hide, even though I had nothing to do with it. I fleetingly entertained the psychic's remark, how I could cause the inn's downfall, till I assured myself it was nonsense. I wished Steve was here. I thought about the weird guest from last year, a fireman who risked burning the place down with his obsession of logs and candles. Hoped he hadn't snuck back in. I peered onto the rack, heat vaporizing my face. There sat a pan of what looked to be over-roasted beets.

As the smoke cleared, a white, short-haired cat appeared near the swinging door. His glaring green eyes pinned to mine. He must be a neighbor's or a stray. No collar. I opened the door and he shot out.

The psychic group had just broken from a meeting. Petra stood staring to one side of me, in a trance-like state. These guys seemed a little creepy. She called me over.

"Stan, every time I pass you, I see someone beside you. A young fellow. He keeps trying to talk to me. Hold on." She put her hand out and stood silent for a moment. "It appears he left this earth too quickly, before his time. I feel a burning sensation in my throat." She held the front of her neck in her palm. "He wants you to know he's at peace now. He's telling you to release him and move on."

I stood dumbfounded. I knew she was speaking of Steve. And I wondered if Mrs. Lyncoff had said something. This sounded too freaky.

"Did you two share a secret?" She didn't wait for me to answer. "Cause he's covering his mouth and showing me a slightly older man standing by his side. It appears this man was somehow involved in these sealed words."

"Something like that. Okay, well, I gotta go." I turned to find a miniature woman glaring, listening. They must all be a combo of Psychics, predicting the future, and Mediums, talking to the dead. Even stranger.

I stepped away feeling ambivalent. Part of me consoled, Petra had spoken to Steve, if that was for real. And part of me saddened, because I missed my friend. How could she know about Cameron, our maître d' who overdosed last year? And that Steve and I kept a secret we'd been with him earlier that night. Her saying they stood side by side creeped me out. All winter, I tried to put their deaths out of my mind. Now it resurfaced, along with the worry of darkness she instilled in me.

To my surprise, I found Mindy polishing silverware in the dining room after I dropped Mr. Mac's tray.

"What are you doing here so early?"

"Just wanted to get a head start," she said.

No one was around, so I hugged her and told her I missed her. She said she missed me, too.

"Here, I'll help you." I buffed the metal until it shined without fingerprints.

God, I longed for her, even if only a week had passed. She was my one and only, and I never wanted to lose her. I admired her smile, as she told me about her drive up here with her friend. How they'd run out of fuel and had to walk to a remote gas station, where crazies worked. They were lucky to get out of there alive. I knew she was being dramatic, but I liked it. She had a way of making the dullest stories seem eventful. You wished you'd been there. I wanted to tell her I loved her again, but decided to hold off for a more appropriate time.

"I can't wait until we go on picnics, up Cadillac Mountain hiking, walking along the rocky beach picking up shells, and sneaking into hotel pools for a swim," I said. These were all things we talked about in Boston. We'd have the whole summer in Bar Harbor to enjoy.

Mindy agreed. "I'm so excited for..." she started just as Riker passed.

"Hey, Dollface," he said. "What's this I hear about sneaking into hotel pools? I'm all in for that."

"It'll be so much fun," she said.

"We'll get a group and go late night. Skinny dip," Riker said.

He wasn't invited in on our plans and I didn't like the way he barged in. My pager dragged me out of the conversation, still hearing Mindy's faint giggles as I approached the front desk.

In bed I reflected on Mindy's interaction with Riker. Her running to him instead of me. And allowing him in on our plans. And why didn't he tell me he knew Mindy? I retraced our last night in Boston, over and over again. I thought it flawless—we ate Italian at a place she'd suggested near her parent's home, shared a bottle of wine, and talked about returning to The Maycliff. She said we should run this place one day, removing all who were in our way. She looked so serious, I laughed. I shared with her I'd like to be maître d' someday. She changed the subject back to us. We kissed endlessly and spent the night together back at my room. I told her I loved her for the first time. And she, me. She stressed how she'd miss me the week we'd be apart. "Dollface" attacked my thoughts, as Riker's shark-infested arm imprinted on my mind. As my eyes slowly opened and closed, I felt someone over me, watching. Although scared to sleep, fatigue embraced me. And as I drifted, a slight humming noise arose.

CHAPTER THREE

James bobbled at the bar laughing with Mrs. Butterfield, sharing his stories about growing up in the area. He was born in the same house he still lives in with his grandmother above the family's convenience store. I'd never seen Mrs. Butterfield so relaxed, her gray do puffier than ever. She sat enjoying her usual stiff martini nibbling on a pimento-stuffed olive. I could see the hairs of Pickering protruding slightly from under the bar ledge. I crumpled old newspaper and threw it and kindling on top of the fire grate, followed by a couple of logs. I lit the paper and watched the flame intensify, crackling louder and louder. The afternoon's light gleamed through the frigid windows. Frank Sinatra's "Fly Me to the Moon" played overhead.

"Stan will get that for you. No problem." James gestured me over with two fingers.

"Stan, dear Mrs. Butterfield needs something from her room. Be a doll and fetch it."

"Sure, what is it, Mrs. Butterfield?"

"It's a little blue bottle sitting on the bathroom vanity. My meds."

I told her of course I would. Bored, I short-stopped it to see Tracy. I peered around a corner and found her entering room twenty-one. When she slipped out to grab something from the linen closet, I crept in and hid under the bed. I could see her feet pacing back and forth as she spread the linens. I strategically waited for the right moment to grab her ankle. I lunged. She screamed and tried to jump back, but trapped, she spanked the ground with a thud. I shimmied out, laughing, still holding her ankle as leverage.

She slapped my hand away. "Not funny."

"Yeah it was. Gotcha." I walked away, feeling pretty chuffed.

"Watch your back, turkey," she said. I waved my hand toward her but didn't turn.

I returned to the bar with Mrs. Butterfield's prescription and she popped a couple of pills on the spot. "Calms the nerves," she said. I grinned.

She asked James what the hum was about last night. James knew nothing of it. Mrs. Butterfield said it started around nine o'clock and got progressively louder throughout the night, not stopping till six in the morning. James had no idea, nor did I. But I admitted I heard the same thing. We guessed it was probably a boat's motor idling all night. And agreed it sounded like a very large boat.

"Are you dining with us this evening?" I asked.

"Why yes, my reservation is early, five o'clock. Would you mind escorting me?"

"Not at all. Just let me know when you're ready."

She chugged the rest of her martini and stood up, Pickering in tow. Mrs. Butterfield had negotiated that the mutt be allowed under the dining table her first night back each year. I walked beside them. At the restaurant entrance, stood Mindy. My eyes lit up.

"Hey, what are you doing here?" I was caught off guard.

"I'm the new maître d'," she smiled.

"Huh? When did that happen?"

Mrs. Butterfield shot me an irritated look.

"Excuse me, Mrs. Butterfield. I'll seat you now," Mindy said.

I stood numb till she returned. "When did this job come up?" I asked.

"Just recently. I started to tell you yesterday, but Riker walked in and you got called away."

Mindy explained Mrs. Lyncoff called her in Boston after I'd left, to discuss this position as maître d'. When Cameron, the maître d' from last year, died, Juan, a local Mexican, replaced him. And while he did an adequate job, he suddenly decided not to return. The boss needed a fresh face, urgently. Mrs. Lyncoff pointed out how hard Mindy had tried and studied, that she had committed herself to the hospitality business, something Mrs. Lyncoff admired. Mindy had earned the position. And she wanted it. She'd shot up from being a waitress last year. I'd worked hard, too, as bellman in both Boston and Bar Harbor. Had Mindy not picked up my telling her in Boston, I was interested in the maître d' position? I wondered why Mindy didn't recommend me instead.

"Can we go to dinner one night this week? So we can get caught up?" I asked.

"Well, dinners may be hard with my new job. Not sure when I'll have off."

"Then maybe lunch or something," I suggested.

Riker strutted by the fountain, hurling a penny at the concrete before it ricocheted into the water. What an idiot. Then he had the audacity to intrude on Mindy and me again, whistling at her as he passed. I followed him, asked what he was doing here. It was my shift. He said he was unclogging a toilet. Mrs. Lyncoff put him in charge of maintenance, as well as bellman, because he was knowledgeable. He'd come from that background, as his father was a janitor at his high school. Wow. New roles and double rolls everywhere, except with me. Hmm.

My pager sounded, so I raced to the front desk to find Chuckie welcoming Dr. and Mrs. Bernstein back. The Bernsteins were from New York, he a plastic surgeon. Mrs. Bernstein's face was slightly wrapped. She must have had some more work done. I delivered the luggage to their room, as they headed straight to dinner to encounter Mrs. Butterfield. I hurried back to see some action. Dr. Bernstein despised that dog.

"Hey, Stanley," James shouted as I passed. He swayed from around the bar and placed a big box in my arms. "Do us a favor and deliver this to the kitchen. Someone put it on my bar by mistake. Thanks hon. And psst…come back afterward."

"Beets," it read. I peered inside the half-empty box on the way to the kitchen and asked Chef where he'd like it set. He motioned with his head, saying nothing. We'd not been on the best of terms, because it angered me he brought the old bellman, Steve, here the last few years and not looked after him when he knew Steve was a manic depressant. Sometime after his death, I let go of that anger. But Chef was still a pain in the ass. I put up with him, though.

I slipped through the swinging door carefully, making sure it didn't hit me in the butt. Last year I'd had a terrible accident spewing lobster bits, salad and red wine all over some once-happy guests. Relishing the smells of mint infused lamb, I stoked the fire in the dining room. Chores of the bellmen included setting all fireplaces throughout the inn and keeping them going.

Dr. Bernstein snapped his fingers at me. "Yes, Dr. Bernstein?"

"Steve, see to it that our room has non-allergenic pillows."

"Yes sir, but it's Stan."

"Oh, right." He sneered as he sipped on his scotch.

Mrs. Butterfield, two tables over, waved at me. I could see her slip something under the table to the fur ball. "Yes, Mrs. Butterfield?"

"I need a couple of dog bones, please. Pickering's peckish."

"Right away."

I short-stopped it by the vacant bar, the lounge infused with smells of pine and burning wood. Mr. Mac occupied an oversized lounge chair in the far corner near the window. Mrs. Lyncoff just rose from the chair beside him. She seemed to check on him often. He now appeared to be talking to someone else, but the chair sat empty. Tony Bennett's "Put on a Happy Face" played overhead.

"So, what's up?" I asked.

"I gotta tell you," James whispered over the bar. He leaned closer. "I was in town today, having lunch with a few friends who work at Aussie's Pub, and jeez, there're rumors going 'round about the strange man, Mr. Mac, over there."

"Rumors like what?"

"Well, we're not exactly sure. Some think he's here to change the town, redevelop it. Others think he's here to buy The Maycliff and turn it into a Holiday Inn. But that doesn't make sense because it wouldn't be the same quality. And looks nothing like a Holiday Inn. What do you think? Seen anything?"

Perplexed, I said nothing. This couldn't be my fault. I hadn't taken any "missteps" to bring the inn down, as that crazy psychic suggested. As I rid the guilt, I told James I only ever see Mr. Mac sitting in the lounge, occasionally jotting something down on his pad of paper. Kind of odd, we both thought.

"Why don't you come with me down to Aussie's tonight for drinks. I'm meeting some of the gang there," he coaxed.

Aussie's Pub was a popular hangout, a hip dive bar with saloon doors and license plates dressing the walls of its dark wood interior. One of the few spots with live entertainment. I yearned to go, but really wanted to see what Mindy was up to after work, so I declined. Said I'd like to another time. He turned to wipe down bottles and I pointed out some white fluff spread on the back of his black trousers. He couldn't reach it, so I bent down and brushed my hand back and forth against his pants and picked at the rest of the lint.

"Stanley?" I heard an invasive voice.

James bounced around as I rose and held out bits of lint for Mrs. Lyncoff to see. She shook her head. I pushed the fluff into my pocket and discreetly slipped by James.

He whispered, "If you change your mind about tonight, you know where to find me." He pulled back and scrunched his neck to one side. I appreciated the offer.

I ran into Mrs. Butterfield heading to her room. "Oh sorry, Mrs. Butterfield. I got caught up. I'll just run and get those bones. Give me just a sec." Her face wrinkled up in a dismissive manner. Said she'd wait at the bar. I walked her to a seat.

"What can I get you, Mrs. Butterfield?" James asked.

"Hmm. Not sure I should have anything." She looked at her watch and pulled Pickering closer. "Actually, it's still early. Maybe just a little nightcap. How about a Tanqueray martini straight up with extra olives?"

"The usual. Coming up."

"And make it a double."

"Yes, ma'am."

I delivered the bones to the bar and ran the pillows to Dr. Bernstein's room.

Mrs. Butterfield was on her second night cap when Dr. Bernstein marched in after dinner. He sat at the opposite end of the bar. Don't know where his wife went, maybe to rest her battle scars. She'd taken her wrapping off after she arrived, and her incisions appeared only faint. It was a good thing the Thompsons hadn't arrived yet, after Mr. Thompson's and Mrs. Bernstein's interlude last year. I thought Dr. Bernstein might kill him.

"Heya Stan," I heard from behind.

I turned to find Tracy and asked why she was here in the evening. She said nightly turndown. Mrs. Lyncoff nixed the gal handling it last year, because she was unreliable, always late. Tracy offered to do it, since she lived the closest of all the maids, ten minutes down the road in Hull's Cove. And the extra money would serve her well.

"James thought you left."

"I did. Went home to grab a bite."

A booming voice thickened the air, the unmistakable Texas drawl. "Well howdy, Stan." I turned just as Mr. Thompson slapped my hand. "Nice to see you again, young man."

"Uh…welcome back, Mr. Thompson." Uh oh. Dr. Bernstein sat in the lounge.

"Do us a favor and drop our bags in the room. Martha and I are gonna enjoy a nip at the bar."

Oh frig. "Of course, Mr. Thompson."

I raced to the room and back, just in time to catch any episodes.

"You'd better goddamn stay away from my wife this trip, Thompson," Dr. Bernstein demanded. Mr. Thompson stayed focused on his drink.

"James," Mrs. Butterfield interrupted. "Where's Pickering?"

"Isn't he on your lap?"

"No. He jumped down and was lying at my feet."

She shot a scowling look at Dr. Bernstein. "Did you do something with my dog?"

"If I was going to do something with that damn rat, I would have fried it in oil a long time ago."

"Well. How insensitive," she frowned. "My poppet is missing."

"Well that calls for another round. Thompson, you're buying."

All drinks freshly poured, James and I searched the premises, calling Pickering everywhere. At last, I heard a whimpering out by the woodpile. The dog stood peeing pink on a log. We thought it was blood till we noticed the chewed-up beet that lay by his side. When I called out his name, he waddled over to me, looking unwell. He let me pick him up, a first. I handed him to Mrs. Butterfield, who had moved from her stool to one of the robust ruby lounge chairs, near Mr. Mac. Her slouch straightened as she grabbed him from my arms. I warned her he had an upset stomach.

Mindy's night had slowed, so she sat in the back doing paperwork. I suggested we hit Aussie's for a drink.

"I already told you, Stan. I'm busy at night."

"Well, I just thought since things quieted early, I'd try."

"Not going to happen."

"Did I...do something wrong?" I asked.

She stared me down. "I just could have used you to bus tables earlier. You need to be available for me. I have this big job now and need to focus more on work. I can't be tied down all the time. We have to cool it a little."

I walked away, my thoughts jumbled. Decided to grab that drink with James. He was still serving the Thompsons and Dr. Bernstein. No one talked. The air lay thick until Mindy strutted in and whispered in James's ear. Mr. Thompson's eyes widened as he stayed glued to her weave. She turned and smiled.

"What was that about?" I quietly asked James.

"Oh nothing. She just asked me to close down her till. She has somewhere to go."

Why didn't she ask me? I know how to shut down the till. And where is she going? Thought she was too busy.

Dr. Bernstein retired for the evening, not excusing himself. Mrs. Thompson followed shortly after, but her husband stayed for one more round. Next year, they should come at different times. The atmosphere stiffened with them together.

James and I trekked to Aussie's after work. I'd thrown on a jacket, but the coolness chilled my cheeks and hands. We found the pub unusually quiet, because the season was just getting started. No live music tonight. U2s "With or Without You" blared throughout. James shared how he yearned to move to Boston, jealous at the chance I had and could not fathom why I returned to Bar Harbor, especially when I'd come from a small town. But Bar Harbor was bigger than my town of Jay, more unique and dynamic. A different set of people. It felt a comfortable change, tourist environment where I met people from all over.

James explained he'd worked in his family's convenience store since he could remember, but the pay wasn't enough to sustain him. So he applied to a local restaurant and bussed tables until some coworker friends, who he referred to as the Opossum family, were caught stealing and they all got booted. Not fair since James didn't do anything wrong. That's when he applied at The Maycliff. He said the Opossum's got a job here at Aussie's, in the back of the house, prepping food and washing dishes. That's who he was meeting for drinks, when they got off shift. Said the kitchen should be closing soon. I'm not sure what happened to James's parents and was afraid to ask. His grandmother ran the store. A couple of beers in, I told him about Mindy and me. How she was my girl.

"No offense. But she seems a little icy with you."

"Yeah, I know. Or rather, I don't know why. We had a great time in Boston."

"My guess is that if you say she was a waitress last year and is suddenly the maître d' now, it's gone to her head."

"I don't think so. She's not like that," I said.

"Girls. Who knows?"

"You seeing anyone?" I asked.

"Don't really want to talk about it."

I got that. The bathroom door pushed open and out walked Riker. He sat at the bar. I felt relieved to see him alone. No bellmen worked at the inn after hours. The front desk had to do bags. He swung his stool around, perusing the area.

"Hey, man," he said, and strutted over toward us, grabbed a chair, swiveled it around backward, and cozied up.

"Where's Mindy?" I asked.

"I don't know, man. I live with the girl. I don't track her every move."

He slugged down his beer. "Well, gotta go." And slid through the swinging saloon doors. I followed shortly behind and left James to wait for the Opossums. Back at the inn, I caught Mindy unexpectedly leaving Mr. Thompson's room.

"Late room service?" I asked.

"Yep. Night, Stan."

My mattress seemed unusually lumpy tonight. I couldn't get comfortable, flipped and flopped, thinking of Mindy. I wished she lay by my side, that we could be passionate like our last night in Boston. Sleep together and wake intertwined, just to start all over again. I couldn't figure out how to reach her, make her want to spend time with me. Her fluctuating moods left me baffled and frustrated. The irritating buzzing noise returned and rattled throughout my body. And I felt aggravated by the unanswered question. What was the key to making a relationship work?

CHAPTER FOUR

I lay in warm sand, crevices molding my body. Everything hurt. The wind blew a slight precipitation through the air, misting my face. I couldn't move. As long as I lay there, nothing could worsen. I focused on the black, white, and beige speckled sand, cupping handfuls and releasing them like a sieve. Not a breath left inside me. Hours passed before darkness closed in. I had to go back.

I played it over and over in my mind. Walking in on Riker and Mindy this morning, arms around each other in the back stairwell, staring into each other's eyes and smiling. They dropped their embrace when they saw me and acted as if it was nothing but a friendly hug. But I knew better. I could sense it.

I passed by the woodpile on the way to my room. Riker sat on a log, smoking and swigging a beer, still on shift.

"Hey man. You doin' all right?"

I said nothing. Just broke through the kitchen door, up the dark stairwell to my room. Screw this. I lay in bed and stared at the ceiling for hours, the hum drilling through my brain.

Morning arose and I decided to confront Mindy, just show up on her doorstep. She denied anything was going on between her and Riker. They were just friends. She agreed to go to lunch with me before our shifts. Finally, I was making ground. We grabbed take-out at Bert's Lobster Pound and ate by the town pier on a park picnic bench. I dipped a chunk of sweet meat into warm melted butter and let it dissolve into my taste buds, a Budweiser washing it down.

"So, how's the new job?" I asked.

"Loving it. I picture myself in a position like Mrs. Lyncoff's someday. Can't wait till school ends and I can do this full time."

"You're pretty lucky she gave you that opportunity. I've got some ideas of my own, too. I'm not going to be a bellman forever, ya know."

"I'm sure."

Although sometimes I felt homesick, there was no way I would return to my stinking town of Jay and end up like one of those reprobates who follow in their father's footsteps. Never leave home. Mindy, on the other hand, thought she might end up in Boston. It's all she knew. This afternoon felt like last winter in her hometown. After lunch, we snuck back to her place for a little rendezvous, just fooled around. Unfortunately, not the whole smorgasbord. Her choice, definitely not mine. I don't know what she was holding out for. It's not like we hadn't had sex before. But I was back on track. Riker, nowhere around. Only his guitar lay on the couch. I shouldn't have been worried earlier. Ridiculous.

I stood on the terrace, blocking the sun's warm stream with my hand, watching the Heli-jet hover and carefully descend upon the back garden, blustering leaves off the maple and birch trees. Two young couples jumped out, probably in their late twenties. The girls in dresses well above their knees. The guys in khaki pants and bright cardigans. I greeted them as the copilot handed me their bags. They waved off their ride.

"That was a nice entrance," I said. The guy in the orange sweater ignored me.

After checking into their connecting rooms, they grabbed two bottles of champagne from their case and popped one on the back terrace, plonking themselves down in the cushioned pink seats, feet on the table.

A fishing boat anchored itself, holding poles overboard. Frosty white seagulls circulated above, screeching their usual tunes. The tide lay low, because the sand bar to Bar Island had exposed itself.

I brought the new guests some nuts and continued wiping down the glass tables, eavesdropping.

"Crap, you totally burnt that guy."

"Dude. He deserved it," the orange one responded.

It sounded like the two guys worked together, Lockholm Aircraft in Palm Beach, Florida, and that the orange guy, who they called Branson, just got promoted over another colleague of theirs they wanted to bury. One of the girls pulled out a game of checkers and brushed everyone's feet off the table. They pushed open their second bottle of Moët and reviewed their plans. Tomorrow would be hang-gliding, then go-carts. The next day, tennis and boating. They only had a few days before the Heli-jet returned, so they had to make the most of it. Branson boasted he had to take advantage of all these new perks.

A limo pulled up front, the driver extracting a stately woman dressed in a red feathered top and snug black leather pants. Pumps and dangly earrings. She must be a model. Her wavy, black hair rested at her ears with streaks of gray that embraced her porcelain face. Her stride made me dizzy.

"Hello, Darling. Here to visit Ms. Malone." Chuckie's eyes protruded. Ms. Malone checked in last night as a long-stay guest. He said Ms. Malone was expecting her, room thirty-six at the end of the hall. By all means, please head up.

She didn't last but a short while, sending her limo driver up to retrieve a large box.

Ms. Malone had stayed in her room since check in but finally surfaced. Her heavy curls lay long and pulled back, revealing her thick black-rimmed glasses. She stood slightly taller than me. It didn't look like she had a big appetite. She reminded me of a school teacher I once had for math. She sat at the bar, savoring a bowl of clams and side of asparagus. Garlic and broth misted the air. I filled in for James on break. And as always, I tried to start polite conversation, especially if the person sat alone. I asked where she was from and if she was enjoying herself, the standard BS.

"Portland, Maine. Just a few hours away. It's lovely here. I usually stay at Shutters Inn, but they were full," she said.

Mr. Thompson popped in and sat beside her, overhearing the conversation.

"Oh, you come up often?" he asked.

"I try to make it up here at least twice during the summer. Sometimes my work is spur of the moment."

"What line of work are you in?" he asked.

"I'm a toy distributor." She slipped in a clam. "European toys."

I piped in. "That's neat. I still have a few wooden trains from childhood I keep in a shoebox under my bed. I love those."

She smiled nicely, just as James rounded the corner and took over. Seemed Ms. Malone began shedding her shell. Shortly after, I passed Mr. Thompson coming out of her room, holding a package.

The young couples still lounged on the terrace, same spots, smoking out of a glass instrument that looked to be a bong. But they called it a hookah pipe and smoked shisha, a form of tobacco, not pot. Branson picked it up on his last trip to Dubai.

Ms. Malone had infused her way in to the group by asking them about it. Fruit flavored smells circulated from the clouds of smoke as she blew out extensively. I heard her joke she could use the device in her work. Branson snapped his fingers at me and asked for a menu and wine list, pronto. He requested an array of dishes be prepared as share plates—various appetizers, steak, lobster, cheese plate, Grande Marnier soufflé. Chef grumbled, which I expected. They stuck with bubbly throughout the night, polishing off numerous bottles. I lost count. Seemed to be going down steadily. Branson toasted Ms. Malone for the umpteenth time, "To room thirty-six."

As day dimmed to dusk, twinkling boats lit areas of the bay and brilliant stars radiated above. Branson said he'd been every-where in the world and never seen a sky so magnificent. Lights ablaze, the Bluenose Ferry, an attractive day cruise ship to Nova Scotia glided in, its sultry manner docking a few doors down. Flickering candles illuminated the friends' carefree features. Nat King Cole's "When I Fall in Love" enhanced the ambiance.

***

Branson, his pink cardigan and crew pranced downstairs, all dolled up after an adventurous day of hang-gliding and go-carts. They'd clearly opened a bottle of something in their room before descending upon us. I caught the pink-stuffed sweater before he dared snap another finger at me, asking what I could get him. They'd be dining outside again in their usual spot. He didn't need a menu. He'd special order from his head. This wasn't going to go over well in the back. And two bottles of Duckhorn, pronto.

The day had gone smoothly until I noticed Mr. Dunlop exiting his car. Oh my god. He's the Mobil inspector, who rates the inn every year. We've always been a five-star property. But last year, he threatened to de-ball me by stripping us of a star, all because I accidentally dropped his luggage down the stairs. Everything scattered, including some foreign object, which he wouldn't let me touch. I wondered why they didn't send a new guy, so he could sneak in, not be identified. But it was to my benefit. I was on this guy. I shot outside to greet him.

"Hello Mr. Dunlop. Nice to see you again." He acknowledged my hello like a starched shirt.

I tried to grab his bag off him. "May I take your bag?"

"Uh. No. Thanks anyways. I've got it." He shooed my hand away. Hell. He shouldn't hold grudges.

"May I park your car?" He declined that offer, too. Said he'd park it himself after he checked in. I opened the door for him. At least he let me do that.

Chuckie recognized Mr. Dunlop by name but couldn't act any more buoyant than he already did. He lived at full capacity. I suggested I at least escort him to his room, but he conveyed he knew the way. To get points, I slipped into Mrs. Lyncoff's office to report the inspector had checked in. I received kudos and a warning not to screw up. Not exactly in those words.

He passed Ms. Malone, the toy salesman, on the stairs as he ascended. They appeared to know each other. I heard him say he'd just come from Shutter's Inn, where she usually stays. Mentioned he'd see her later, as he trotted up, new bounce to his step.

Ms. Malone joined Branson's celebratory party out on the terrace. I perused the area, making sure everything stayed in place. Tables wiped down, fireplaces set, flowers on desk, shirt tucked in and pager on. Then I waited for Mr. Dunlop to come down from his room. What would I say? How could I make a good impression? I felt antsy. My skin began to itch. I stood in a trance till Branson yelled for me. He called me "hey," as if it were my name. Needed matches. Oh frig, not the shisha with Mr. Dunlop here.

As Mr. Dunlop descended the stairs, I formed a wide smile ready to hit him with. But he didn't seem to notice. He rushed by me and joined Ms. Malone and the group of elites. He had his pad with him and jotted something down. I felt sure it was about the hookah pipe. Oh god, the humming noise. It would start at nine. He'd surely enter that into his notes. That wouldn't be my fault. There's no way I could head that off. I just didn't want him to look for something to go wrong, since he already had a bug up his ass about me.

Mrs. Butterfield hovered, complaining to Chuckie at the desk. "Ever since Pickering got into those beets, he's not been well. He has the runs. Can Chef make him some soup or something to ease his tummy?"

"I'll check with him when he gets in."

Mr. Thompson walked by with Mrs. Bernstein, Roxy. Towels in hand. They stopped by the desk, inquiring about the hum last night. Chuckie cackled in ignorance. He knew nothing.

"Odd," he said. "Maybe it was something electrical." His eyes wandered side to side. "Well, hopefully it won't happen tonight. Also, Mrs. Bernstein should have a package waiting for her here from Ms. Malone."

"You sure do," he chortled, handing Roxy the box. "Ms. Malone's a busy lady."

Having had a fling last year, I wondered where their spouses were. Dr. Bernstein warned him last night and I hoped they didn't get caught together.

"Stan, tell my wife, Martha, I'll be down at the rocks, poking around. She doesn't like squirtin' clams and slimy seaweed. Best she wait here. I'll be back in a jiffy."

"Yes, sir, Mr. Thompson."

Mr. Dunlop's eyes and ears followed every scene. He sat in a perfect spot to view the back lawn, front door, and reception desk. Perspiration formed on my forehead. I kept my clammy hands tightly clasped behind my back.

Mr. Thompson grabbed the box from Roxy and handed her a penny, kept one for himself and led her out to the fountain. They cast their desire quickly, before heading around back. I peered out a terrace window as they came into view again. From a distance, I saw Mr. Thompson massaging oil over Roxy's back as she giggled and squirmed. They disappeared beyond the trees.

Laughter drew my attention to croquet set up on the back lawn. Dr. Bernstein and Mrs. Thompson played a game of it. He stood behind her, holding her cupped hands on the club. "One, two, three," they swung together and hit the ball just side swiping the ring. They high-fived. What was going on here? The couples were mixed up. Not sure I should bother telling Mrs. Thompson where her husband was.

"Psst," James motioned me to the bar, with his two flapping fingers. I eased my way over with a stern face, as if we talked business. "Hey, I saw Mr. Mac leave the lounge today. Well, the back of him anyway. He strolled across the front lawn, holding something. I tried to follow, but Mrs. Lyncoff called me back. One of my friends at Aussie's said he went in there the other day, had a drink and asked some questions about the area. Don't you think that's strange? You think he is going to turn this place into a Holiday Inn?"

"No way. He's just a strange old man. That's all," I whispered out of earshot.

Mrs. Butterfield sat on a stool holding a diaper-wrapped Pickering. An inquisitive look pierced James's face.

"Upset tummy," she said.

James served Pickering's soup to him at the bar. The dog sat content, paws on ledge, slurping the pale broth. I weaved between Mr. Dunlop and Pickering to try and camouflage the fur ball from view. Last year, we got in big trouble for having the dog in the restaurant. Against health standards.

Classical music washed over the mood and murmurs volumized. Chuckie buzzed me to deliver dinner to Mr. Mac in his set corner of the lounge. Mrs. Lyncoff finally purchased silver plate covers in place of last year's saran wrap. I lifted its lid to reveal a scrumptious mushroom topped tenderloin, escorted by potatoes au gratin. The shallots and peppercorn fumes led my mouth to water and stomach growl. I set his usual glass of ice water tableside. He gleamed and thanked me for my service.

Ms. Malone had spoofed herself up today. She'd gone from school teacher to slightly shy of escort. She certainly seemed to be making the rounds and her new young playmates always in for the whole shebang. She must be pretty good at her job to make friends that easily. High in sales. They'd all lean in and whisper momentarily, then furiously howl back. Over and over again. You'd think no one else was around. But there were several other tables trying to enjoy cocktails on the terrace, and the dining room was full. I'm sure they could hear this crowd outside. Mr. Dunlop didn't participate, just observed. I couldn't read his poker face. Meanwhile, more steamed in the kitchen than just clams. Chef tossed Branson's seafood platter on the serving station. One of the scallops flew off and shot to the floor. I reorganized the shrimp, lobster, and crab as it slid when it hit the counter. Pinky and his followers anticipated a third bottle by the time I served their first course. It felt darker to me tonight, as if the stars didn't shine as bright and the boats were not as well lit.

Chortling arose from the croquet area again. I looked in dim light for Dr. Bernstein and Mrs. Thompson. Although I could faintly see one body pressed behind the other, I recognized the voices: Mindy and Riker.

CHAPTER FIVE

The following day's temperature rose several degrees, enough to strip Branson of his cardigan and into a purple polo shirt and white shorts. And plenty to make me sweat thinking of Mindy and Riker merged together last night. Racket in hand, the foursome headed out for a morning of tennis.

Mr. Dunlop enjoyed breakfast with Ms. Malone in the dining room. I had off, thank goodness, so the inspector became Riker's problem. I strolled down to Nick's, a popular local spot in town, undressed with lumpy soda fountain stools and tattered booths. The best pancakes and eggs at unmatchable prices. This was the place I first learned about The Maycliff, overhearing two construction workers talking about it last year. How they might get work at the inn. That's why I pursued it. I was out of options at the time and needed a job. A year having passed, I contemplated what I could do to move up in the inn, something beyond bellman. Maybe bartender or front desk manager in charge of Chuckie. I needed to formulate a plan, so Mindy would notice.

Mindy and I agreed to meet at noon for a walk around Witch Hole, one of the carriage path trails built by the Rockefeller family. I slipped my hand into hers as we strolled along the little watering holes, cyclists cruising by us. The sun weighed heavily down. Black capped chickadees chirped from the pines.

I mentioned that I saw her and Riker playing croquet last night. She just brushed it off, saying they took a couple of shots while on break. Her eyes folded, fleetingly focusing on mine before looking away. Then she shook her head as if I was a bumbling fool. I shouldn't have mentioned anything. I decided not to make a big deal of it and let it go.

We'd come to a fork in the road. "Hey, wanna go this way?" I asked.

"Sure."

I found a hidden pocket in the woods and swooped Mindy into my arms, kissing her passionately. She clung to me with fiery emotion. "There's a spot I discovered nearby. Follow me." I pulled her behind me, as I cleared the branches, stopping at a big carved out tree trunk. I lay her down, gently caressing her neck. The spark between us intensified, stillness in the air. Even the leaves went quiet. This was the moment we would rekindle. I heard nothing. Until she said we had to go.

This hardly seemed fair. I wondered why we had to leave so abruptly in the heat of our lust. I felt irritable. I only ever rendezvoused with Penthouse pets. And that was getting dull.

I wished I'd been on shift this evening, just so I could be near Mindy. I thought about her all evening. I decided to swing down to the restaurant to see her.

"What are you doing down here, Stanley?" Mrs. Lyncoff asked.

"Nothing. Just thought I'd see what was happening."

"Well, you're not dressed. So please disappear and go to your room or somewhere else."

"Yes, ma'am."

Mindy stood next to Riker—watching, listening.

I noticed Mr. Dunlop sitting alone in the dining room, his eyes observing me up and down. Surely, he'd understand I was off duty. But that mattered little to me right now. I walked away, head tilted. I played in my mind how I could do something special for Mindy. Really get her attention.

I passed by Mrs. Butterfield. She sat alone at the bar.

"Where's Pickering?"

"He's still not well. Sleeping in the room. I've come to get more soup from Chef. And I lay awake most nights from that noise. Could you see what's causing it?"

"I'll ask Mrs. Lyncoff. And I'll get the soup for you," I offered.

Chef grumbled when I asked, and threw a bowl in front of me, broth splashing against the side.

"And take this to Mr. Mac. He's been waiting awhile." I'm not working, but okay. I hoped Mrs. Lyncoff didn't catch me again. I only tried to help. I dropped the bowl to Mrs. Butterfield and the tray to Mr. Mac, who lounged at his table, muttering to himself. Something he did often. He gratefully nodded. Although I only half cared, I wished I wore better than a t-shirt and jeans when Mr. Dunlop looked over. On the way past the front desk, Chuckie nabbed me to drop a package to Dr. Bernstein's room. James pulled me aside on my way down.

"My friend Mo, who works at the Town Council, said The Maycliff would be turned into a year-round spa. The plans are going in front of the committee sometime in October for a vote."

"Well I don't know how they'd keep this place going year-round, with the snow and all. And who would want to come to a dead cold ghost town?" Maybe this was the inn's demise. It would suffocate, trying to stay open. All because of a stinking psychic. I wanted to tell James what she said, that I could shatter the inn. But decided it would make it too real. In my mind, it never happened. At least that's what I told myself.

"Mo says people with a lot of money who want to hide away, lose weight, spa treatments, and maybe some cosmetic surgery. Or maybe those who want to have affairs. No one would find them here. Bet we'd get a lot from New York. Could be good for us. Work year-round," he said.

"I think they'd have to hire professional staff. People in the spa business," I said.

"They still need someone to bartend and lift bags."

"Not sure alcohol would be part of the reduction in weight program. But you're right. Maybe," I said.

James told me Mo knew everything in town. Her nickname was Moroccan Mo. One, because of her big maracas and two, because she'd basically slept with everyone in town, guys and girls. A native Mainer, like him. He said her dad, Bert, runs the oldest lobster pound in town near the pier. Rumor has it you could catch more than crabs with Mo. But James claimed he loved her no-boloney attitude. She remained one of his best friends. James switched the blender on, focusing on his creation. A shadow swept by me. I turned. Nothing. "Mary?" I whispered. It felt somewhat comforting, yet a little disturbing. The image of the nanny's brutal death sometimes haunted me. My body tingled from the head down.

James poured the icy white concoction into four lime-rimmed margarita glasses and placed them on a tray. "Do us a favor and deliver this to Mr. Thompson's room."

Ms. Malone stole a seat and ordered a bourbon. Mr. Thompson suddenly appeared, grabbing her shoulders from behind and whispering in her ear. She turned slightly as he massaged the area before strutting off. I don't know where he went because he wasn't in his room when I got there.

Roxy, Dr. Bernstein's wife, answered the door. She told me where to set the drinks and thanked me without a tip. Dr. Bernstein emerged from the bathroom in his underpants.

"What in the hell is all the ruckus about at night? I can't sleep with that constant engine noise," he complained.

I told him I was looking into it. Actually, though, I'd forgotten to mention it to Mrs. Lyncoff. I'd do so first thing in the morning. But why were the Bernsteins in the Thompson's room, half undressed? And where were the Thompsons? All I knew was they were getting something I wasn't. And that didn't seem right. I was the one in my prime. I scratched my arms and the back of my neck and gave my legs a shake.

A scream bellowed down the hallway. Mrs. Butterfield ran out of her room, frantic. I raced to her.

"What's wrong?"

"It's Pickering. He's not moving. I gave him the soup." I thought how Chef despised that dog and wondered whether he'd poisoned it.

"Help!" she pleaded.

I flew through the door and, against my will tried to resuscitate the thing with CPR—breathing into his tiny, gooey mouth. Ugh. Then pushing five times on his little chest. I repeated the method several times. Bellman turned doctor. Pickering coughed, rolled to his side, and spat out pink fluids. Mr. Dunlop stood at the front of her open door. He must have seen everything. Pickering bounced to his feet and jumped into Mrs. Butterfield's arms.

"I think he's fine now," I said, wiping the saliva from my mouth.

"Thank you, dearie. My poor baby. I need to get you home and to a real doctor." She kissed his nose.

I backed out the door, nearly running into Tracy. Mr. Dunlop had vanished.

"What's up?" I asked.

"Was going to ask you the same. You're not supposed to be working tonight."

"I know. I'm not, really. But, kinda," I said.

"Will you help me turn down the last room, so I can get out of here? People wouldn't leave their rooms, so I got a late start."

"Sure."

We turned down the bed and chatted about our day. I looked around waiting for something to pop out at me. Nothing. I helped her tidy the bathroom and align fresh towels on the rack. Cleared the trash.

"Night, Stan." Her eyes gleamed as she closed the door. That was a fast exit.

I followed behind, but the knob wouldn't turn. I twisted harder. Banged on the door but no answer. Kept at it, calling Tracy. I thought I heard Riker's voice, but then silence. I sat on the edge of the bed for what seemed endless time, sensing the vibration of the deafening humming noise, until I heard fiddling at the door. I bounced up as Mr. Dunlop and Ms. Malone entered, package in hand. I pretended I'd delivered fresh towels and was just leaving, although not dressed in uniform and a late hour for turndown. My whole body trembled. I said only hi, no eye contact, as if not to notice he wasn't alone. He pushed me out the door, hanging the DO NOT DISTURB sign. Oh my god, even the inspector. The hallway left me with only an abandoned chair and Riker fleeing around the corner with Mindy.

CHAPTER SIX

Eggs Benedict, oatmeal with fresh berries, two coffees, and an orange juice. Pretty simple order. Although he usually rose at the crack of dawn, it didn't surprise me Mr. Dunlop woke so late. There were distractions.

The tray looked meticulous, everything in its place and draped with pink linen. I double-checked the ketchup, jam, salt & pepper, two water glasses, cutlery, and a fresh cut pink rose in a crystal bud vase. I knocked on his door. He was quick to answer, instructing I set it on the little table by the window. While I switched all items off the tray, he asked about the loud humming noise last night. I told him I believed it was a boat, a very large boat. I didn't really know, but at least it couldn't be our fault that way. I said Mrs. Lyncoff would ask it to be moved elsewhere. He argued he didn't see any boats out there, to which I didn't know what to say. Except, hmm. He went on to complain about the heat last night. It was hard to sleep between the noise and the heat. He requested a fan. I promised to look.

I asked if he would like me to remove the plate covers, to which he nodded. And there, on that perfect table, sat an Eggs Benedict and an omelet. Before he could say anything, I acknowledged the mistake, apologized, and said I'd be right back with the oatmeal. He masked any reaction. The bathroom door remained closed.

As I tore down the stairs, Mrs. Lyncoff's words of caution reverberated through my head, "Don't screw up." I should have paid attention to the order, but I was distracted by the details. The important thing now was speed. How fast could I get back to his room without his Eggs Benedict getting cold? Clearly, he still had company.

I noticed his opened pad sitting bedside, guessing he'd just written me up. The bathroom door remained shut. I apologized profusely again and shot out. He shared two words with me: "thanks" and "goodbye."

I couldn't find a fan but would look again when I returned. I pulled the van around the drive. The Thompsons and Bernsteins wanted a lift to Jordan Pond House for popovers and tea. I didn't understand how they were now getting along. And Branson and his tag team requested a ride to Sand Beach.

They all spoke of this unexpected weather and how difficult it was to sleep last night with the heat and noise. Mr. Thompson seemed fascinated with the line of work Branson was in. Lockholm Aviation handled serious business, military contracts. Branson arched back, telling the Texan of his promotion as Project Manager, specializing in missile defense systems engineering. The two conversed most the trip. Mr. Thompson asked if he could tour the facilities if he came to Palm Beach. Branson stressed it was pretty covert, but he'd try to gain him access.

Branson shook Mr. Thompson's hand. Said it was nice talking and jumped out, sporting tie dye swim trunks, a lime green polo, and topsiders. His friend in a similar get up. The girls dressed in bikinis, short wraps, and elevated flip flops.

They had to trek down a long flight of stairs to reach the beach; it surrounds mountains of rock. I'm not sure they realized how cold the Atlantic stood, fifty degrees year-round. Maybe with the heat of today it would be bearable to swim.

Mr. Thompson invited me to join at the table, rather than waiting in the hot vehicle. It didn't make sense to drop them and return because of the distance. They'd be done by the time I reached home. I gratefully accepted. I'd stay for a quick bite then leave them on their own. The steam from breaking open the popover warmed my face. The smells of home. Butter and jam melted as soon as they touched the bready puff. I scarfed down the two popovers and excused myself to peruse the gift shop. It was everything Maine imaginable, from cookbooks to ornaments, clothing, kitchenware, and food. I bought some nice silver earrings for Mindy. No reason, really. Just thought they'd look good on her and she'd like them.

Mr. Thompson asked me to drive by Thunder Hole on the way home. A spot where big waves crash against rock and water is forced through a cave's crevice, causing a thunderous noise. Particularly prevalent at low and high tides, and the tide sat about at capacity now. I'd never been here, just heard about it. We parked and I led my group down to the safety viewing area, following the signs. Most tourists stood far, not taking advantage of the observation deck. One wave after another rolled in fast and boom, slammed the rock with brutal force, shooting massive amounts of water forty feet high, accompanied by its powerful roar. We stood entranced, unaware of its magnitude. It towered over us and slammed down like a mini tsunami. We only had time to grab the railing, so as not to lose our footing. We were drenched, every bit of us. Oops. I apologized repeatedly. Mr. Thompson bent over laughing, his wife not so much.

Dr. Bernstein did not appear amused either, but Roxy giggled. That seemed enough of a tour for today. We waddled our heavy bodies back to our ride. I personally found it refreshing in the heat of the day. The temperature's significant rise was unusual for June, normally to be expected in August. We wrung out our clothes as best we could before heading home.

I arrived back to find Mr. Dunlop waiting for a lift to the pharmacy. I slid open the door. Mr. Thompson tipped his head at Mr. Dunlop. The soaked guests jumped out of the van, and Mr. Dunlop hopped into one of the wet seats, then out. He shook his head and asked for a towel. I said, of course, and excused myself to the linen closet. Mrs. Lyncoff sidetracked me. She told me to go by the hardware store to pick up fans. Complaints were pouring in because of the heat. At least I knew we had none or they were in use. Places weren't built with A/C in Maine, because it was rarely needed. She scoffed at my being wet, didn't want to know why. Just told me to change.

Luckily, the van had A/C. I told Mr. Dunlop I'd be picking up a fan for him in town. I dropped him at the pharmacy and ran to the hardware store. All but three fans had sold out. I grabbed the rest and threw them in the trunk. When we arrived back at the inn, I set up two in his room: one by his bedside and one in the general area, oscillating. All it really seemed to do was move hot air around, though. I left Mr. Dunlop's room with him lying down fan on face, eyes closed, moaning how unbearable it was. Thankfully, he'd be checking out in the morning. I couldn't believe he stayed so long. Maybe because of the incident last year, he increased the number of days. I just had to get through one more night.

I found Mr. Mac in his usual spot and asked how he was handling the heat. Not well, he said. I told him not to worry, I'd put a fan in his room. I thought it important he get the last one. Mrs. Butterfield crossed my mind as well. But she seemed a little hardier.

I hoped the temperature dropped soon. Mrs. Lyncoff had arranged a pianist and singer to play in the lounge tonight. I think she did so to impress Mr. Dunlop. Let's hope he came out of his room. The heat seemed to be draining everyone and making some cranky.

Since the hardware store was sold out of electric fans, Mrs. Lyncoff sent Riker to pick up a box of Chinese wooden fans at the five and dime. We'd put them in all the guest rooms and on lounge tables. She felt it was better than nothing. James and Mindy were setting up early with a banquet table for hors d'oeuvres. They waved me over to help. I pulled Mindy aside and gave her the earrings. Her eyes and mouth opened wide. She took off the ones she wore and replaced them with mine. James gave me a thumbs-up and mimicked kisses behind her back.

"Jeez, aren't those the cat's meow," James said, reaching out to touch them. "I'm impressed, Stanley. You have more style than I thought." He tapped my hand.

She hugged me hard, while I slipped the A-Okay signal to James.

"What's this about?" Mindy asked.

"Nothing. I just thought you'd like them."

"I love them! You've never bought me jewelry before. It's so special." Her eyes sparkled and her smile broadened. She squeezed me again and kissed my cheek.

Wow. I should do this more often. I didn't expect this kind of reaction. Maybe she'd warm up to me again, like in Boston. We dropped our embrace and focused back on work.

The chaffing dishes arranged, we lit the fuel underneath for Chef's warm delights. There was plenty of space left on the table for cold appetizers, as well. The food would be complimentary, like a happy hour, but longer. If guests came in for the food and live music, they'd surely pay to drink.

Riker returned, and we set a number of fans on each table, in addition to the guest rooms. Chef brought out a dish of coconut shrimp, drizzled with chili sauce and topped with parsley. He requested our help. We went back and forth to the kitchen, grabbing dishes till the table was filled. It looked enticing, adorned with a warm dish of Oysters Rockefeller, lobster toasts with avocado, crab quiche, puff pastries stuffed with cream cheese and prosciutto, chicken wings, beef tenderloin canapés, deviled eggs, smoked salmon, and desserts. I felt starved. My stomach rumbled. I snuck a canapé when Chef retired to the kitchen. The juicy, savory meat melted between my gums. And the rich taste of a dark chocolate petit four raced my adrenaline. James and Mindy followed suit. We snuck more from other dishes and rearranged them, so it didn't look like anything was missing, just in case Chef or Mrs. Lyncoff did a final spot check. We couldn't go all night staring at this stuff on an empty stomach. That just wasn't right. We devoured enough to hold us over. The rest we'd enjoy at the end of the night as leftovers.

Chuckie asked Riker to pick up Branson's group at Sand Beach. They'd be waiting at the edge of the road. Riker grabbed a whole row of pointed lobster toasts and hid them in a cloth napkin. Mindy teased she caught him. Riker stopped and touched her left earring, whispering something in her ear. She crunched her neck to one side as if ticklish.

"Catch you later," he said.

"Sure will," Mindy bellowed back.

Riker swooped by me on the way out. "You trying to buy her?" he muttered. His smug look angered me.

Mindy slipped beside me, reiterating how she loved surprise gifts, as I observed Riker stuffing a lobster toast in his mouth as he drove off.

A few guests already occupied seats and started to dive into the delicacies. I asked Mr. Mac what he'd like and fixed him a side plate. I did the same for Mrs. Butterfield, who sat propped on a stool. The pianist arrived and set up her music and mike. Her tight knit black dress danced up her legs, as she bent. She started to sing Ella Fitzgerald's rendition of "Let's Fall in Love." Mindy glanced at me in between serving cocktails.

Ms. Malone helped herself to the buffet and grabbed a table alone. And the Bernsteins and Thompsons, now dry, dove into the food and nestled together at their own spot. Mr. Thompson excused himself and swung by Ms. Malone's for a quick chat. All the windows remained open for air flow, with the evening, still warm. Mr. Dunlop entered the room with Ella's "Love Me or Leave Me," scouring tables till he noticed Ms. Malone and joined in. She'd already made him a plate. I helped Mindy serve drinks and bus tables. She kept touching her earrings all night, her dimples more prominent when she looked at me. Mr. Dunlop asked for a Dewar's on the rocks, as Ms. Malone cooled him with a pink flowery fan, while nursing her bourbon. Most guests took advantage of their colorful, floral apparatus, a scent of sandalwood in the air.

A few guests made it to the dining room, where the music could also be heard. But most made the appies their meal and plowed down cocktails. The evening started to cool and become bearable. Branson arrived late. His DO NOT DISTURB sign had been on his door for hours. His girlfriend clung to his royal blue cardigan, as he carried his own bottle into the lounge, acknowledging his friends by hurling the Moët up.

He sidestepped Ms. Malone's table and whispered something, before joining the others. He wasn't supposed to bring in his own booze. The whole point was to make money on alcohol. But we just let it slide, knowing a fuss would make it worse. And we didn't want a scene with Mr. Dunlop around.

The Thompsons and Bernsteins went up for seconds and thirds. They seemed to be having a grand old time. The lofty Houstonian slipped over to Branson's table and stood for a chat. Mr. Mac looked content, probably his kind of music. Same with Mrs. Butterfield. I hoped Mr. Dunlop didn't notice Pickering under the bar ledge. James asked me to fix him a plate, so I snuck one for him and helped nibble off it.

Irritability had transformed to serenity. People conversed, drinks streamed, delicacies devoured, in an atmosphere of love songs, crackling fires, and candlelit tables. Everyone stopped complaining about the weather and raved about the evening. But, I don't know how they felt once the vibrational drone unmasked itself at bedtime. I fell asleep with my ears sandwiched between my pillow, feeling proud I'd bought those earrings for Mindy but annoyed with Riker's comment I was buying her and that his grubby hands had touched them.

CHAPTER SEVEN

The town picked up as June unfolded. Mr. Dunlop brought his own bag down and pulled his car up himself. I steered clear, as he talked to Mrs. Lyncoff on the drive. I was off duty and not dressed anyway. They talked briefly before he leapt in his car and drove off. I tried to read Mrs. Lyncoff's face, but it held deadpan.

Branson and his groupies stood on the back lawn as the Heli-jet eased its way down, the sun vaguely peering through the clouds. Branson, back into his orange, clung to a bottle of bubbly and four plastic cups. I guess for the long ride home. As the chopper lifted, I acknowledged I didn't mind seeing their backsides.

James had introduced me to an old friend of his who worked at the five and dime on Main Street. I often swung by when in town. Jerry always seemed to be working, local guy who was a comic buff and always pushed the magazines on me. That and penny candy. He sat sucking on a fire-ball, hot cinnamon jaw breaker. His tongue stained red against his rich skin. A tone slightly lighter than the Africans that visited last year.

"What do you have for me today, Jerry?"

"We have this new Batman comic in. And there's a special on the penny candies. Ten percent off every two dollars spent."

"I don't think I need that many sweets. Just a few." I grabbed a bag and loaded twenty pieces into it—gummy fish, milk duds, candy cigarettes, and a few bazookas.

"Hey, I hear your inn's up for sale."

"No, it's not."

"Well that's the word around town. People say it's going downhill. Owners are selling it for financial reasons."

My judgment frayed with the thought of the psychic. Had I done something to cause this? I needed to defend my position.

"No way. I've only heard they may turn it into a spa and keep it open year-round. But that'll only make it more appealing."

Jerry focused back on his comic, sliding his glasses up with his forefinger. It was as if I now stood alone.

"Gotta go. See ya tomorrow."

"Later, Stan."

The jazzy sound of the local band resonated from across the road at the Town Green. The old members swayed in the gazebo, as they played "When the Saints Go Marching In." People picnicked on blankets across the lawn with their cold cuts and sodas. Some listened from benches. Seemed there was nowhere else anyone needed to be but here. In the crowd I spotted James across the way moving his hips to the beat and belting out the words to the song. A girl stood beside him, clapping to the rhythm. I crossed the street to join.

"Hey. Want some candy, little boy?" I offered up the bag.

"Sure." He dove in. "I just love these town bands. Makes you feel like you're always on vacation." Orange gummy stuck in his teeth. And he continued to jiggle. "This is a friend of mine, the one I told you worked at the town council, Mo."

"Hey there," I said, waving my hand slightly. "Maybe you can clear the air. Jerry at the five and dime said The Maycliff is up for sale. Is that true?"

"I don't know anything about that," Mo said. "Just know an application's been filed for some development." She clapped in my face. "I heard spa, but I don't know. I haven't seen any plans."

"Hmm. Oh, damn, there's the Bernsteins and the Thompsons. What the hell? They're always together now." They walked out of a restaurant, arm and arm with their proper spouses, looking as if they were having a grand old time. "What's with them?"

James just laughed. I hid my face, turning and looking down, as I swallowed the last of my Milk Dud. Didn't want them to see me. I'd get stuck in an awkward conversation. At least at the inn I could offer them something to avoid full-on awareness of their relationship. "Guess I'd better get back for my shift. Riker will be getting off soon. Nice meeting you, Mo. I'll see you later, James?"

"That you will. Be up shortly."

Mrs. Butterfield sat on the edge of the fountain, holding one hand tightly onto Pickering's leash. She tossed a coin backward over her shoulder. I waved before sliding through the back entrance, greeted by the white cat perched on the stairs. "Scoot," I said. His sharp green eyes pierced through mine. "Scoot," I repeated. He didn't move. I fumbled by him on the way to my room to change. I didn't like to spend long on those spooky stairs where Mary was killed. Steve used to try to scare me on them. When I returned, the cat was gone.

The smell of onions and garlic penetrated the air, making me hungry. I short-cut through the kitchen, where Chef hovered over the stove, stirring a long, wooden spoon in a big pot.

"Have many reservations tonight?" I asked.

"I don't know. Bring me the book." His eyes didn't waiver.

I noticed the box of beets on the counter. "You cooking with beets this year?" I asked.

He turned and glanced. "I'm trying to, but somebody keeps swiping them."

I left to retrieve the reservation book. Chuckie and Riker stood whispering to each other until they saw me and stopped. I asked them what was up, but they claimed nothing. Norma bounced down the stairs holding some papers. "We have another group coming in boys, small one. A team of doctors. Psychiatrists and their spouses."

If only they could analyze Chuckie while they were here. That could take more than one visit, though.

"They'll be arriving tomorrow at check in and dining in the restaurant, early evening. Look after them for me please everyone. Oh, and Mrs. Lyncoff has arranged an acoustical engineer to visit tonight to check out the noise issue. Stanley, please show him where the sound comes from."

Chuckie asked Norma a number of questions, including what Mr. Dunlop said about our rating. My ears intensified. Norma said he'd written several recommendations, but his over-all stay proved enjoyable. We remained five-star. I took a deep breath of relief. Everything hadn't been exactly perfect. Thank god for Ms. Malone. Hopefully, she'd return next year. I left with the reservation book and popped it on the serving station in the kitchen. Chef silently grabbed it. The beets were gone.

I pushed through the swinging kitchen door to the dining room. Mrs. Butterfield sat at a window table, sipping gin. I noticed a hairy thing sticking out from under the table. Although Pickering was only allowed in the dining room the first night's stay, I wasn't going to squeal. She took her pills out of her purse and popped a few, swigging them down with her cocktail.

Mindy looked stunning in her blue dress, all dolled up with the earrings I'd given her. When I told her how nice she looked, she reiterated how much she loved the present. Rarely did anyone give her a gift. She glided through the room seemingly flawless as she seated guests. She remained too busy to chat long. But I'd catch her later. Chuckie buzzed me back to the desk, just having finished with an angry guest, trying to calm him regarding the mysterious nightly noise. He said the Thompsons and Bernsteins wanted a picnic on the lawn. He asked me to turn in their order, set up a blanket, candle, and wine cooler, and when their food was ready, let him know. They wanted a bottle of Stag's Leap Chardonnay and a couple of Glenlivets to start.

Just before nine, the acoustical engineer appeared, and I showed him to the water. Almost on the dot of nine, the humming started. He removed the fancy equipment from his bag, popped on his mega headphones and fiddled with some knobs, turning them left then right. I stayed with him awhile, curious what he'd find. He was surprised the noise was becoming progressively louder. He scratched his head in confusion. Said it sounded very odd, like nothing he'd heard before. I left him to continue recording the sounds. He said he'd see his own way out when done and analyze the readings back at his lab.

Late evening, I caught the Thompsons sneaking out of the Bernstein's room, accidentally knocking the DO NOT DISTURB sign off the knob. It felt a bumbling greeting. He seemed unusually relaxed and she, giddy.

"Oh, Stan....what are you doin' here so late?" He kept talking before I had a chance to answer. "Hey, thanks for that picnic today. It was a damn good spread. Enjoyed a speck too much hooch, though."

"My pleasure. I see you're here all week, so hopefully we can catch up."

"No, change of plans. Heading out a couple days early to Martha's Vineyard with the Bernsteins."

"Oh. That's nice. Well, goodnight. See you tomorrow."

Guess they'd become pals. As much as I liked Mr. Thompson, this was just friggin' weird.

***

Chef was in one of his moods. Flipping his hands about, yelling at Mindy. "What the hell? Get the goddamn table set for these guys."

"Don't talk to me like that. We're setting it now," she growled back.

I wanted to stick up for Mindy, although she was doing a fine job. I offered my assistance, but she just got mad. Once the Psychiatrists seated themselves, Chef pumped the meals out fast, too fast. It became an uncomfortable speed, almost pushing them out the door.

"Jeez, like what's with that?" James asked, flicking his hand back.

"Don't know. But it's unfortunately his typical behavior."

Riker whizzed by on his way to fix a loose faucet. I saw him gently slap Mindy on the ass as he passed. She turned in an irritated manner. Good for her.

One of the docs asked Mindy to slow the pace, so she confronted Chef with the group's complaint, and he exploded. Threw off his apron and stomped out of the kitchen.

I followed him for Mindy's sake. The limo lady had just pulled up to visit her friend, Ms. Malone, always leaving with a large box. I stood just outside Mrs. Lyncoff's office, where I overheard Chef rant about Mindy. Mrs. Lyncoff calmed him and ordered him back to work, promising to talk to Mindy tomorrow. I later filled Mindy in, but she didn't seem grateful for my assistance. James noticed the look on her face and simply shook his head at me as she walked away.

"Why do you hang on to her like that? Let her abuse you?"

"I'm not letting her abuse me. I'm just trying to help her out," I said.

"Well if you ask me, she doesn't seem to want your help."

"Maybe not." But deep down I knew she needed it.

A few psychiatrists dominated the conversation, talked incessantly about issues they encountered with their clients. The skinny doc at the end of the table twitched, repeatedly turning his head and checking his shoulder. His wife seemed equally agitated.

Dr. Perth clearly took charge of the group as he weaved his way back from the bathroom, bumping into me and excusing himself. "How you doing?" he slurred, as he plonked himself down next to his wife. She looked pissed off. "Bottom line is, I just tell my patients what they want to hear. That usually shuts them up." He raised his glass.

The only female doc was middle-aged and mainly listened, but the few words she spoke had specific intent. Articulate in manner, she found her job rewarding, helping those in need. Her husband kept his distance.

Dr. Perth brought up the noise issue. Had anyone heard it? They all acknowledged they had. "Sounds like a B-1 Bomber," he said. "Weird it's only at night. Makes it hard to sleep." That's one subject they all agreed upon.

Mindy checked in on the group to see if they cared for anything else. The female doc graciously declined. But Dr. Perth insisted on more rounds, said it might aid his sleep. I decided to help her serve, but Dr. Perth distracted me, pulled me aside. Wanted to hear my story.

"No story, really. Just from a small town and grew up with four sisters. Trying to figure out what I want to do. For now, it's hospitality."

"And why do you think you're cut out for the business?" Dr. Perth asked.

"Well I'm a hard worker, for one. And I enjoy being around people."

"You know, most people don't end up in the business in which they start or get their degree in. And what you think you might be interested in may be a choice you make because it's an easy one. Maybe you don't want to push yourself or face failure. You need to search deep to figure out what you really desire." He poked at my chest. "You don't want to end up like any of the crack-pots we see."

The skinny one didn't seem part of the group or conversation, his mind clearly elsewhere. He stood up, wiped his seat, sat back down again. Brushed his fingers through his hair. Scratched his chin, silently belched and left the room without a goodnight. His wife followed.

I missed my chance helping Mindy, struggling to be polite to Dr. Perth. Riker had grasped the opportunity. They walked in together, Mindy holding the tray of cocktails, Riker looking like a thug.

In the back of the house, Chef had mellowed. I wanted to throw him in with the pack of lions, get him some head therapy. I heard him apologize to Mindy, and she insisted it was okay. I stayed to help her clean, and she seemed to appreciate it. She hugged me goodnight. I beamed until I saw her and Riker walking up the drive on their way home. She turned and blew me a discreet kiss behind Riker's back.

My stomach sank. I didn't know if that kiss made me feel good or bad. I wished I could talk to Steve, get some relationship advice, and wondered if he hovered by my side. I kept rewinding the tape of episodes involving Riker. I couldn't sleep, so I decided to peruse the kitchen for a snack. I snuck to the fridge in the darkness and came across a pint of crabmeat in a plastic container. The temptation got the better of me, and I woofed down a good portion. Mrs. Lyncoff had offered room and board, although I knew that didn't include seafood. I felt deserving of it, though. A little perk now and again. As I put the container back, the lights flicked on. My eyes widened, hoping it wasn't Mrs. Lyncoff. I didn't see anyone. I heard a slight rustling in the other room and slowly peered around. "Hello?" A screech echoed, then something shot at my feet as glass shattered. The white cat had jumped off the counter, knocking Mrs. Lyncoff's remaining twin china vase to the floor. Oh crap. His sharp eyes focused on me before he vanished. In the silence, I quickly kicked the remnants under the counter, hoping the boss would forget about it. Or not care since it no longer had a match. I flipped the light switch and got the hell out of there. I went the long way to my room up the main stairs because it was the closest escape. As I approached Mr. Mac's room, the door clicked shut.

CHAPTER EIGHT

The plush Maycliff minivan rounded the town pier, and I scooped up the doctors. They'd taken a whale-watching boat out late morning. We passed Aussie's Pub and headed for the baseball field, where the vintage car show was taking place. Mrs. Lyncoff had given all the guests at the inn free tickets to the event. I dropped the group and found the closest parking I could, far down the street. On my way back, I slipped into the five and dime for a pack of gum. Jerry was ringing out a customer, his teeth stained from a fireball. Bert, Moroccan Mo's father, twirled on a stool, enjoying his usual root beer float at the old-fashioned soda fountain. Bert's Lobster Pound in town remained an open-air dive, less expensive than the others that surfaced later. That's where I ate when I splurged on lobster and clams. The patron decides the weight-range, usually one to two pounds, and chooses which lobster he'll sacrifice out of the tank, watching the critter be sentenced to death, as its dropped into the boiling water. That always puts me off until my plate is up. Mrs. Lyncoff ordered all the inn's lobsters through Bert, and he sometimes personally delivered them, rather than sending one of his guys. I no longer attempted to talk to him. He never remembered you outside his place and only talked orders inside. I slapped my Trident down on the counter.

"Fifty cents," Jerry said. "But I'll throw in a magazine for another buck."

"No thanks. Just the gum. I've got to head to the car show."

"That's where I'm going when I get off soon. There's a nineteen sixty-four Aston Martin I wanna check out."

"Sounds cool. See ya there."

The day had woken clear but windy. Tourists and locals crowded the many displays. An old-fashioned band, the one that played the Town Green across from the five and dime, kicked out the tunes of Billie Holiday's "All of Me." Mrs. Lyncoff passed behind a car holding the arm of a man in a top hat; couldn't see his face. The docs were scattered about and courteous as they passed.

"Mindy!" I shouted. I felt glad to see her by herself. "Hey." I hurried to her. "You should have told me you were coming."

"Well I just decided."

"You here alone?"

"Kind of," she said.

"You wanna hang out?"

"Well, I would. But I'm meeting my old roommates here. We're having a kind of reunion today." She folded her arms and lifted her shoulders as if the wind chilled her.

"Oh, all right," I said. "Then I'll see you back at the inn later."

"Sounds good. See ya, Stan." She gave a slight wave.

James stood right behind me when I turned, so I hung out with him and later Jerry when he arrived. Jerry knew everything about cars. He seemed like a walking encyclopedia. James dragged me in different directions the whole afternoon. Jerked me one way then the other while the brain gave us a run-down. Didn't even need to talk to the car's owner. We stopped at one of the hot-dog stands for lunch and sat on a rock, watching the crowds.

Jerry and James only had one hotdog to my two. We slurped the rest of our sodas and leapt up to graze the grounds again.

James kept yanking on my shirt. "Stop pulling me. I want to look at this cool Bentley, nineteen thirty."

"Come on. There's so much more to see." He tried to grab me again, but I pulled back.

On the other side of the classic black gem my eyes fell upon Mindy and Riker. They rounded the car and strutted by quickly. But I caught them.

"Hey, where's the rest of the gang?" I asked.

"Uh, we don't know. They haven't shown yet," Mindy said. Riker's expression infuriated me.

"I see." I looked at Mindy, but she turned slightly. Her hair blew in her face and Riker brushed it away. It felt as if I was punched in the gut and left winded. My mind lay blank. I couldn't believe what I was seeing. Mindy with that jackass and him touching her. I wanted to say something but didn't want to play the fool either. I wished to crawl in a hole and hide.

James piped in. "Let's all hang out."

Riker stared down him and Jerry. "Nah, we promised those guys we'd meet up. We're going to go look for them now."

"Okay, see you later, Mindy," I said. My reaction sluggish and automated, I pulled James away. Jerry followed.

"What's with that?" I asked, trying to act like it hadn't put a dagger through me.

"I told you," James said.

"Don't say that. She'd planned to meet her old roommates here. It's a reunion," I said. James just rolled his eyes. "That idiot just hangs around her, because he has no friends."

James made a big to-do out of them hanging out together and I told him to stop. I felt crappy enough. I dreaded going back to work and thought about playing sick. I could hibernate in my room all night.

"Boo," said Tracy as she crept up behind me. I wasn't in the mood. She and the girls had just finished their shift.

"Is the whole inn here?" James asked.

"Pretty much, I think," Tracy said. "Hey, why aren't you hanging out with Mindy? I just saw her."

"With a group?" I asked.

"No, just Riker."

Tracy felt my anguish. She jerked me by the shirt, pulling me away from the guys.

"Hey, you have to open your eyes. Mindy's not good for you. I mean, come on. Look what she's doing," Tracy said.

"They're just old friends. And they're meeting up with all the roommates," I said.

"Really, Stan? Okay. If that's what you want to believe. It's your decision."

Things just seemed to get worse. I felt attacked. I didn't want to hear any of this. Why did they have to put that nonsense in my head? No one seemed to understand. I just wanted to leave. I checked my watch.

Dr. Perth stood engrossed in conversation with Ms. Malone at our arranged meeting place for the ride back, while his wife talked to the lady doc. We waited for all to gather. Some stayed for the night entertainment—a live band with beer and burger stands. Jerry slipped me a rolled-up magazine on my way out. Said he just finished reading it, and it was mine now. I appreciated that. James in tow, we headed toward the inn.

Mrs. Butterfield sat in her designated spot at the bar, sipping on the usual and glancing back at Mr. Mac. Pickering sniffed the area and strutted out from under the bar. He wore an

English cap, clearly designed for dogs, and a blazer with a fake tie sewn on, along with a diaper. The Bernsteins sat at a distant cocktail table with the Thompsons. Their skin contact felt gross. All four of them. Mrs. Lyncoff had hired a fill-in to cover bags and drinks for the day. Give us a break. He left, and we resumed our roles. I wondered when Mindy would get back.

"Thompson. Quick drink and then let's head to dinner." I heard Dr. Bernstein say.

Mrs. Butterfield whispered over the bar to James.

"No problem, Mrs. Butterfield. I've got you covered."

I pulled James aside for the scoop. Mrs. Butterfield asked him to suggest to Mr. Mac dining with her one evening. She admitted she fancied him.

Chuckie squeezed Joan's hand as she left the front desk. Looked like he tried to be discreet but wasn't. Then he buzzed me to the desk. Ms. Malone just dropped some sample giveaways at the desk to be included in the welcome packages Dr. Perth arranged. I guessed they were brain-teasing games or puzzles for fun. Chuckie asked I deliver the packages to all the docs' rooms while they dined. I darted around and back down.

"Done," I said.

I strolled into the restaurant to find Joan working the door and asked where Mindy was. Apparently, Mindy asked Mrs. Lyncoff for the night off. Joan offered to cover. I said nothing. Just walked away. Wonder why she wanted the night off so badly? She never did that. Did she really like old cars or hanging out with Riker? The ache double-stabbed me.

The Thompsons and Bernsteins headed for dinner, which left only Mrs. Butterfield at the bar and Mr. Mac in his lounge chair. I felt sorry for Mr. Mac, sitting alone all the time. Perhaps he calculated costs of new management. Or how exactly he planned to run the place as a corporate hotel. Maybe he'd bring in a new chef. My eyes sparked at the thought. I approached him and offered a cup of tea or glass of wine. Wouldn't be a bad thing to get on his good side. He thanked me but declined. Just stared out the window. Mrs. Butterfield kept a keen eye his way. But I don't think he noticed her or maybe just not interested.

A couple, mid-thirties I'd guess, stepped out of their car and knelt down in front of the sacred bath, splashing water on different body parts. They remained at this place of worship for an extended period. As they rose, the man plopped one in the fountain. Was everyone superstitious? I shook my head. Chuckie greeted the bejeweled couple as they entered. "Good evening. Checking in?"

"We are." The fellow nodded. They weren't dressed in traditional dishdasha or burqa garb, but her eyes peered as if she was.

"My goodness. I see you came all the way from Saudi Arabia. What brings you here?"

The man didn't respond, so Chuckie kept talking. "Please sign here," he said.

I escorted the mysterious couple to their room, mesmerized by the extraordinary diamonds choking their fingers. I tightened my spiel, because they didn't seem too interested. Simply requested a plate of dates and tea be served to their room at sundown. They knelt down in the bathroom just as I left.

I slipped into the broom closet outside the men's room, where the pay phone hid. Sat down on the stool while Mindy's number rang and rang. Hung up, coin dropped. I tried again. Looking up, I could see a shadow close in on me. "Yes, Mrs. Lyncoff?" She motioned me out of there, shaking her head. Discouraged, I closed the door and returned to my front post.

Just looking at Chuckie aggravated me. And his chatter made it worse. He said Riker snuck out a bottle of wine earlier to share with Mindy this evening. Those two were tight. Really good friends.

Night slammed down on me. I don't know what was worse, the noise outside or the racket in my head. Why wasn't my girl by my side? Hardly fair. I couldn't get any time with her and much past a hug.

CHAPTER NINE

D r. Perth bounced down the stairs. He greeted me hello, shaking my hand and patting my back. Then caught up with the skinny doc, wrapping his arm around skinny's shoulder. The two strolled to the parlor like old chums. Skinny seemed calm compared to yesterday, wore a grin past Boston. The lady doc kissed her husband suggestively, as she headed for work and he headed for town. The mood had changed with the whole group. They all seemed so touchy-feely in public, which I found off-putting.

Mr. Thompson, being the friendly guy he was, introduced himself to everyone at the inn. He slipped by the Saudi's table and plonked himself down a few minutes. The Thompsons and the Bernsteins appeared ecstatic about their day, not bothered by droplets of rain. They left holding hands, all of them, with the two ladies in between.

Breakfast was smokin' busy, with everyone coming in at once. I wished Steve was here to help. He was great under pressure. I'd last stoked the fire before the rush and it held strong, crackling with intensity. Classical music remained muffled by the crowd's murmurs and the calm atmosphere.

I could sense the beady eyes of the Islamic woman staring at me. I felt she listened intensely to people's conversations.

The man remained still, gazing out the window. I checked on them to see if they needed anything, like a coffee. The man shook his head politely. Explained it was their holy month of Ramadan, so they couldn't eat or drink till dusk. They must fast. But they did ask me to check on a gift that should have been left for them at the front desk.

Mr. Mac disguised himself behind a spread newspaper. Mrs. Butterfield joined in the room sliding into a big, comfy chair with Pickering, whose lip started to curl. The low methodical growl coupled with a staring contest between him and the white cat, who suddenly appeared on the bar top. No one seemed to notice the feline, even when he jumped down and disappeared behind the bar, other than Pickering, who suddenly went quiet. I retrieved Mrs. Butterfield's pot of tea. She suggested no dog biscuits this morning, as Pickering's digestion remained off. And they'd be dining with Mr. Mac in the parlor this evening.

A raggedy looking group trudged through the screen door and plonked themselves down at the bar. Said they were friends of James.

"He's not in till four," I said.

"That's okay. We don't need him to get sloshed," one guy blurted, his beer gut hanging over his jeans.

"Oh, you guys must be the Opossum family. I mean, James refers to you as that. Says you three are always hanging out together."

A scrawny girl with piercings throughout her face stood up and gave me a high five. "That's us. Can you fix us Bloody Marys please, double shots?"

"Coming up."

Mrs. Lyncoff strutted toward me, her right eyebrow arched and her eyes widened. She whispered in my ear, asking if these were my friends. I told her no. They're just local town folk coming in for a drink. The wrinkle between her eyes creased deeper as she waited for me to expand. Irritated, she ignored our guests and walked out.

"Man, who's that bag?" the big gutted guy asked.

"The manager."

"She's intense."

Beer Gut had slid behind the bar, helping himself and the other two Opossums to another round.

"Hey, where's that creeper James keeps telling us about?" he asked.

"Shhh…he's in the corner," I said. Of course, they all turned to look.

The Middle Easterners slipped out of the room, one into the ladies' room and other the men's, in time for their call to prayer. That reminded me to check on their gift. I picked it up just as the limo with the exotic lady rolled up to visit her friend, Ms. Malone. The Arabic couple occupied the bathrooms for some time while other guests eagerly waited. I knocked on both doors but no answer. Finally, the woman came out; her eyes gazed at me but showed little expression. She carried her shoes and waited outside the men's room. Her husband swept past as she followed. They returned to their original spot only to find the package tabletop and escaped to their room.

Riker came flying in, winded. "Hey man, can't work tonight."

"What? Why not?"

"Something came up."

"Well, I don't wanna work your shift. I've been here all day."

"Sorry, nothing I can do. You're the only sub. Later, bro."

What the hell? Before I could think of a comeback, he was gone. Maybe it wasn't a bad thing after all. At least I could see

Mindy without Mrs. Lyncoff telling me off for getting in the way, not on duty. That is, if Mindy didn't ask for another night off. I couldn't help but wonder if anything happened between those two last night after drinking. Mindy didn't hold her liquor well.

I mixed another round of drinks for the Opossums. They talked about a band playing tonight at Aussie's Pub, "Under City Lights." It's the hottest local band around, in from Bangor. Entry by ticket only.

"What kind of band is it?" I asked.

"Kind of pop rock, if you know what I mean. They have a really cool sound, great beat," Beer Gut said.

"Any tickets left?"

"Yep, I'm helping the band out. I have twenty to sell, ten bucks a pop. Nine-thirty showtime. There's a warm-up band before. I'm the soundman, like I am for a lot of local bands. Gonna come?"

"That's kinda steep. Ten bucks," I said.

"Includes a drink."

"Sure, why not? I'll take two." This seemed a great excuse to get Mindy out. She worked too hard.

Piercings wrapped her arm around Beer Gut, gently stroking his ear. The third Opossum riddled with tattoos, slouched in his chair, listening to the conversation, but not saying a word, just occasionally laughing to himself.

"Got anything to eat?" Beer Gut asked. I handed him a menu, but he squawked at the prices. "Just the free nuts," he requested.

"The Opossum family!" James enthusiastically bellowed. He shimmied in with open arms and hugged each one, expressing his excitement for tonight with little bounces and compact claps. A tendency of his. It allowed my escape to ready Mr. Mac and Mrs. Butterfield's parlor dinner. I offered

Mrs. Butterfield another pot of water for her tea on my way out, but she declined. She had to freshen up.

The docs' meeting had broken for the day, and they stood outside the parlor mingling. Their spouses just back from town. They all agreed they wanted downtime, so the evening would be spent with their significant others, doing their own thing. Dr. Perth grabbed his wife's hand and kissed it. She looked smitten. The couples disappeared into their rooms, hooking their DO NOT DISTURB signs. I tried to shut off my brain, not imagine the goings-on behind the scenes. But I couldn't escape it. It planted itself in my face with the main areas of the inn empty and the guests saucy room-service calls. I longed for Mindy. Where was she?

Tracy arrived early for turndown. She short-stopped it by the fountain, tossing a penny high into the air just nicking its side. Then rummaged through the grass to collect it, before trying again. If she wasn't jetting it like a rocket, she'd have better aim. I punched through the door.

"Guess luck isn't in the cards, huh?" I provoked.

"I'll get it," she said. "It's no fun just plopping it in. Might as well make a game of it. And anyway, the higher it goes the stronger the wish. The more apt it is to come true."

"Where'd you hear that hogwash?"

"I didn't. I just made it up," she said as the shiny metal pelleted through the water. "Got it! You should have a go."

"Nah. I don't believe in that stuff."

"Suit yourself. It's your destiny."

We talked our way to the linen closet, where she lit up a cigarette and munched on Godiva chocolates meant for the pillows at turndown. "Hey, come join me." She patted the upside-down milk crate next to hers.

"Just for a sec. I gotta get back."

One of Tracy's sisters walked in. "Sam's helping me out tonight." Sam grinned and took a seat. The maids being a family affair, Mrs. Lyncoff stressed not to upset any of them. If you upset one, we could lose the whole crew, she said.

"Ya know, I think Mrs. Lyncoff has a boyfriend," Tracy grinned.

"Why's that?"

"I overheard her whispering on the phone, telling the person she loved them, and she always had."

"So, that doesn't mean anything. Could have been anyone," I said.

"No. It was her expression, too. Hard to imagine her with anyone," Tracy said.

"Well. It's really not our business." Although I wondered what kind of man she'd be with. Then I remembered the man in the top hat, walking through the park with Mrs. Lyncoff. Could that be him? However, I wasn't going to give Tracy any fuel.

Tracy already knew of the dinner tonight with Mrs. Butterfield and Mr. Mac when I told her my plans of setting up the parlor. That triggered her recent findings. The maids were instructed to clean Mr. Mac's room only once a week on Friday mornings as he lounged in his usual spot. She said, this week, she came across an old black and white photo on his bedside table of three children on horseback, one much younger than the other two. She wondered who they were. Maybe his grandkids, I suggested.

She also said there sat two big locked trunks in Ms. Malone's room. She was dying to know what they contained. I told her to mind her own business and called her a snoop.

She asked me what was going on with the Thompsons and Bernsteins. She spotted Dr. Bernstein with Mr. Thompson's wife on the drive, and they weren't just acting like friends. Dr. Bernstein didn't even seem grumpy anymore, she said.

I shrugged my shoulders. "Guess they're just happy," I said.

Tracy babbled on about her worry of the inn selling, where that would leave her and her family. I assured her that Mrs. Lyncoff would have a place for them. We wouldn't all just instantly lose our jobs. I hoped that to be true. Tracy might never speak to me again. I reminded her it's hard to find good staff. She seemed somewhat comforted by what I said. Sam glanced up fleetingly, half smiling.

I had to get going on the room set up, so I darted out. Chef's good mood surprised me, as he handed over a cheese platter and champagne on ice. "Keep your dirty paws off the plate," he said. "Oh, and pop the cork just before five."

"Got it." I lit the paper and stoked the kindling till the fire came to life, blistering fiercely. Let the old-fashioned radio warm up till I could focus on an easy listening station. Quarter of five, I picked up their lobster entrees and popped the bubbly, before disappearing back to the restaurant.

"Mindy, hey. Guess what?" She stood, perusing the reservation book, her face beaming.

"What?"

"I have tickets to "Under City Lights" tonight, at Aussie's. Thought we could go."

"I love that band. Great. What time?"

"Nine-thirty start. I'll wait for you if you're running late. And we'll walk together." She agreed.

Multiple room service deliveries kept me running all night. Most of the docs answered in their bathrobes and seemed unusually sparky. Some relaxed in bed with a cigarette. I made great tips. People became awfully generous, one gave thirty percent. My last room service called at nine o'clock, Ms. Malone. She yelled from the bathroom to leave the tray on the table, which I did. I could hear her bath water running. All sorts of toys spread across her bed and she had various boxes set aside and personally labeled, including one for Mrs. Butterfield. The toys were unusual. A feather duster. I guess for kids playing house. And a horse whip for their make-believe riding. I picked up a spiny rubbery thing, trying to figure out what it was. I turned it all directions. It had a motor. I switched the button and it jiggled around. Was it a futuristic toy car? I wondered how it worked. I carried it over to the toy chest, peering inside. There were boat paddles and various boxes labeled sleek, soft, easy to control. She also sold costumes with a bunch of holes throughout. But my mouth dropped open, as I spotted a package with a shocking photo on it, advertising different speeds and promoting zestiness. I abruptly released the prickly item I held and rubbed my hand fiercely on my pants. Eww…what had I touched? The bath water stopped running, so I scrammed.

I scurried to the men's room and did a thorough scrub. Sweet Ms. Malone? All those package deliveries, I thought. Wow. No wonder. Stupefied, I found Mindy in the restaurant. I wanted to share my findings with her on our walk to town but didn't know how to approach it. I fumbled around the intimacy subject, wanting to know why she'd cut me off this summer. But the words didn't form. If I broached it, she might think that was the only reason I dated her.

The whole gang, except Joan, scattered about the event— James, the Opossums, Riker, Chuckie, Tracy, and Sam. I held Mindy's hand as we squeezed through the crowd looking for seats. We found one place left at the bar, where I insisted Mindy sit while I stood beside her. The band played Bryan Adams's "In the Heat of The Night."

I shouted through the music. "Remember our last night in Boston when this song played on the radio? Wasn't that the best night ever?" I wanted to provoke memories, spending the night together. Mindy agreed with some hesitation.

"Stan, I need to talk to you about something." She grabbed my hand.

"Sure, anything. What's on your mind?"

"Well, you know how I feel about you." She looked intensely into my eyes as if a hatchet was coming my way. My chest beat with a thud.

"You really upset me that night in Boston."

"How? What'd I do?" Panic struck me as I tried to remember.

"You know."

"No. I don't. Tell me," I insisted.

"I shouldn't have to tell you. That's the point," she said.

Riker mysteriously appeared and wrapped his arm around Mindy. She dropped my hand. "Hey, doll," he said.

"Hey, Riker." She peeled his arm off.

The band moved from well-known artists to playing their original songs, but the music loudened, making it hard to have a conversation. We all nodded and shouted a few words of insignificance at one another. James huddled in, followed by Tracy and Sam. Tracy stepped back and let Sam sidle up.

The musicians took a break, but now there were too many people around for Mindy and me to finish our conversation. So we just continued our small talk until last call. I wanted desperately to walk Mindy back, but as she and Riker shared a house together, it didn't make sense. What started out a promising night ended in a lonely walk home, wondering what I'd done wrong in Boston.

CHAPTER TEN

I arrived back at the inn, slightly intoxicated, to find the Saudis chowing down a feast at one of the tables in the closed dining room. They had lobster, steak, cheese, dates, soup, cookies, and cake; even wine and a bottle of whisky sat at their table.

The man nodded when he noticed me, stood up and shook my hand, introducing himself as Kamal. His demeanor had changed, I first thought due to the food. Then I noticed Ms. Malone getting up to leave. Even his wife's eyes smiled. I couldn't really offer them anything, as the kitchen and bar were closed, so I politely vanished to my room. And they seemed sufficiently supplied with a banquet. I lay alone in my room with the enormous droning vibrating through my head. I started to wonder if it was coming from room thirty-six, Ms. Malone's room. I felt agitated. I thought about the missed opportunity to talk to Mindy and tried to figure out why she now kept me at a distance. I squashed the pillow over my head in hopes I'd silence my mind.

The night dissolved into another day on the job, this time at the front desk. Chuckie called in sick, so I subbed. Mrs. Lyncoff told me that she would be having another acoustical engineer by to analyze the sound. The first guy turned out to be a quack.

Mrs. Lyncoff retained Riker for the morning bellman shift. People came in off the street throughout the day inquiring about rates. Most walked out, but I managed to sell a few rooms. The phones periodically rang, but there came a brief flurry when I couldn't keep up. Some of the inquirers became impatient and angry over the wait time. Just hung up. But I could only multi-task so much. A lady from the chamber of commerce called. They're responsible for guiding tourists and recommending hotels and restaurants and things to do. She said The Maycliff's ratings were off the charts. They'd been flooded with calls asking about our property. She wanted to know what we were doing to make our guests so happy. But I couldn't answer that. I didn't know how to. And it might make us sound like a brothel. That would certainly get my ass fired if I started that rumor.

"Riker." He stood looking down at his shoes, shuffling his feet around. "Riker!"

"Huh?"

"You have a room-service delivery. Here." I handed him a piece of paper with the order. Room service requests were high. I rarely saw guests out anymore. Even the Thompsons and Bernsteins ordered up before they checked out. I found this annoying.

Mr. T slapped me another hefty Texas tip before he left. Ms. Malone checked out afterward. Riker helped her down with her big trunks that turned this place into a pleasure palace.

When Riker returned, I instructed him to polish the banister and vacuum the front area.

"Who said?"

"I said. The front desk is in charge of the bellmen."

I came out from behind the desk and stretched. Finally, Kamal and his wife left their room. They'd had their DO NOT DISTURB sign on all morning. Tracy couldn't get in any stayover rooms to clean. The couple sat peacefully on the terrace, catching glimpses at each other. Hummingbirds fluttered over the large stone planters, filled with pink petunias, their tiny beaks dipping in to pollinate. And white butterflies flittered about, more than usual.

I told Riker when he finished he needed to Windex all the outdoor tables and wipe down the cushions. Then chop some wood and kindling and stack it on the side.

"Hey, enough already," he said.

"Oh, and Mrs. Butterfield called down. She wants Pickering walked as soon as possible. And…I need a cranberry juice, please." I felt thirsty.

"Get your own juice."

"I can't leave the front desk."

"Well then, you'll have to wait, I guess," he said.

I nabbed Tracy as she swept by and asked her for a juice. She happily complied. It tasted good and cold, and I thoroughly enjoyed it until I chugged to the bottom and found I'd partially swallowed something slimy. I heaved the gruesome thing, engulfed in red, at a most inappropriate time, just as Mrs. Lyncoff passed. The shell-less snail hit her chest and dropped to the ground. Wet, dark cranberry remains stained her white blouse. My body heated as my mouth widened to speak, but nothing materialized.

"Stanley," she firmly stated.

"Yes, ma'am," I answered timidly. Tracy's smirk turned away to contain her laughter.

"What are you up to now?"

"I'm so sorry, Mrs. Lyncoff. I didn't know there was a snail in my drink. And I just reacted."

Her face laced with annoyance. "Clean it up."

"Yes, ma'am."

Mrs. Lyncoff walked away mumbling, "Just look at my blouse. I'm a mess." She twisted back and looked atop the desk. "And change those chrysanthemums to my china vase. You know I don't like that one."

What do I do about the vase? And how do I explain it was the cat? I'd have to think on it.

"Thanks, Tracy." She grinned. "I should have guessed you were up to something while you stood by watching me drink. You trying to get me fired?"

"No way," Tracy said. "Work would be dull."

"Now you owe me one for getting me in trouble."

"Anything," she said.

"Can you get me a list of chores you need done in your rooms, like lightbulbs out, loose fixtures, whatever? The longer, the better. Riker doesn't have enough to do around here."

"Oh, I see. Sure. Happy to help. I always keep a running list." She reached in her pocket. "But I'll draft a few more items." As she scribbled on her note pad, I observed through the window the new dishwasher guy chopping wood. Unbelievable. Riker makes the dishwasher do his work, while he stands watching and smoking a cigarette. We never could keep a dishwasher. They always quit. And Riker's probably why.

When lazy ass resurfaced, I handed over Tracy's list to keep him busy and save me from doing this stuff later. I followed up with a call to Chef to see if he needed anything. He said as a matter of fact he did. He wanted the reservation book and some condiments chopped. No problem, I told him. I started an additional list for Riker.

Check-ins started piling in all at once, four couples. I buzzed Riker to come back and assist with bags. He ran up and down the stairs, sweating. I also made him clean up the cranberry, which he assumed was a guest accident. I reminded him I couldn't leave the desk. I suited this role as a clerk.

"Hey Mindy." She walked in, looking for the reservation book, but I told her Chef already had it. "Great band last night, huh?"

"Yeah, it was."

"Hey, can we finish our conversation sometime?" I asked.

"Nah, let's just leave it. Doesn't really matter anymore," she said.

I wasn't sure if she meant it doesn't matter because she's changed her tune about me or it doesn't matter because she's let go of it. I hoped it was the latter but would anxiously have to wait it out. I just couldn't get my head around what I'd done wrong in Boston on such a perfect night. The words of the psychic reverberated through my mind, threatening personal challenges and scoffing that I had a girlfriend.

Mindy's face lit up. "Hi, Riker. You got up early this morning."

"Yeah, had to cover for Stan."

"That's because I had to cover for your friend, Chuckie," I piped in.

Riker ignored me and turned his attention back to Mindy. "You think you can steal me something to eat without Chef seeing? I'm starving."

"Sure," she said. "I'll see you later, Stan. Gotta get to work."

"Later, Sweetie." She gave me an inquisitive look. Guess I overstepped it but just wanted to mark my territory.

Riker followed. "Wait Riker. You need to..." Just as I was conjuring something up, Mrs. Butterfield descended the stairs. "Stanley, no one's come to walk Pickering yet."

"I'm sorry Mrs. Butterfield. Riker's right here."

He must have forgotten with all the chores I thrust upon him. He grabbed the dog and side-swiped the fountain, where James and his five and dime friend stood. Mrs. Butterfield and I looked on as James handed his buddy a coin. Jerry stood about fifteen feet from the splash pool, aiming precisely and repetitively before flicking his wrist. As his good luck charm danced in the water, he bounced up and down before thrusting his arms up in victory, closing with a high-five to James. Edged together, they shimmied through the screen door. Jerry announced he'd come in for a drink as he set a bag of candy in front of me. I peered in and counted five pieces as James greeted Mrs. Butterfield and offered her a cocktail. She said she'd be delighted. She'd just have a little nip. James coddled her, scooping her arm and pressing his cheek against hers as they strolled toward the bar.

I thanked Jerry for the candy. "No problem. We missed you today. Hiked up Cadillac Mountain. Found an intense trail, short and steep. We wanted you to come, but James said you had to work. What are you doing on the front desk?"

I told him I was filling in for Chuckie. He asked if I had a Band-Aid for his blister on his heel. I scouted the desk and drawers but nothing until I opened the cabinet below. There lay a big box that read Beets. What the hell?

"What?" Jerry asked.

"Oh nothing. What are beets doing under the desk?"

"Beats me," he said.

"Wow. A comedian." I opened the lid, expecting to find some missing beets, but the box had been turned into a first aid kit. I handed Jerry a Band-Aid and told him to scram.

"Whoa, I'm going. Thirsty anyway."

I suddenly felt the warmth of a body behind me, relieved someone arrived to take over, but I turned into empty space.

Norma called down, requesting I stay for the evening shift. I felt trapped. Chef descended upon me, reservation book in hand, showing me we only had a few slots left for dinner, to be careful committing to a time. We were short-staffed.

I fleetingly turned as a red Porsche 911 roared to a stop. Moments later, a voice bellowed from the doorway, greeting Chef as he walked by.

"Why, Mr. Thompson. You're back. Did you forget something?" I asked.

"No. Change of plans again," he said.

"Where's…?" I curtailed the wife question when I saw a petite frame, topped mustard-blonde hidden beside him.

I stared across at the stone statuette of the woman on the marble table, beside the stairs. Her eyes melded into her body in an eerie manor. But at the moment, it felt comforting.

"You going to check us in?" Mr. Thompson asked, not introducing his lady friend.

"Of course."

I fumbled about the papers, consumed with his quick turnaround. He'd just departed. I wondered where he left his wife and if she joined the Bernsteins alone in Martha's Vineyard, if he was getting divorced and this lady friend was his mistress. It couldn't be his sister, the way he wrapped his arm around her waist. My nerves rattled. An uneasy, weird sensation like I was somehow the screw-up here, the crazy one that wouldn't notice he wasn't with his wife. No one seemed to raise an eyebrow, except me. Not even Mrs. Lyncoff as she passed by and greeted them.

Kamal and his wife returned from dinner, as I handed Mr. Thompson the key. His chest opened like a flamingo as he offered his hand to Kamal, saying it was nice to see him again. Kamal raved about their meal to him. After not eating all day, they splurged. Now, they just wanted to lie down. First time I'd seen him open up so much. He expressed how much they enjoyed the sweet couple, Mindy and Riker. Found them entertaining, warm, and welcoming. I started to correct Kamal, tell him they weren't a couple. But Mr. Thompson spoke up, insisting their new friends join them for a drink. Kamal brushed off his fatigue and eagerly complied.

Joan arrived early and relieved me of duty. I parked Mr. Thompson's awesome rental, careful not to ding it. Then checked on the restaurant looking for Mindy, but it had closed early. No late reservations, I guess. Chef still hung around, looking at stock. Didn't seem to notice me. I joined James at the bar, where a beer awaited me. Mr. Thompson's buoyant voice inquired about oil reserves in the Middle East. Kamal's reply sounded analytical and drawn out. Mr. Thompson leaned closer. Their conversation moved to a whisper, their focus unbreakable till Mr. Thompson motioned for another round. Chef joined at the bar for a glass of red wine. His even temper gave me a break, allowing a toast between us. I asked him if he'd seen Mindy. He said she and Riker left early tonight. One of the waitresses closed up.

CHAPTER ELEVEN

Riker had the morning shift, an opportunity for me to sleep in. But I couldn't. Hadn't actually slept all night because of the droning, inside and out. I grabbed a coffee in the kitchen, jumped back onto the serving counter, legs dangling. Chef barged in and asked what I was doing. Just leaving, I said. I hopped down. As I started out the door, he praised my spreading out the restaurant reservations nicely. He'd mentioned it last night. Said most front desk clerks mess it up. Normally, that would have lifted my day.

"Hey, can you help me with a few things?" Chef asked.

"Well I'm not working. But sure. What do you need?"

"A big delivery just came out back and I need the food put away."

"No problem." I shrugged.

I carried box after box and plonked them down on the kitchen counter.

"Chef?"

"Yes?" His Quebec accent sounded so formal.

"I probably shouldn't ask this. But do you ever talk to Steve's parents? I was wondering how they were doing."

"His mother passed away a few months after he did. Maybe it was the broken heart, maybe the alcohol, or a combination. His dad is struggling."

The boxes felt heavier to me now, my legs suddenly weak. If the roles were reversed, how would my parents have handled the news? For a brief moment, I wished to be home.

"I'm sorry about your wife," I said. "Steve told me about the cancer last summer."

"Thanks, Stan. It's been tough. She was a great lady."

I cleared the last of the boxes and asked Chef if there was anything else before I headed to town to find Mindy. I knocked on the big, dilapidated door until she answered and asked if we could talk. I told her what Chef and Kamal said last night.

"Stan, you have to stop this. It's insane. I told you before there's nothing going on. We're just friends. We share the same house. I knew him last year. If I wanted to be with him, I would. I love you."

At that moment, I pulled her close, holding her head between my hands. "I'm sorry. Forgive me. I must be overworked and not thinking straight. I just worry about you." Her hand led me to the bedroom. My guard down, I felt free of all inhibitions, ready for this moment. Passion filtered through my every vessel. The beat of my heart ran loud and fast. I was lost in it. But then, she abruptly stopped. And just wanted to be cuddled. It's not that I didn't want to hold her, because I did. But why was she tormenting me like this? Pulling me close then pushing me away. Teasing me. And how come every other person at the inn had it so easy, got lucky? I lay on my back, one arm wrapped around her, rapidly jolting my knees, staring at the ceiling.

Beneath a blanket of white, we sauntered back to the inn. I held Mindy's waist to keep her warm and close, stealing pecks along the way.

Chuckie greeted us as Mindy grabbed the reservation book, squeezed my hand and headed to the restaurant.

"Glad you're back. It turned into a long day yesterday," I said.

"I had a bad head cold. Better now," Chuckie said.

A man skipped a penny into the pond before bursting through the screen door, taking off his ball-cap and tossing down his overstuffed bag. "Oi mate. Where's a thirsty man get a beer 'round here?"

"Around the corner in the Pine Room. It's our bar and lounge," Chuckie said.

"First I gotta check in." His eyes surveyed the area. "This place is a beaut."

"Stan can show you to your room and take your bag, Mr..."

"Name's Simon. No Mister, please. Nah thanks, I'll drop it myself." He signed the papers and shot up the stairs.

Kamal and his wife sat with Chef reviewing the menu for the upcoming days. Their family would be arriving this evening in time for the four days of Eid, the sacrificial feast. Festivities would begin in the morning. Eid, he explained, was the celebration at the end of Ramadan. They would have a call to prayer five times a day and specific food served throughout. They spoke of beef, kabobs, fried liver, something called Sheer Khurma, rice dishes, sweets, dates, and a variety of sodas. Eid, I overheard him, was the most important of all the Muslim celebrations.

Simon, already down from his room, towered over the three, acknowledging them with G'day and a nod as he passed. A look of bewilderment stained Kamal's face as the man from downunder shimmied up to the bar. James passed him a beer. I stood restocking bar glasses.

"You from Australia?" James asked.

"Nah, mate. I live in Sydney, Australia. But I'm from New Zealand." He chugged his beer. "So, what's a bloke to do 'round here for fun? I have a couple of days before I start work," Simon said.

"Well, there's loads. Depends what you're looking for," James said.

"Adventure."

"Okay. There's bungee jumping, hang-gliding, hiking to the top of Cadillac Mountain, swimming in the Atlantic. That'll get your blood thinned quickly with the frigid water."

"I think I'll steer clear of the ocean. Got stung by a bluey a few months back," Simon boasted.

"What's a bluey?" James asked.

"Bluebottle Jellyfish. The little bugger nabbed me at Bondi Beach. The toxic mixture shoots through your body and stings like a mother."

"That sounds dangerous," I fused in.

"Bloody right. But there's far worse. The Box Jellyfish paralyses and affects breathing. A mate of mine had a heart attack from one. Bloke nearly died. The Eastern Brown snake paralyses too and causes unstoppable bleeding. Then we have the Funnel Web, a male spider with a fatal bite. Have to watch they aren't hidin' in your shoes. Can't leave them outside. We've got the Bull Shark, crocodiles, and all sorts of good creatures."

"Jeez," James said.

"I'd like to go there one day but sounds risky," I said.

"Nah, you just learn what to look out for," the kiwi confided. He nodded to James. "I'll take another."

"Absolutely." James offered him a bar menu, but he waved it off.

I was buzzed to the front desk, as the pack of Saudi relatives arrived, all in either black or white, the women fully covered. Even the children wore the traditional dress. The women and children stood off to one side across the hall. I guessed about thirty in the group.

I escorted one family up the stairs, carrying a heavy load of bags. The dishdasha-clothed man followed, with his wife and several children many steps beneath. The man showed respect as I told him about the inn. I echoed the same with the rest of the family.

Pickering jaunted past, down the stairs. I turned to look for Mrs. Butterfield, but she wasn't around. It appeared Pickering took a little stroll on his own. Chuckie called him over and picked him up. While Mrs. Butterfield napped, Chuckie agreed to dog sit. His idea of overseeing the dog was delegating to me, starting with a walk. Pickering changed back to his old ways, growling at the sight of me. He'd already forgotten how I saved him from the beets and resuscitated his lifeless body. Narrowly out the front door, he decided to stop and take a dump. I tried pulling his leash, but he wouldn't budge.

"Stanley!" I heard a shout. Mrs. Lyncoff stood just inside the screen door, hands on hips, lip curling.

***

Two separate prayer rooms had been established. The men kneeled in the parlor and the women and children in a guest room booked especially for their holy time. Following their hour of prayer, they resided in the restaurant for a special feast. Simon passed through in shorts and a t-shirt, camera wrapped around his neck. One of the waitresses offered him a seat, but he declined.

"Having a dingo's breakfast this morning. Going on a hike," the kiwi responded.

"Dingo's breakfast?" she questioned.

"A yawn, a leak, and a good look 'round. G'day."

As Simon swept out the door, the Opossum family arrived for Sunday brunch and Bloody Marys. Mrs. Lyncoff shot her scathing look at me.

Chuckie called me over to escort Mrs. Butterfield down from her room, while Riker pulled up the van to take her to the airport.

"We're sorry to see you go, Mrs. Butterfield," Chuckie announced.

"Thanks, dearie. Well, I'd like to return this year in the fall. Let's book something now." I waited as Chuckie made the arrangements. I'll bet she was returning to see Mr. Mac. They seemed to enjoy their dinner. Simon stood chatting with Mr. Thompson on the front drive before the kiwi slapped him on the back and shook his hand. I bid Mrs. Butterfield goodbye. Her healthy tip remedied all the trouble her little varmint caused me. My eyes darted to Mr. Thompson's red hot-rod peeling up the drive.

Seeing Riker reminded me I needed to move up. Now that Mindy was maître d', a position I would have liked, I had to pick something else. I could see myself on the front desk, doing a better job than Chuckie. I decided I needed to shine whenever filling in for him, especially when Mrs. Lyncoff came around.

"Hey Stan." Sam looked away. "Tracy wants to see you when you get a chance. She's in the linen closet."

"What's it about?"

"Not sure," she mumbled.

"Kay. I'll be there in a minute."

But I didn't plan to go see Tracy, because I knew what it was about. I'd hung posters of naked men all over her linen closet last night, and placed the blow-up she'd given me in a rather disrespectful position, involving a big beet. She sent her minion, Sam, to lure me into some trap of her own. No way I'd fall for that. I'd just pretend I got sidetracked.

An array of dishes swept along the extended Sunday brunch table—Chef's famous clam chowder, lobster thermidor, beef brisket, and lemon dill chicken all aligned in chafing dishes. Various salads, cheeses, fruit, and streams of devilish desserts, like crème brûlée and blueberry pie dressed the end of the banquet table.

James worked the bar, pumping out Mimosas. Kamal stepped outside the festivities to have James slip a little whisky in his coke. They spoke loudly, half in English and half in Arabic, about the hajj in Mecca, who had traveled there already and who planned a future journey. Kamal quickly downed his coke and raised his finger for me to approach. He placed his arm around my shoulders.

"Stan, have you ever heard of the hajj in Mecca?"

"No, sir. I haven't."

"It's an annual Islamic Pilgrimage to the most holy Muslim city, Mecca. A religious mandate that all Muslims must carry out at least once in their lifetime. We must make the journey to Mecca."

"Have you done that?" I asked.

"No, I plan to in the next few years." He looked up to the skies then back at me. "Do me a favor and keep my drink refilled."

"Absolutely," I said.

The Opossum family had finished brunch and moved to the bar. James told jokes, which kept them laughing. Then he moved to charades. "Hey Stan, you do one," he said. "We're doing movies."

"Nah."

"Come on," he coaxed. "Don't be a drag."

I reluctantly decided to do *A Fish Called Wanda*. I held my nose and shimmied up and down, swimming with my right arm, until Mrs. Lyncoff caught me and pulled me into her office.

"Stanley, just what do you think you're doing, horsing around at the bar with those unscrupulous guests? We have a full house."

"I'm sorry. They asked me to join in. And I tried not to, but they insisted. And…"

She swept her finger left to right to silence me. "I've heard enough. You have to up your game. You're slipping again."

"Yes, ma'am," I shrugged as I removed myself from her icy chair.

Mr. Thompson had just pulled his Porsche up front and asked me to park it as he and his lady friend ripped up the stairs to their room. I slipped in. It felt good. I slowly put pressure on the peddle, didn't want to zoom off. Eased around the circle and carefully into a wide spot. Couldn't let anything scratch this baby. I kept admiring the ruby as I backed away.

James tried to grab me again, but I refused. Said he'd gotten me in enough trouble already. He told me not to worry. Seemed Mrs. L liked to act tough as old boots. They continued with their charades as Kamal brushed in and placed his empty glass on the bar.

"We're going to salah, prayer that is. We'll be back." The group of bodies draped in white led the way, with a formation in black following a healthy distance behind with children.

Simon plonked himself down at the bar. "How ya goin'?" he addressed the Opossums. "I'll take a coldie please, James."

"Coming up. How was your hike?" James asked.

"Crickey, it was great. Outstanding views at the peak."

Simon had the Opossums mesmerized with his stories, first about the bluey then how he once fought off a crocodile. How he got himself lost in the bush a few years back and had to survive on berries and bugs till he found his way out.

Beer Gut told his version of heroism, how he once ran into a black bear in the woods. Could have lost his life. Had to navigate his way around the bear, raise his arms and pretend he was big, till the bear ran the other way.

"No way. You've got to be kidding," James piped in. "Those are the smallest, most docile bears around. They wouldn't harm a flea."

That shut Beer Gut down. Piercings slapped her friend on the back and called him a fool. Their tattoo buddy grinned.

Simon laughed. "I'm just messin' with you. I'm no Crocodile Dundee. But I did get stung by a bluey. I grew up mostly around sheep in New Zealand, where there's more of them than us. There's an old Kiwi saying, 'Where men are men and sheep are scared.' And you don't want to know what that means. Not my lifestyle, I assure you. Even if sheep were the last ones on earth."

I excused myself to assist the second acoustical engineer, which reminded Simon what a bad sleep he had. Said it sounded like a loud generator going all night. He joked we must be doing something illegal down by the water. The second sound guy did much the same as the first, leaving with a similar puzzled look after assessing the situation for two hours. He'd get back to Mrs. Lyncoff as soon as possible.

***

As the season picked up, Riker and I started overlapping our shifts to keep up with the busyness. I decided to offer Chuckie a break on the desk, brush up on my skills. He looked stunned when I asked. Normally he had to hunt me down. I'd make sure Mrs. Lyncoff noticed me, and when the time lay right, I'd march into her office and ask for the job. Mindy would be thrilled.

Norma appeared with a plateful of cookies and offered me one. "These are from Mr. Mac. A token of appreciation to the staff," she said. A really nice gesture, I first thought. I didn't realize he noticed what we did, but maybe he was trying to butter up the staff he'd be taking over if he was indeed going to turn this into a Holiday Inn. Norma stood munching on a cookie as she offered some to passersby. I spoke exceptionally loud and embellished politeness to guests. Norma had ears and a voice with boundless influence.

Kamal swept by, leading the trailing group back to the feast and festivities of Eid. Norma graciously acknowledged them and continued through the inn on behalf of Mr. Mac's own mission of thanks.

"Hey, Mindy." My eyes grew wide. I held the reservation book toward her. She grabbed my hand slightly and retracted with an air kiss. I decided now would be a good time to share my plans with her about moving to front desk clerk. She thought that a great idea and encouraged me to do so. Said I'd be perfect for it. Raised voices from the bar bellowed through the inn as we stared out the window.

Riker stood outside, talking to Chuckie and having a smoke. He took his time finishing his cigarette then dropped it and grounded the butt with his toe, leaving it. A pack of crows danced above the hazy day, their irritating screeches relentless. I remained fixated, imagining a scene from Alfred Hitchcock's *The Birds*. I waited for the ravens to dive in on them. And suddenly, one did. My adrenaline shot up, eyes widened. It plunged hard and I focused in anticipation as it went straight for the cigarette butt, picked it up, then dropped it. Those guys didn't even flinch. Disenchanted, I observed Chuckie grab a coin out of his pocket, set it on his fist, and flick his thumb up, admiring the copper belly flop into the water.

I wanted to stall them. Mrs. Lyncoff often passed by on her way for tea this time of day, and two guests had just walked up to the desk. But Chuckie sideswiped me, taking over. I wedged my way under the stairwell, blank expression. Mrs. Lyncoff patrolled by just as Riker escorted some guests to their room, entertaining them to laughter. Mindy looked on.

"Stanley?" My eyes remained attentive. "The vase."

CHAPTER TWELVE

The parade remained a big deal in this little town, July fourth. Mrs. Lyncoff had designed a Maycliff float, which Riker built. He didn't want to go on it though, so I took his place. He preferred to drive the truck that pulled the float. A small table dressed in fancy white linen set the stage with fresh flowers, a candle-looking light and red wine glasses. All glued down, so they didn't slide. Mindy played the diner and I the waiter. The backdrop of the float resembled a bookshelf and fireplace, with an oversized comfy chair. Mrs. Lyncoff insisted we bring Mr. Mac for the ride. He could be a guest of the inn sitting in the chair, sipping on tea. I'm not sure he wanted to be a part of it, but he agreed. Glued paintings of waves and boats with big, bold The Maycliff Inn signs surrounded the float. Nat King Cole's "Mona Lisa" played on the hidden portable tape deck.

I bought a white button down earlier in the week and threw on my black bellman pants. The restaurant lent me a bow tie. This felt uplifting. The four of us headed down early to get in line. The town flooded with tourists and locals standing outside their stores and restaurants, beaming with pride. Foldable chairs lined the streets. The production a little more involved than the old car show.

Mindy dressed up, hair high and immaculate. Her costume earrings and necklace sparkled against her fuchsia formal, appearing as an elite guest. Her striking red lipstick pronounced. I held out a tray as if to serve her lobster, fake of course. It lay on a bed of seaweed for presentation. We grinned and had some fun with this, as we strolled through town, the crowd cheering. Every so often, Mindy and I would throw silver-wrapped Hershey chocolate kisses into the crowd. The spectators loved it, hands in the air trying to catch them. Riker jolted when driving, because the Coconut float in front, which carried one enormous coconut, kept swiftly braking. The large fruit appeared wobbly, as if it might fall. But we reshuffled and managed to keep our balance. I could hear Jerry, James and the Opossum family shout out as we passed the five and dime. We threw a handful of chocolates their way, extra hard. Grabbing them from the ground, they fired back at us, one hitting Mr. Mac on the forehead.

"You okay, Mr. Mac?" I asked. He insisted he was fine, and threw the sweet back into the crowd. Beer Gut tried to hit us with a few water balloons. But he missed and hit an onlooker, who seemed rather perturbed.

Kids on bicycles trailed behind us, ringing their handlebar bells. Some had wagons trailing behind, with their own little homemade float. One little girl had a beach scene with Barbie dolls. A young boy had rockets, dirt, and planes. Occasionally, we'd fling a few chocolates back, but they'd get too excited trying to catch them and nearly fall off their bikes. I peered at the policeman's float behind the kids on bikes. They danced to Reggae, draped with shell necklaces and straw hats over their uniforms. The town's fire truck trailed behind, blasting their horn. I could see Bert's Lobster Pound float turn a corner ahead, with Mo shaking her stuff. Bert just sat there, on the edge of a big claw, not waving or anything.

Sam rested on Tracy's shoulders, flapping her arms, sandwiched snuggly amongst the crowd. Their spot too far away to hear their chants. Blowers hailed, confetti tossed, candies spewed. All kinds of music played at once. Screams of joy and praise dominated the scene. People clapped, dogs barked, kids cried. The scene made up of everything a small town was about.

Riker jerked the damn float, I think on purpose. My left leg rose and right arm shot out, struggling to keep balance, but I couldn't gain control. The lobster darted off the plate and shot into the crowd, striking Mindy's coifed hair on its venture, leaving only the seaweed to dress her deflated do. At this point, the parade could not end fast enough. She grabbed the slimy substance in one big scoop and threw it at me hard. I took the hit, because I knew things would be far worse if I dodged it. She looked the other way the rest of the trip, arms folded. Mr. Mac clearly enjoyed our unrehearsed episode. I could sense a gleam in his approving eyes and devilish grin.

Back at the inn, there was no time to dismantle the float. We had to get to work. Mr. Mac dozed off in his lounge chair. It must have been a long day for him.

"You going to the fireworks tonight?" Chuckie asked guests checking in. They arranged to have dinner in town, then head to the pier to watch the show. Chuckie shared, he and some workmates planned a picnic in the park under the fireworks.

When the guests dispersed, I asked Chuckie who planned on going to the picnic. I hadn't thought about evening arrangements. He said a bunch of them, like Riker, James, Mindy, Tracy, Jerry, and a few others in town.

Why hadn't I heard about this? No one mentioned it to me. Maybe they assumed I knew. I told Chuckie I'd be joining as soon as I got off shift. I left the front desk and found Mindy in the restaurant. Her pissy mood only slightly subdued, she said she thought I'd heard about the evening's plans. Chuckie organized it and Riker had been telling everyone. She asked Norma to replace her early this evening. Although Norma generally worked days, handling conferences, she occasionally enjoyed filling in evenings to suss what went on. I offered to walk Mindy to town if I got off in time. She shrugged.

I caught up with James. He griped he couldn't meet the gang till after the fireworks. He had to bartend till ten. We'd walk together if I couldn't go earlier with Mindy. As it turned out, I couldn't. Jerry met us along the way, big bagful of candy in hand. Although we missed the show, the group still huddled around the picnic blanket. I sat between Mindy and Riker, making Riker shove over. He pushed into Sam, which annoyed her. Tracy put her arm around Sam and told her not to worry. I grabbed a few beers from the ice chest and handed one to James and Jerry, slugging the other down myself. Jerry opened his bag of candy and passed it around.

Riker nodded as he unwrapped the handkerchief he pulled from his pocket and shoved a wad of tobacco in his gums. Then passed it to Chuckie.

Although the fireworks had long ended, Simon appeared in the distance, dangling a brown bagged bottle. He stopped short of our blanket. "Heya mates." And took a swig from the paper bag. "Mind if I join you lot?"

"No, not at all," Chuckie cackled. "Glad you could make it. Didn't think you would." Chuckie had apparently invited Simon to our gathering.

"What's goin' on with that creepy inn?" Simon asked.

"What do you mean?" I asked.

"I put my shoes by the bedside last night, crawled in for a kip, and when I woke, my thongs were by the door facing out, as if someone was asking me to leave. And I swear I didn't do it. And no one else could have."

"That's weird," I said.

"Yeah, freaked me out."

I filled Simon in on the Mary stories, the friendly ghost that remained in the inn but had no plans of harming anyone. Maybe not he said, but clearly she wanted him out of there. Tracy piped in and said Mary particularly favored his room, eleven.

"Maybe I should switch rooms. I pushed my thongs to the side and peered out the door. It was nearly midnight and there stood a man, staring out the window. I called to the bloke to make sure he was okay but nothing. Crikey."

"That had to be Mr. Mac," I said. "He's a little different."

Simon swigged down the last of his drink, jolting the bottle upside down in his mouth to make sure he got every last drop. Asked about a pub to get a pint. Aussies stood across the street, so we ventured over. "Under City Lights" played their rendition of Bon Jovi's "You Give Love A Bad Name." No cover, because it was late enough in the evening. A crowd jammed together dancing in front of the band. Mr. Thompson and his lady sat wedged at the end of the bar. He raised his glass and nodded us over.

The song ended and the crowd on the dance floor dismantled, focusing their attention toward the door. Only a clumsy glass fleetingly shattered the stillness. Kamal stretched by the entryway, arms lifted up and out as he proceeded in, his wife behind. The room remained breathless, till the band started up again. Simon approached them and insisted they join us.

"My friends," Kamal politely greeted us.

Eyes of the room devoured us, even though the noise level had risen.

Mr. Thompson lifted his hand from his lady's knee and rose. "Kamal. Nice to see you again."

"Likewise, my friend."

"Can I get you a whiskey?" Mr. Thompson asked.

"Please." Kamal nodded. He turned to Simon. "And you my friend, where are you from, Australia?"

"No, mate. I'm no Aussie," the kiwi hastily corrected. "I'm from Auckland."

"Hmm," Kamal nodded. "I've never been to what you people call down under. Perhaps I will visit there one day."

Simon asked Kamal what attracted his group all the way to Maine. He said his uncle had a recent cataract operation in New York, and they came to be with him. Said he's still in recovery and must return to New York for more tests before heading home. The family must stay together at Eid, celebrate and pray with loved ones. Simon discreetly asked how many wives he had. Kamal said just the one, who'd be producing a boy in winter. He had no intention of marrying another at the moment. He shared his brother had four, all of whom must be treated equally, no favoritism. That gets expensive. His wife's eyes remained steady.

"Good god, I couldn't handle the one Shelia. Divorced her years back. Your brother's a strong man, Kamal." Simon slapped him on the back, slammed down his drink and motioned for another.

Riker approached Mindy and asked her for a dance.

"No, we're just going up there," I interrupted.

"Good on ya," Simon said, stealing my seat as I rose.

I didn't really like to dance, but I pulled Mindy off her stool and onto the floor. She looked like a great dancer, well balanced, rhythmic. I felt a little awkward but figured people were drunk enough by now they wouldn't notice. Thankfully a slow song came on. This would bring us closer, maybe jog some memories of hers. Entice her to get chummy.

The bartender appeared to motion me over. I looked around and back at him. He kept swirling his arm. I grabbed Mindy's hand and headed to the bar.

"You want me?"

"Yeah, you have a call."

"How do you know it's for me?" I asked.

"She described you."

Described me how? And who'd be calling me here? It was Mrs. Lyncoff. Joan felt too sick to stay for her night audit shift, so she desperately needed me to fill in. I didn't want to leave.

"Maybe I should walk you home first," I suggested.

"No, that's okay. You'd better just go. Mrs. Lyncoff sounds in a panic from what you said."

"I'll walk her home," Riker offered.

I could tell Mindy wanted to stay and looked at me for approval. And Riker coaxed her on.

"Do what you want," I said. She excitedly pecked my lips and thanked me.

On the way home, I kept thinking how irritating Riker was. He acted like a hot-shot. "You have a black shadow hovering over you," echoed through my mind. That damn psychic.

Joan anxiously awaited my arrival, halfway out the door already. She hadn't joined us, because she wasn't much for fireworks, so she offered to cover Chuckie's shift. But she felt a bad bug coming on, couldn't stay for night audit. Just said

Mrs. Lyncoff asked to clean up after Kamal and his family finished. Take care of the dishes and food and make sure the area returned presentable for breakfast. She couldn't have been that sick, because she stopped to worship what she probably hoped was the fountain of youth, tossing her good fortune. Little did she know it wouldn't help.

The humming noise had ramped up, but the sound muffled by the Saudi group who remained in the lounge—mingling, laughing, and eating. Although I couldn't understand much of what they said, mostly talking in Arabic now, it was obvious they were having a good time. One of them motioned me over and asked in English to bring more sodas and another cheese platter with fruit. I wasn't supposed to go digging through the kitchen but didn't want to refuse either. I scrounged around till I could put a platter together, presentable enough to serve. Another asked me for a cup of tea, which sent a frenzy of requests for the warm concoction. Lemon, honey, brown sugar, mint, chamomile. Everyone liked it a certain way. I despised tea drinkers. Too much work with all the choices of tea and condiments on the side, tea pots, cups, and saucers. All that stuff. Coffee drinkers were simple. Regular or decaf, cream and sugar.

Kamal and his wife snuck through the back and down the hall with Mr. Thompson and Simon. I wished them a nice evening and hoped they'd enjoyed their time in town.

Kamal shushed me with his finger to his lips. "Stanley, please bring me a refreshment."

"Umm…I'm not supposed to serve liquor after one a.m.," I said. "It's the law."

His eyes squinted in seriousness, before he joined the gathering. Mr. Thompson also requested a drink for himself and Simon. They'd be at the bar. His lady friend must have gone to bed.

Well, I guess no one's to know. I can ring it in tomorrow. I served Kamal his usual and his wife a coke. One of his group asked me to pass food around. And several requested cold sodas or more hot tea. Kamal formed a pathway to the bar to replenish. I heard him telling Mr. Thompson he ran one of the largest development companies in Saudi. They seemed to enjoy each other's company. I retrieved more cakes and cleared whatever dishes I could as I went along. Last I remember glancing at the clock, it read 3:30 a.m.

I awoke to Mrs. Lyncoff's voice praising Riker for a job well done. At first, I thought I was dreaming. Riker stood behind the desk, giving a guest directions. I must have fallen asleep in one of the lounge chairs. I rubbed my eyes and looked around. The room stood a mess with dirty dishes, tea cups, coke cans, withered cheese, and dried-out meats. Breakfast would start in thirty minutes, as the wait staff scurried to clean up and set tables.

Mrs. Lyncoff pulled me aside and scolded me for not complying with her orders. I tried to explain what all went on, but she just swiped her finger left to right. I looked up at Riker and what was to be my next job and shrugged. Chuckie bounced in and relieved Riker of duty.

Mrs. Lyncoff danced by them. "Good teamwork." Chuckie gleamed. Riker gloated. I cringed.

I shuffled toward the kitchen, heading to my room for sleep. Light penetrated through the window catching my eye. I looked closer at the streak across the lawn. Simon lay sprawled on his back, hands behind head and binder by his side, soaking in the rays.

Chef intercepted and summoned me to help with a set up. Although dreary, I obeyed, trailing him back to the kitchen.

A small conference, Pfizal Chemical, had returned. They came every year, arriving last night before Joan escaped her shift. They liked to bring up their own bags. Therefore, Mrs. Lyncoff didn't schedule a bellman. Their first meeting was early this morning and Chef needed Riker and me to set up. Just as Steve and I always did, we ran to the dark, musty basement and carried the tables up the stairs, covering them with white linens, pads and pencils. I reluctantly tried to strike a conversation with Riker, but he seemed pissed off.

I found out later through James, who heard from Chuckie, that Riker couldn't stand pharmaceutical companies, because his father was addicted to prescription drugs for years. It changed his whole personality and most likely contributed to his early death. Said those companies push drugs at any cost. The more dependent on their drugs, the more cash in their greedy pockets. They con doctors into believing in their drugs, so they prescribe them to patients. And they purposely promote paranoia through advertising, making you believe you have an ailment, just so you buy their product. According to James, Chuckie griped, "It was a full house win for those scoundrels, making them filthy rich, while the rest of us sorry souls become psychotic and broke."

A tawny brunette with tortoise-shell glasses stood behind the front desk when I walked in the door. Her high ponytail bounced as she nodded at Chuckie's blathering. She turned her head and grinned at me warmly. I froze. I knew I didn't know her, but for some reason, I was very happy to see her.

The girl turned back to Chuckie's bumbling while Riker looked on. She was obviously the new clerk. Would this mean Chuckie wouldn't need me to cover so much? I wanted that position. If I'd known Mrs. Lyncoff planned to hire another clerk, I would have asked for the job. She could have hired a new bellman, instead.

I noticed Mr. Mac struggling down the stairs, nearly tripping. I leapt over a number of steps to reach him quickly, while Riker raced past us to a guest walking out with a suitcase. Riker nearly knocked us both to the ground to get to the departing guest, hungry for a tip.

"I've got you, Mr. Mac," I said. "Take it easy. One step at a time." I kept my arm wrapped around his, and we slowly descended the stairs.

"You're a good boy, Stan. Thank you."

"My pleasure," I said.

As we reached the bottom, Mr. Mac asked who the lovely young lady was. The new girl seemed to be watching us and flashed an intriguing smile against her bronzed frame.

"I'd like to meet her," he said. I walked him over to the desk.

"Mr. Mac," he said, holding out his hand.

"A pleasure to meet you." She reached back. "I'm Juliette."

"Your eyes are the color of the most brilliant day. Unique and perfect." He winked.

"Thank you," she said faintly.

"I'm Stan." I reached my hand out to receive a gentle squeeze back.

"Nice to meet you, too, Stan."

Riker walked back in, shoving a wad of ones into his pocket. Juliette briefly looked at him then back at me. She seemed swallowed up next to Chuckie. I knew the season lay in full swing, and the desk had become hectic, hard for one person to handle at prime time. And while I desperately wanted the position, Juliette seemed to fit the roll in every way. She even looked like a Juliette.

CHAPTER THIRTEEN

I picked some flowers from the garden and caught Mindy up the drive as she walked down for work. "For you," I said. Her eyes brightened as she excitedly thanked me.

"What's this for?" she asked.

"Just cause," I said.

I steered her to a big rock on the side of the drive, hidden behind a tree and put my arm around her.

"I'm just happy we're together again this summer," I said.

"Me too." She leaned her head on my chest. I squeezed tighter.

"You know. We should camp out one night, since the weather's warmed up. Jerry has sleeping bags and a tent we can borrow. Just the two of us. Sound good?"

"Sounds great. We'll just have to figure out a time when we're not working too late or have to be in so early. But it might be more fun to get a group of us to go."

The sound of a motorcycle squealing around the corner broke the moment. I looked up to find Riker peeling down the drive. He hadn't seen us. We agreed we'd better get to work. I held Mindy's hand the whole way down the drive and she stayed close.

Before we parted ways and she headed to the restaurant, she squeezed my hand firmly. I squeezed hers back.

I checked on James at the bar to find Riker standing in front of Jerry, pushing his finger at Jerry's chest, calling him a no-good squirt.

"What's going on?" I asked.

"Nothing. He's just a wuss. I tried to grab a piece of candy out of his bag, and he closed it. Jerk."

"Leave him alone," James said.

"Oh, the other squirt is going to defend this guy?"

"Back off, Riker," I said.

Riker stuck his face in mine. Held his arm up as if he was going to pummel me. I stood still, although tense inside. I didn't want to fight this guy. But if he hit me, that would only make him look bad to Mindy. We heard Mrs. Lyncoff's voice coming.

Riker implanted his face closer into mine. "You'll never get that front desk job."

Stunned, I said nothing. He glared into my eyes for one last jab before backing off and barging out the door. I couldn't believe what I'd heard.

A towering man stood pacing at the front, in the spotlight of the afternoon sun. Mrs. Lyncoff galloped down the steps and outside. She must have pulled him elsewhere, because I lost view. What was that about?

Norma descended, focusing on a lady at the front desk. "Good afternoon. I'm Norma. So nice to finally meet you and have your group stay with us. We're delighted. I see Juliette and Chuckie have taken care of your check in. This is Stan. He'll be assisting you with your bags." The guest returned the cordial remarks.

I escorted the lady officer, in full uniform, to her room. She'd organized the team of police officers for the conference.

They drove in from Rhode Island. Newport. Gun on hip, her no-nonsense walk followed beside me. Riker remained on duty as well and between the two of us, we assisted all the officers to their rooms. Eleven of them. Tracy had just exited the lady officer's room and nudged me as we passed. I hoped she hadn't rigged anything.

The lady officer wasn't long in her room before she returned to the front. The tall man who had spoken with Mrs. Lyncoff earlier plunged through the front door, shouting at the lady officer in charge. Mrs. Lyncoff raced onto the scene at the same time Chef bolted from the kitchen and Mindy from the dining room. Everyone's face froze in observation.

"What are you doing here, Joe?" The lady officer jolted.

"I warned you not to leave me," he said.

"I didn't want to, but…but I had no choice."

Chuckie started to reach for the phone. "Don't touch that," he said, noticing Chuckie from the corner of his eye. Chuckie carefully put the phone down.

Riker walked in the front door and didn't flinch.

"You had a choice all right. Twenty years and this is what I get? I lost my badge because of you. My child. And you just move on as if it means nothing? What the hell's gotten into you anyway? You seeing someone?"

"No, Joe. Now please, just calm down." She motioned her hand gently downward as anger sieged his face.

"Joe, if you want to talk, let's go outside."

My body was now an inferno. I couldn't tell if he held a gun. Riker tried to interrupt like a tough guy, but the disgruntled man held his hand out not to come any closer. Mrs. Lyncoff wouldn't have anything of it. She warned that he either leave immediately or she'd have him escorted off the premises. He continued shouting profanity at his ex, his face disdained. In a jack rabbit instance, Riker hopped the guy she called Joe and smashed him to the floor, his concrete load pinning him face down. Riker's forearm pressed against the back of Joe's neck. He tried to roll his body side to side and free himself. He used momentum to flip himself over as Riker grabbed him in a headlock. He jabbed Riker in the gut, enough to clear himself. Joe started to rise when two cops bolted in the room, grabbed him from behind, and restrained him.

"Just calm down," one of the cops said.

"Get off," the man shouted. "I'm fine. I'll leave."

The cops slowly and carefully released their grip. The man stared at his ex and staggered toward the door. "You're going to regret this," he said before the door pushed open.

Mindy ran to Riker and helped him up, kissing him on the lips in front of everyone and wrapping her arms around him snuggly.

"You could have been badly hurt," she said.

My body went numb and my thoughts blank. I couldn't look away, although I tried.

Juliette looked shook up. It was only her second day on the job and she was subjected to this.

"You okay?" I asked.

"I guess so," she said, as she curled herself into me for protection. Although I felt listless, I held her firmly, Mindy looking on.

"It's all right. This isn't our normal everyday appearance." I tried to cheer her up with some humor.

"I hope not," Juliette said.

Mindy uncoiled herself from Riker. Her face frowned my way before walking off. I held Juliette a bit longer until she felt ready to be released. She quietly thanked me.

The lady cop, highly apologetic, uncomfortably slipped into a lounge chair next to some fellow officers. They spoke of how he must have followed her to the conference, thinking he could get away with violating his restraining order in another state.

Cocktails started early and evaporated swiftly as they conversed over the unfortunate situation. James said, if this were marriage, he'd just stay clear of it.

Mr. Thompson trotted downstairs just as the air had calmed. He missed the whole thing. He discreetly pulled me aside and asked me to take him to town in his car. He needed me to then hide the car, make it invisible just for the day. He confessed his wife knew he'd rented a red Porsche, and she might come looking for him. He asked I keep this between the two of us.

Peculiar as it sounded, I agreed it was no problem at all. The timing worked well, as my shift was ending, so I could drop Mr. Thompson and the car and go wherever I wanted. I lowered the sun visor to shield the day's brightness and cautiously drove the Hawaiian-clothed Southerner to the town pier, mindful of full stops and other cars along the way. His lady friend had gone to town earlier to shop. She stood flailing her arms above her hat, waving us down by the boat dock. They planned to catch a dinner cruise around the islands. They'd call for a ride back sometime late evening.

I took the car for a spin around town, looking for places to hide it. I thought about going up Cadillac Mountain, but it would be way too far for me to walk back to the inn from there. Having done a few loops, I tracked back along the water's edge and about to pass Bridge Street, the hidden drive that goes to the uninhabited Bar Island. On an impulse, I took a sharp right and drove down the bumpy road, dust flying up the windows, until I landed at the sandbar. The bar is only exposed at low tide and bridges a path to Bar Island. It's the only time you can walk or drive across, so I decided to take advantage, zip there and back. I did worry about the car getting dirty, but I could hose it down back at the inn later. I felt the urge to stop alongside another car about halfway along the bar. I climbed out. The tide was rising and washing in all sorts of interesting organisms. I searched around for sand dollars and starfish. A few others did the same, some collecting clams and crabs.

I strolled along the water's edge, finding neat shells, cleaning them off in the water and placing them in my rolled shirt. I built quite a collection. The robust scent of salt penetrated the surroundings, amongst drifting seagulls and boats sailing their unique course. Distracted, I reached the island, perusing the sign about island trails. I wandered on one of them. It took me up and around to the other side of the island with awesome views. A couple stood snapping scenic photos from different spots and angles of the island. They stopped to take a break and knelt down amongst a slew of blueberry bushes, picking the sweet berries and popping them in their mouth. I joined nearby, nibbling until my stomach despised the fruit. They started a conversation, saying they were from Nantucket, renting a cabin nearby for the summer.

"Looks like a nice camera you have," I said.

"Yes, we're trying to capture a great photo," the woman said. "There's a contest in the Bar Harbor Times for best photo of the area. Gets front page coverage. The prize is a two-night's stay at Shutters Inn. You heard of it?"

"As a matter of fact, I have."

"Anyway, we'd better get going. We have to cross the bar and shoot some pictures from land before it starts to get dark," the woman said.

"Good luck," I said. "Hope you win."

Fatigued, I sat down on the ground for a little rest in the sun. I rubbed my fingers along the dirt, making zigzag designs. My mind kept replaying the cop scene with Mindy running to Riker, hugging and kissing him. And in front of everyone. I wondered if other girls did that to their boyfriends. She should have raced to me in a situation like that. And she never saw how Riker acted like a bully toward Jerry. My head beat like a drum. It crushed me that Mindy told him I wanted to work on the front desk. I confided in her. He was the worst person she could have blabbed to. What did she see in that guy, that hoodlum, that so-called friend? I couldn't control my mind. It ran like a broken record.

I dragged myself up and brushed my pants off, walked to the edge near the path down. I could see the town pier and various mansions waterside. I spotted The Maycliff, but the distance was too great to see if anyone stood outside. I glanced at my watch. Hadn't realized the time. I had to find a hiding place for the car.

When I reached the billboard of island trails, my feet were wet. My head a garbled mess, I studied the sign as if it could save me, saturated with warnings of a fast-rising tide. Three quarters of the Porsche's shiny body exposed itself, while the remainder was devoured by the water's evil body. A payphone sat beside the sign for those who got caught on the island. I called Jerry urgently. He'd know what to do, being a car buff. He said he'd borrow lobster Bert's truck and tow it if need be. He'd get there as fast as he could.

I trudged through the water with intense resistance, panting fiercely until I reached the red bombshell. I opened the door with great force, water pouring in. I tried to turn it over, but not a click. Plowing my way to the back of the car,

I attempted pushing it from behind. But it wouldn't budge. I anxiously watched as the Atlantic's hungry belly swallowed up the ruby bit by bit. There I stood, stranded and in very deep crap, contemplating my fate, wondering how I would get out of this one. I knew Mr. Thompson wanted his car hidden but not like this.

Jerry finally arrived. He parked the truck and pushed his way to me with a long rope.

"Thanks for saving me, Jerry."

"I haven't yet," he said, "but I'll do my best. And thanks to you for saving me from that bully, Riker, earlier."

Jerry hinged up the car and told me to stay with it. Help push. He floored the truck to some success. At least we had movement from the car. I kept shoving at the backend, hoping to make a difference. Our attempts were productive, and we slowly edged our way to land. We hastily opened the doors, allowing water to pour out.

I hopped in the truck alongside Jerry.

"How'd you get yourself into this mess?" he asked.

"Long story," I said. "Can you help me clean it up? We can hide it in the delivery area of the inn by the garage."

"Course I will. I brought all my tools. Everything we need, including a water vac."

We made the woodpile our operational table and Jerry got to work. I wasn't sure how saltwater would take to its shiny red paint or the inside seats, not to mention the mechanical system. Would it even start? My other option would have been to let it drown and say it was stolen. Seaweed coated its once luxurious body. And remnants of salt glued to its sultry frame. I rubbed my hand across its rough, gritty exterior. The car door appeared stuck, but I yanked till it opened with an unhealthy, thunderous creak. I climbed in the wet, slimy machine. Everything felt sticky and consumed by smells of salt and fish. The car wouldn't even turn over. Deader than dead, like me.

Jerry did all he could until dark and said he'd be back in the morning to continue. Fingers and ego shriveled, I crept down the back stairs, poking around corners for Mr. Thompson, shuffling quickly from one area to the next like the Pink Panther. I peered through the peek-a-boo window on the swinging kitchen door, and there he sat, oblivious. I shot the other way, avoiding him at all costs. I hoped Mr. Thompson didn't want his car tomorrow or ask where I'd hidden it.

Mindy caught me creeping around. Frightened the hell out of me. Her subdued greeting and strained smile only triggered the cop scene again. She looked tired to me and her hair a little unraveled.

CHAPTER FOURTEEN

Jerry was back working on the car by the time I got going. We had a quick chat before I tended to my bellman duties. "You better today?" I asked Juliette, stopping at the desk.

"Much," she said. "Thanks for consoling me. That was a scary way to start a new job."

"Like I said, it was unusual. Nothing like that should happen again."

Her soft lips broadened.

Chuckie claimed he needed a break, since I was there. Asked me to stay and help Juliette, as she was still new. Couldn't leave her alone. I didn't mind. Chef had a load in his arms walking across the front lawn. He paused to admire his reflection in the glassy domain, adjusting his hold and allowing a bit of hope to slip from his fingers.

As check-in time approached, the desk heated up. Juliette swiftly answered calls, handling questions with great precision and balancing people on hold. A man walked in off the streets and she calmly relayed the rates. He'd be delighted to stay, so she proceeded to check him in, while simultaneously on a call. I reached for the phone, but she insisted she had it. I stood, amazed at her sense of control.

When things quieted down, I asked her where she was from. I could tell she wasn't from around here.

"I'm originally from Montreal. But my family and I moved to Stowe, Vermont, a few years ago," she said.

"How'd you end up here so late in the season?" I was curious how she got my job.

"Well, I'm a camp counselor in the summers in Stowe. But one of the programs just ended and this opportunity suddenly came up. A friend of mine told me about this job. And I thought it would be a nice change. I'd heard about Bar Harbor. So I applied for the job last week. And Mrs. Lyncoff called and accepted me right away."

My head numbed. "Oh, well that's good," I said, but didn't really mean it. "So, you going back to Stowe at the end of season?"

"Absolutely. I teach ski school in the winters, little kids. I love watching those tots all bundled up, snow-plowing down the mountain. They're so cute. And they're always so happy being out in the fresh air," she said. "What about you?"

Mrs. Lyncoff passed, her facial expression smudged. "I'll tell you later," I whispered.

Chuckie returned, looking baffled as he stood by Juliette. Told her she was doing a good job. He appeared even more like a dead weight now. This could be a good thing for Mrs. Lyncoff to see.

I snuck in an early check out room, while Tracy busied herself cleaning another. I'd picked up some tools and a couple of bottles of bubble bath when last in town. I turned off the water valves and dismantled the sink and tub faucets, emptying a bottle into both. Replaced the fixtures and did the same for the toilet, removing its lid. Tidied up and snuck into the hallway. She'd never rid all those bubbles. I tossed the empty bottles in her maid's cart, hiding them beneath tissue. I patiently waited till she exited the room she cleaned and stuck my face into hers singing "Tiny Bubbles." Don Ho would be proud. Tracy didn't have a clue what I'd planted. I disguised my smirk. Although she carried a look of bewilderment, so maybe she suspected something.

Within the hour, Tracy strutted down the hallway with the pack of girls, her arms wrapped around a heavy load. Sam focused on the box. Tracy could not believe what she'd heard about the ruckus with that ex-cop. She wished she'd been around to witness it. Sounded like more action than the average day. She gloated I'd missed a ton of fun the other night at Aussie's. After I left, she and Kamal had a dance. She even got him to do a couple of shots. Apparently, some good-looking guy chased after Sam all night. She grinned. Sam kept her head low.

"If you and Mindy ever break up…." Tracy started. Sam walked away.

"Gotta go," I interrupted. I thought it best to ignore Tracy. I had no interest in Sam, but I didn't want to hurt her feelings either. No mention of the bubbles. She just slammed the box she held into my arms and asked I deliver it to the kitchen.

"What is it?" I asked.

"Says Beets. I just found it lying outside the delivery area, so I figured it belonged to the kitchen."

"Kay. I'll drop it off."

Passing the lounge, I saw Simon had retreated from the lawn and sat chatting with Kamal. Mr. Mac content with his water in the corner, scribbling on his notepad. Simon caught my eye and nodded me over, asking for a black coffee, while Kamal requested a cup of Earl Grey tea. Simon unfolded his binder, and the two began flipping through it, as the Kiwi navigated the way.

I set the box on the bar and found my hands covered in a black tar-like substance. That damn Tracy. Mindy startled me from behind, while I scrubbed with warm soapy water. She popped her head over the back of my shoulder.

"What's up?" she asked.

I brushed her off my shoulder and kept scrubbing, but it wouldn't dissolve. I stuck paper towels to the box's underside to prevent more rubbing off. Mindy went on about her business.

Serving their warm drinks with grayish, sticky hands, I curiously eavesdropped. Mr. Thompson joined in for a coffee, politely reminding me to get his keys. I developed a sudden ache on my side after acknowledging I would. Kamal said his original success was in oil. A family business. It allowed him to step into development. His company, Alsayed & Sons, now built hotels, monumental buildings, metro lines, medical buildings, industrial projects, and major housing complexes throughout the Middle East. They toasted. Mr. Thompson responded with his own triumphant story in the oil business. How he had owned an oil company in Houston, hit a couple of big wells, and sold the business a few years ago. He told everyone that story. Steve and I used to joke about it.

I delivered the box to the empty kitchen and peered in Chef's office closet, jumping back when I noticed the white cat sleeping in his chair. I must have startled him, because his hiss echoed when he heard me, his bulging eyes widening.

"Hey, little fellow." I waved my hand at him. His heavy eyelids gently closed.

Chef bolted through the door just as I was leaving. He shot me a grin, threw some bags down on the counter, and stepped into his office.

"Oh, the cat's in there," I said.

"What cat?" he asked.

I looked around. The cat was gone.

I blew through the door to find Mrs. Lyncoff on the other side, talking to Norma and a guest.

"Here's our bellman now." She introduced me.

I reached out my hand to shake his. "What's on your hands?" Mrs. Lyncoff asked in disgust.

"Oh, they just got a little dirty," I said.

Mrs. Lyncoff apologized profusely to the guest and instructed me to go wash up immediately. I passed the Islamic group, who appeared to have just checked out. They must have brought their own bags down, as most guests did. Kamal led the procession of black and white gowns out the door, saying his goodbyes. He and his wife would be staying.

The front desk cleared. Chuckie leaned on the counter, smirking. Juliette looked picturesque, always sporting a contagious smile. I don't know how she stood next to that oaf all day. James strutted in with Jerry by his side. Those two always hung out together on their time off. Same interests. Jerry brought me a used Archie book and a few gummy worms. Knew I liked those.

"Ew, what's with your hands?" Jerry asked.

"Just Tracy, playing another prank." He and James laughed, while Juliette tried to contain her amusement.

I stuck my hands in my pockets, passing Mrs. Lyncoff. She nodded in acknowledgment.

It came time to clock out at the front desk. But Chuckie asked me to visit Mr. Mac in the lounge. I questioned why, but he didn't know. Just said Mr. Mac requested me.

"What can I do for you, Mr. Mac?"

"I would like some pictures of the stone lady by the stairwell. Could you take a few good ones for me if you don't mind?"

"Absolutely. Of course. I don't have a camera, but I'll find one."

"Thank you, Stanley." I started to leave. "And by the way, you're doing a fine job here." I wondered how he could suggest that. He didn't see all that I did. But it made me feel recognized.

I borrowed a camera from Mrs. Lyncoff and walked to town to get the photos developed. If you requested a rush, they were ready in two hours, so I waited. When I returned to the lounge, Mr. Mac was gone. I knocked on his door. He didn't answer, so I slipped into his empty room and left the package on his bed, just as my beeper sounded.

Sirens intensified as the truck closed in. Two paramedics jumped out of the ambulance and flew through the doors with a stretcher. They raced to the bar and back, body laid out. An oxygen mask on his face. I assumed Mr. Mac, but at closer look, it was James. The medical professionals fled, slamming the trunk door until diverted. Even the paramedics couldn't resist the well. They flung one in before leaping in their seats.

"What's going on?" I pushed Chuckie.

"Have no idea," he said.

"Cover for me," I said. I grabbed Jerry by the car and we swiped a couple of rusty old bikes that sat in the delivery area all summer. I don't know whose they were. And we rode as fast as we could to the town hospital. We urged the nurse to let us see James, but she made us wait till he stabilized. She wouldn't even tell us what was wrong. An hour trailed by before they allowed access.

James's cheeks rested plump and red, suffocated by little bumps over his face, neck and arms. "What happened?" I asked.

"They think it was an allergic reaction."

"What are you allergic to?" Jerry asked.

"Nothing that I know of. But they jabbed me with an EpiPen. My throat swelled up, and I couldn't breathe. Chef apparently

129

found me gasping over the bar and called for help. The nurse made a list of what I'd eaten, drank, and touched today. They ruled out poison ivy. They're just testing everything now. I only ate beans on toast earlier, which I always do. And some pickled beets and onions Chef left out in the kitchen."

"Well that would have made anyone sick. Pickled beets," I said.

James said the doc wanted him to stay till they found the cause and the swelling subsided. He needed me to cover for him on the bar. Jerry said he'd stay. I scrubbed my hands raw in the hospital sink before I left, leaving only a few spots of black.

"Stan, by the way, the car's good to go. All dried out and in working order. I was just going to give it a last vacuum and spray some more mildew and fragrance stuff in it."

"I'll take care of that. You're the best, Jerry. I can't believe you managed to get it all back together. Thanks a ton," I said. "Really. You saved me."

"What car?" asked James. He looked bewildered.

"Mr. Thompson's," Jerry said. "I'll explain in a minute. You just rest."

"I was back at the inn at the crack of dawn today, Stan. Luckily, we got it out of the ocean fast enough or we couldn't have done it."

"Ocean?" James questioned.

"Just relax," Jerry said, patting James's hands.

Mindy raced out of the inn to greet me on the drive. She wrapped her arms soothingly around me and stroked my back, saying she'd heard about James. Hoped he'd be all right. They weren't fans of each other, so I was surprised she showed so much emotion. I didn't want to let go, but knew I probably should. I told her about the allergic reaction and that they'd probably keep him overnight.

"Chef told me he found James just in time," she said. "He could have died."

"I know. He was extremely lucky. Thank god," I said.

"What can I do to help?" Her embrace tightened, as I gently brushed back her hair.

"Why don't we go to the hospital after work and see how he's doing," I suggested. I noticed Juliette gazing out the window as if she studied the trees.

"Okay. That's a good idea. Let's do just that. Come find me in the restaurant and we'll..."

Chuckie poked his head out the screen door, interrupting. "Okay, enough. The bar's hopping. Time to get back to work."

My eyes squinted in his direction, laser-sharp enough to cut. I wished he'd vanish off the friggin' earth. That might be worth throwing a penny in for.

I walked right in the front door to Mr. Thompson.

"Just the guy I wanted to see," he said. "May I get the keys to my car, please?"

"Of course. I'll just run and grab them. I was just about to quickly vacuum it out, then I'll pull it up."

"Why thank you, Stan. That's very kind."

I finished the last of the restoration and pulled the car into the lot. Mr. Thompson was at the bar with his lady friend.

I placed the pristine keys in his hand.

"Where'd you end up hiding it?" he whispered.

"It's a secret," I murmured back.

He laughed while he picked up "The Bar Harbor Times" from the counter to read.

"Look at this fool. Ha. Got his Porsche stuck in a heap of water," Mr. Thompson delighted.

His lady chuckled alongside him, peering over his shoulder. I hesitantly glanced down. A photo of the seaweed-covered beauty laced the front page, with a big warning to visitors, "What Not to Do in Bar Harbor." It got worse when I noticed the picture had me beside the car. But thankfully, it didn't capture my face. My back was turned.

I stepped behind the bar to cover for James, but I'd be on the wrong side of it. I needed a drink, a big one. But Mrs. Lyncoff's keen eye rounded the corner, and her finger hooked me in. I trailed her to the office, passing Riker hovering over Juliette. She pushed him away. Her compassionate glimpse my way soothed me.

CHAPTER FIFTEEN

id Mrs. Lyncoff find out about the car? Would she fire me? I sat down in her frosty chair, anticipating the bite. She wanted to discuss the noise issue, to my surprise.

"We can't carry on with this aggravating noise that keeps the guests up all night," she said. "We've never experienced this before."

By this time, she'd had three acoustical engineers check out the noise, because she thought the first two were nuts. But with the last confirmation, she gave in. All three came to the same conclusion.

"As crazy as it sounds, the noise is mating fish," she said.

"Huh?"

"It's Midshipmen fish. The male fish hum, or sing, at night to attract their female counterparts to mate. They mate from May through October and then retreat back to the far depths of the ocean. Midshipmen generally hum from nine p.m. to six a.m. These fish obviously migrated here for some reason this year. Maybe the storm we had before the season began washed them in. Or they discovered the Bluenose Ferry's running motor, which soothed them. Something's caused them to migrate here."

This was some weird-ass stuff. And how could fish sound so loud and motorized? Mrs. Lyncoff didn't have the answer to that. She assumed there were hundreds of them vibrating down there.

"So, what do we do about them?" I asked.

"The experts I've spoken to don't really have a solution, other than trying light, since they hum when it's dark. Or they suggested we try other pitches of sound to counter theirs and hopefully drive them away. It's going to be trial and error. Anyway, I've bought a pool light I'd like you to hook up and test. I need you to handle this, rather than Riker, since you live on the property and are around at night."

The bellman—a maid, doctor, desk clerk, bartender, waiter, driver, and now fish-fighter. And for fish having sex. The goddamn fish get more action than I do. I begrudgingly grabbed the pool light and extension cord.

I descended the stairs to find Riker's arm wrapped around Juliette. She looked uncomfortable. Mindy seemed pissed off, her scathing glare digging into Juliette's virtuous eyes. Juliette appeared caged. I felt sorry for her.

"What's up, Mindy?" I asked.

"Oh, Stan, am I glad to see you." She hugged me.

"What's going on?"

"Nothing. I just came to get the reservation book. Come on. Let's walk together." She pulled me away, as her head shot back briefly. Mindy reminded me we were to go see James at the hospital after work. I remembered, though. I told her I had to get to the lounge now to cover for him.

Riker had just left Juliette alone as I passed the desk.

"I'm sorry about him," I said to her.

"That's okay. He's kind of in my face. But I can handle it," Juliette said. "I've worked with people like that before."

"Well, you let me know any time he's really bothering you, and I'll put a stop to it," I said.

"Thanks, Stan. I really appreciate it."

"Of course," I said. "I have to go tend the bar now. But, I'll see you in a bit." I started to walk off. "Oh, and if you ever need a break, just holler."

"I will," she pleasantly replied.

A number of guests swarmed the bar. Chef had covered the drinks in the meantime and patted me on the back to take charge before disappearing to the kitchen. Simon stood entertaining the pharmaceutical crowd with his well-crafted stories. Norma enjoyed a glass of red with Jasmine, the lady who'd arranged Pfizal's visit. The thirsty crowd kept the drinks flowing. I'd become pretty suave at bartending, as most people ordered simple concoctions. Norma must have noticed my competence. Hopefully, she'd spread that information to Mrs. Lyncoff. The group suddenly rose at once to head to dinner, Norma as their escort. Simon vaulted onto a bar stool in the now subdued lounge, ordered a beer and chugged it, slamming down the glass. I served him another.

"Hey, Stan, any empty rooms tonight?" Simon asked.

"Not sure. I can check. You want to move?"

"Thinkin' about it, mate. Either the maids keep moving things in my room, or your friend, Mary, is."

I checked with Juliette, but with the conference in, it was a full house. Simon brushed it off. Said he only planned to stay another week, so he could tough it out.

He asked about my background. I told him I was from a little nearby town, called Jay. I had four sisters, who drove me crazy. But mostly, I just couldn't stay in my little town where no one advanced. They all followed their parents' trails, ended up in the same line of work, and married their high school sweetheart. That wasn't for me, I said. I had bigger dreams than falling into my dad's small building supply company.

Simon agreed. "You get one crack at it. I ended up an architect, my passion." His eyes strolled the premises with admiration.

A young couple snuck in and sat at the end of the bar, introducing himself and his newly wed wife, Emma. They'd flown in from Kentucky this morning for her best friend's wedding.

"Well, congratulations. Let me buy you a celebratory drink," Simon insisted.

The two beamed as they observed me tossing rum, lime, sugar, and strawberries into the blender and letting it rip. I poured the daiquiris into chilled glasses, adding a plump strawberry to their rim. They thanked Simon.

"No worries," he said, before excusing himself from the bar. I noticed him shake Mr. Mac's hand, but he stood blocking the old man, so I couldn't see Mr. Mac's expression. A few minutes in, Simon left.

I pointed out The Maycliff was a great place for weddings. "We have one tomorrow," I said, "about a hundred people. Are those your friends?"

"Yes. I'm the maid of honor."

Emma said the bride played her maid of honor a couple of months ago. I told her we get lots of honeymooners here and asked if Chuckie knew, because newlyweds are given a complimentary bottle of champagne. Emma said it iced in their room upon arrival with a nice note. Such a thoughtful idea, she acknowledged.

I popped in the kitchen, looking for bar nuts. Chef stood hunched, cranking out the group's meal, spooning a dollop of basil mint sauce on each lamp chop. No time to disturb him.

I smiled at Mindy as I passed her. She grinned. To my surprise, James had slipped in behind the bar, while Jerry slid on a stool.

"What are you doing here? Thought they weren't letting you out?" I asked.

"They said I was good to go. The swelling's gone down enough. I'm out of danger."

"What was the cause?"

"Beets," he said. "Jeez. Apparently, I'm allergic." James laughed.

"I thought it was a cinnamon jaw breaker you'd eaten, like Jerry, that stained your tongue earlier," I said.

"Oh yuck. Bad taste. No way. Told Jerry to stop eating them."

"I only eat them when he's not around," Jerry said, as he tilted his neck.

Riker raced in, asking for a beer. But James said he couldn't give him alcohol while on duty.

"Okay. Then look the other way," Riker said. He snatched one from the fridge and swigged it.

"So thirsty. I've been running around fixing things in rooms—clogged toilets, curtains off track. They're always coming off the rod 'cause people yank them. Oh, and someone locked themselves out and lost both keys. No spares left. So, I had to rekey it for them. One of those days. Now I have to go check out a leak in one of the rooms. Calls keep coming."

"Hey, Riker," I said. "I don't think Juliette likes you wrapping your arm around her. She's new and all. I'd let her alone."

He leaned back to get the last drop from the bottle then shoved it at James. "To hell with that," he mouthed in my face, before disappearing. James shrugged. I shook my head.

Chuckie paged me to the desk, Riker standing beside him. Chuckie fled for the bathroom, shouting for me to cover with Juliette. Of course, I would. Mrs. Lyncoff marched toward us as

Riker overbearingly announced he was going to fix yet another problem. No phones rang. No people walked in. We just stood there as Mrs. Lyncoff passed.

"Hey, I'll be right back," I told Juliette.

I ran to the bar and poured the leftover Strawberry Daiquiri for Juliette to try, discreetly sneaking it to the desk.

"Here, have a sip," I said.

Her eyes widened with anticipation as her lips grasped the rim. "Yum," she said. "It's delicious, thanks."

"One of my specialties," I said. "There's more where that came from."

Juliette laughed. "How'd you learn to bartend? I wish I knew how."

"I'll teach you. It's easy. One of the bartenders last year showed me some drinks. But you really just learn as you go along. Look drinks up in the cocktail book. I'll make you a banana Daiquiri next time or a Pina Colada."

"I'd love that," Juliette said.

She asked if I didn't mind if she took at quick break to use the bathroom. I told her of course not.

Once out of sight, the phone abruptly rang. Then another line jingled. And another, until all three lines were going. In walked someone from the street inquiring about a room. And a guest stood requesting a wake-up call. I couldn't figure out whom to address first. So, I played hot potato. Bounced them around till all went silent, and the only one left was Mrs. Lyncoff, standing, watching. My left eye fluttered.

Before nine, I took the long extension cord and pushed it into an outdoor plug, crossed the garden, stopping halfway. The cord wouldn't reach. Friggin' thing. I left it and scrounged around for more extensions in the garage. After ripping through drawers and cabinets, I found two under a pile and attached them. I shimmied the pool light down to the ocean, where the sound generated. The waves hit aggressively, so I couldn't keep the light still. It kept banging against the rocks. I waited and waited. Laid down on the small concrete parapet, listening for any subdued sound. It felt as though the drilling penetrated through the concrete, vibrating my head. I lay there over an hour, thinking about those arrogant fish and the little party they enjoyed down there, a friggin' orgy. My mind throbbed. The humming continued. The light made no difference, didn't disrupt their festivities. I pulled up the equipment and wrapped the cords around tight. And retracted to my room, the humming still rumbling through my brain. It wouldn't quit. I grabbed under the bed and yanked out my Penthouse magazines. Seemed everyone had company but me.

***

We had the wedding to prepare for. Some of the attendees checked in before three, which worked out because the pharmaceutical company had an early departure. So the maids could get in the rooms first thing. Sometimes, they had to wait till late afternoon to clean, especially since Ms. Malone's visit.

Chef called Riker and me in once the wedding guests headed to the church. He had a beet reduction simmering on the stovetop. Tracy strolled in and squeezed the back of my neck. Jerry had given me a bottle popper that had been stuffed in his pocket, the kind you hold the neck of the small, plastic bottle upside down and pull the string. I grabbed it from my pants and looked at it momentarily before deciding to shoot it over Tracy's head. She giggled as the confetti streamed down on her, till it hit Chef's pan and became, "oh crap" for the both of us. Chef slammed down the phone, grabbed the pan and threw it in the sink, watching it sizzle under the hot water. Mrs. Lyncoff must have been standing in the corner for a while because she did not look pleased. Tracy went on her way, colored specks weaved through her hair. Riker's smug face remained taut.

Chef's focus turned to the tiered wedding cake, hovering over it and fussing. Said the bride and groom insisted on buttercream icing, but he warned them, when it's hot out, the buttercream melts. Told them we have no air conditioning. He repeatedly reapplied the icing, obviously frustrated. The four layers kept trying to slide off one another. This could be disastrous. He made me stand in the walk-in fridge, trying to hold it together with toothpicks. It wasn't working too well. The second tier from top was about to slide off, so I had to put my hands around the sides to stop it. I shouted for Chef. He grumbled something in French as he fixed it once again and instructed me not to move. But my hands turned blue, trembling. I struggled to keep still as I slowly became an ice sculpture.

Once the cake became stable, Chef released me. I stood by the stove, rubbing my hands together, trying to thaw out. Mindy shot in and said the wedding party had arrived. Her eyes engaged mine for an extended second.

"Stan, come on. You can help," she said, as I followed.

The bride and groom had a ceremonial toast by the fountain, tossing their magical cent into the thirsty water in hopes their marriage wasn't doomed like most. As if Abraham Lincoln could save them. The crowd gathered on the terrace. James stood serving a trayful of choices—red, white, champagne, or club soda upon arrival. Mindy handed me a similar tray and asked me to pass some drinks around. We covered the room proficiently and I felt proud to be by her side. An assortment of hors d'oeuvres garnished the cocktail tables. The sun lay heavily upon the crowd as they nibbled, drank, and mingled. We repoured drinks as they emptied. I became transfixed on a lobster boat motoring up to its orange and yellow buoy, pulling up the trap. It must have been empty, because the fisherman tossed it back in with a thud. Colorful sails brushed by in the distance. A trickle of sweat formed on my forehead. Mindy called me over to help serve the entrees. She said the group should be sitting down shortly. Chef drizzled a white wine sauce on the crab-stuffed sole and garnished the plates with capers, parsley, and a flower-shaped lemon.

While the guests enjoyed their meals, Chef brought the now balanced cake out for display on a round table outside the dining room. The white icing looked so creamy and smooth. The plastic bride and groom stood immaculately on the top tier.

Riker reappeared and hastily told me to pick up the dinner tray in Mr. Mac's room. Riker had an urgent call in another room, an overflowing toilet. There was no answer when I knocked, so I just entered and grabbed his tray. As I sprang down the stairs, Mr. Mac steadily walked up.

"Hey there, Mr. Mac."

"Why, hello, Stan," he said. His eyes remained focused on his path. I hopped over the last two stairs, turned and looked up, watching his every exhausting step. It weighed me down.

Focusing back toward the kitchen, my mouth cracked open. The tiers of the wedding cake were all sliding in different directions. I dropped the tray on the marble table that carried the lady statue and shot to the cake, trying to hold it together with the serving fork and knife, set tableside.

"Mindy," I whispered. "Psst." I tried to get her attention. I couldn't move for fear the cake would fall. She ran over, trying to help. But she put her fingers in the cake. That didn't look good.

"Don't do that," I said. "They might see." I blocked my back toward the dining room, so the guests couldn't witness the disaster.

"Well, what do you want me to do? Let it fall?"

"Let's bring it to the kitchen," I suggested.

We carefully carried the lopsided cake to Chef, who cursed his way to French.

"What in the sam hell? Goddamn guests never listen to me!" he shouted. He stuck me back in the fridge, while the sugary structure mended. Meanwhile, Mindy bought time with the wedding party. Finally, the Leaning Tower of Pisa was rebuilt and we were released, the cake and I. This round I didn't have time to thaw out. I had to shoot straight to the front, where the bride and groom awaited photos of the cake ceremony. The cake lasted till the knife slid in. The top layer couldn't stay strong. It skated off and smashed onto the floor. The plastic bride and groom broke apart. Not a good sign. The gasp of the crowd turned the room quiet. Until the bride shouted it meant, good luck. What a line. They all snickered, releasing the tension. Chef brought three large plates and dismantled the cake for easy serving. I cleaned up the mess.

Dancing followed in the lounge. Drinks circulated all night. I went out the service exit to the terrace, a hidden area where I liked to take a break. But the groom occupied the space, kissing Emma, his wife's best friend.

CHAPTER SIXTEEN

I couldn't bear to look at Emma or the groom. They stood with their significant others hugging one another, saying their goodbyes. But Emma slithered toward me, whispering it wasn't what I thought. They were just good friends, having a moment. And maybe they'd gotten a little carried away, but it meant nothing. I shrugged my shoulders as if indifferent. After all, it really wasn't any of my business. But I would never do that to Mindy. Then the vision of her and Riker stabbed me again. But they hugged, not kissed. The words of the psychic suggesting something astray with Mindy and me resurfaced.

When the crowd dispersed, Chuckie hovered over the hushed desk.

"Hey Juliette," I said. "How's it going? You taking charge here?"

"No." She softly tapped my arm. I held my gaze. "But it's going great. I'm having fun. That was a nice wedding party visit. Livened the place up."

"That it did. But I'm glad they're…"

Chuckie interrupted. "Guess who's in trouble?"

I sighed. "Now what, Chuckie?"

"Someone cleared Mr. Mac's dinner last night before he'd had a chance to finish it. And I know it wasn't Riker, because he was busy fixing a leak."

I said nothing and marched upstairs to the office. Norma let me in, but Mrs. Lyncoff had gone to town. Reluctantly, I explained to Norma, Riker told me to clear his tray. She assured me she'd convey the message to her boss when she returned. She then handed me a few gadgets to test different decibel levels on the fish, see if it drove them away.

I trudged back to the linen closet, knocked on the door and pushed through the empty room. I needed a distraction. I waited and waited till I heard someone coming. Tracy was well overdue for a payback. As the door cracked open, I yelled "Boo!" loudly and stuck my face into hers. The extended scream belted out, and I stepped back, elated with the reaction. Until I saw it was Sam's euphoric expression. I explained I'd intended it for Tracy and prudently slipped away.

Simon's binder swiped me as he swept by. My pager went off just as he asked if Mr. Mac was in the lounge. I guessed, probably. Jerry trailed behind James, who arrived for his afternoon shift, but Jerry didn't stay long. After he left, I could tell James wasn't himself. He seemed down, like something bothered him.

"You all right?" I asked.

"Sort of," he said.

"What's the matter?"

At first, he claimed nothing. Then he pulled me aside and hesitantly started to speak. I could tell he grasped for every right word. And that it felt painful for him to share whatever rested on his mind. Finally, his words formed and he confided that he and Jerry had been an item for two years now. He said he was only telling me now, because he needed someone to talk to. Jerry's jealousy was driving him insane. Silence embraced the moment as he studied my face, but my expression lay still.

I told him it didn't matter. It wouldn't change anything between us, what I thought of him. He was still my friend. I'd suspected something between the two for quite some time. They appeared so tight. I liked them both. Actually, I felt relieved he'd shared this with me. So I didn't have to pretend I didn't know or suspect.

"Anyone who looks at me, except you, blasts him into a frenzy. And he won't let it go. Has to know how I feel and what I'm thinking at all times. I don't know what to do," he said.

I suggested he try to talk it over with him, so Jerry doesn't feel so insecure. I said that's what I would do with Mindy. He agreed he'd try. I sensed a heavy weight lifted once he unveiled his secret. He thanked me for being a good friend.

I returned to my post by the front door. Riker strutted in, leaned over the reception desk with his face implanted in his hands, and stared at Juliette. He hovered there a prolonged time, bragging about his talents as a musician and offering to play for her some night. Chuckie's dense expression looked on. Juliette didn't appear too interested, struggling to be polite. That thrilled me. Sam shadowed behind Tracy as they passed, Tracy twiddling her fingers at me.

Simon lifted himself from Mr. Mac's table, binder under arm, and shook his hand with the other. Mrs. Lyncoff replaced Simon, sitting down briefly, until Mindy served him what looked to be a beet salad. I decided I best apologize for his dinner removal last night and explain. He told me not to worry one bit. He actually didn't have an appetite last night. It only came up, because Chuckie asked him how he enjoyed his meal.

Mr. Mac's focus turned to Mr. Thompson, who just arrived back from a jaunt in town with his lady friend, Kamal, and his wife as they retreated to a lounge table for drinks.

Oil seemed to dominate the topic of conversation. Kamal insisted Mr. Thompson visit him in Saudi. He'd show him all his developments and expose him to some fabulous sites and restaurants. Mr. Thompson sounded delighted and reciprocated with an open invitation to Texas. He called Mindy over for another round, pressing his hand against her well-curved backside. An irritable twitch jolted me.

I rose when I'd lost Mr. Mac's attention and noticed light resonating behind him. Seemed odd how it hovered there. I tried to figure out how sun could beam like that.

I followed Mindy to the bar while she placed their order.

"Ya know, I was thinking you shouldn't return to Boston this year for school."

"Why not? I want to," she said.

"Well, I thought we could go somewhere different. Like maybe New York. Surely there's a good hospitality school there."

"I can't get accepted this late. Plus, where would we live?" Her demeanor warmed. "Would be fun, though. But I can't do that."

"Can we just discuss it Friday after work? We still on for Sand Beach then?"

"Oh, I forgot about that. Riker asked a bunch of us to go to the movies. Why don't you join?"

"No, not interested. We already had plans."

She grabbed my hands and insisted she was sorry and could cancel. I told her to forget about it. We'd do it another time.

Chuckie buzzed me to fill in for him at the desk again with Juliette. She didn't seem to need assistance, but Chuckie felt she did. Don't know why. She could run circles around him. The distance between us seemed smaller than it was. I kept thinking I should speak to Mrs. Lyncoff and convey my extreme interest in the front desk. Juliette and I would make a strong team.

Riker motored in. "Hey guys." Juliette had her hand resting on the desk. He patted it twice and pointed his finger at her as if cocking a gun. "Where's Chuckie?"

"On break," I said. "Don't know where, but he walked out the door with Joan."

"That slick SOB. Don't expect him back for a while," Riker blurted before strutting back in the same direction. "He'll be in the bush."

"What are they doing in the bush?" Juliette asked.

"You know. It."

Juliette covered her open mouth. She touched the back of my hand ever so gently with her fingertips. Warm sparks shot through me.

"Last year, they got caught doing it in the unmade guest rooms. So they had to find another spot."

Juliette's surprised look turned into a giggle.

I hadn't seen Mindy standing nearby. Wonder how long she'd been there?

Mindy interrupted, coming to get the restaurant reservation book. She grabbed my head and kissed my cheek, completely ignoring Juliette, then detoured outside to talk to Riker. She looked mad. I explained to Juliette that was my girlfriend and we'd been dating since last fall.

"I assumed so," Juliette said. "She's pretty."

The desk remained quiet; no phones rang or guests walked in.

"You know, I see you helping Mr. Mac, often," she said. "That's awfully nice of you."

"Well. He's a good man," I said.

"He is," she agreed.

"So, you glad you came to Bar Harbor?" I asked.

"Yes, I am. The real reason I came was because of a break-up. I...I...was with the wrong guy." She paused and took a breath. "And I'm staying with the friend who told me about this job. She comes here every summer to work. She's a big help, very supportive."

I told her I was sorry about her break-up and confided in her my story of how I ended up here from my little town, the pressures I felt and desire to get away on my own. She seemed to get it.

Mrs. Lyncoff marched to the desk.

"Stanley, I need you in my office right away. Chuckie has accused you of something, which quite honestly, could be your last straw. I'll be up. I need to talk to Juliette for a minute."

Accused me of what? I didn't do anything.

I sat in her office, peering out the window, restlessly waiting. Mrs. Lyncoff stormed up the drive and into the bush. I could see her yelling through the branches. Chuckie hobbled out, yanking up his pants that sat at his ankles and hanging onto his shirt. Not a nice sight. Then Joan ran out with some gadget wrapped around her waist. Looked like something from Ms. Malone's room. Other than that object, she was completely in the buff, all clothes in hand. Mrs. Lyncoff covered her eyes and turned her back toward them as they struggled to dress quickly. Cars slowed as they passed up the drive. I wanted to burst out laughing, but Norma would have my hide. She couldn't see what was going on from her desk. I watched the whole show, beginning to end. I didn't care if I got fired. This was worth it.

Mrs. Lyncoff burst through the door. "What are you still doing here?"

"I thought you wanted to talk to me," I said.

"No. Just go," she said.

Chuckie and Joan scrambled behind the desk gathering their belongings, while Juliette busied herself on the phone. Chuckie's face steamed with exasperation. His stuff lay spread out, and he was flinging it all around, hurling words foreign to him. Joan stuffed her gizmo in her purse, along with some other weird items. Juliette looked at me as if it was hard to concentrate on her call. I could understand. There was a lot of commotion around her. Wow. I guess they were as good as fired. I felt ecstatic. One, for getting rid of Chuckie, and two, for having a real shot at the front desk. I'd talk to Mrs. Lyncoff in the morning. I didn't think now would be a good time. She needed to cool off.

Well after evening's fall, I tromped the decibel gadget and sound machine outside and hooked them up. Dragged them to the garden's edge, carefully climbing down the embankment to the water's slippery surroundings. With the lower tide, I spotted a large concrete pipe in the vicinity of the sound. I guessed it to be a storm drainage pipe that runs into the ocean. It appeared this pipe acted like a conduit. The noise resonated through the large channel up into the house. Made perfect sense. No wonder it resulted in such a powerful uproar. I plunged the hydrophone into the fish's habitat, popping on my headphones. I turned the controls gradually to see if the slightest increase or decrease in sound and intensity made a difference. The humming actually caused a strong vibration, more evident with this equipment. I housed myself on a seaweed ridden rock, barnacles poking through my pants. I lay down uncomfortably and gazed up at the intense stars, trying to count them. I envisioned boiling a Midshipmen in the Big Dipper. A couple of hours elapsed, and no recognizable change. I felt tired, wanted to go to sleep. I'd have to try again another night. I trudged up the hill, one hand on dirt, clinging to any foreseeable weeds for support, heavy equipment wrapped around my arm and shoulder. Seemed easier to get down than up. I plunked my weary self onto the hardened bed, annoyingly attentive to the mating fish reverberating through my skull. I plugged my fingers into my ears to no avail. My whole body shook. I cursed the fish to sleep.

CHAPTER SEVENTEEN

I raced to the office to find Mrs. Lyncoff and express my interest in the front desk position. Mrs. Lyncoff said she'd already contemplated it and would switch Riker and me up on the desk with Juliette during peak hours, until she figured something else out. She had a replacement coming in for Joan.

In the afternoon when James arrived I pulled him aside to fill him in. He already knew everything. I relished in the memory of Steve shaking his head in disbelief that Chuckie would be so desirable.

"They deserved it. But, I'm surprised she'd fire them in peak season," I said.

"Oh, from what I heard, she was madder than hell."

"She was. I saw her," I said.

I looked around. A few guests engaged in conversation over an afternoon cocktail, while Mr. Mac read the paper and sipped coffee. The white cat curled by his side. Oh damn, the vase, I remembered. What to do about it?

Check-in time arrived, so I assisted Juliette on the front desk. New guests emerged via the puddle. A rabbi and his wife, pitching their faith. The registration address read Atlanta, Georgia. His kippah atop his head and extended gray beard covered any readable expression. After check-in and a restaurant reservation, I escorted them to their room. I relayed tonight the chef planned something different, a barbeque on the patio, which would be nice on such a great day. His wife said that sounded lovely.

Simon brushed by me on the way down. I asked how Mary was doing. He said, "Spot on." He'd gotten used to her. It'd become a game, wondering where his shoes would end up in the morning. Usually by the door.

"It's not the first woman that's tried to run me off," he said.

Riker bolted through the door, late for his shift. I scoped the area for Mrs. Lyncoff, hoping she'd bear witness, but nothing. He marched into the kitchen, solely addressing Juliette on his way, only to return minutes later, munching on a croissant. Stood his post by the stairwell with half a mouthful hanging out.

"Hey, Stan," Tracy waved as she approached the desk. "I heard about Chuckie and Joan. Can't believe it. You must be pleased."

"More than a little," I smiled.

The whole staff gossiped all day and weeks following about Chuckie and Joan's firing. Riker seemed to care less, even though they appeared tight.

"How's it going?" Tracy asked. "Juliette's doing a good job, huh?" She left no room for an answer. "Juliette, how's it working next to this guy? You got a handle on him?"

"Good," Juliette replied awkwardly.

"Stop it, Tracy."

"Well, I got a handle on him," Tracy gloated as she pranced off.

Riker grabbed a pack of Marlboros out of his pocket, smacked the top against his wrist till one popped out. He pushed through the screen door, lit his cigarette, and leisurely ascended the drive.

"What the hell. Where's he going?" I asked.

"I don't know," Juliette said.

"He's such a jerk," I said. Juliette just laughed.

The desk calm, Juliette and I had nothing else to do but talk.

"So, what other things do you like to do besides skiing?" I asked.

"Really, I just love the mountains in any form. In the winter, I stand at the top and the air is incredibly fresh. I look around at this open space and feel really free. And when I ski down, I'm invigorated. And in the summer, I love to hike the mountains. It's a different sensation, because it's warm and you're not in all that gear. But it's just as amazing at the peak. That sense of freedom. Kind of like that scene in the *Sound of Music*, where she's on top of the mountain, twirling around. Feels that good. It's a different world up there. I also like to paint, mostly scenery. So of course, the mountains."

I could tell she worked out a lot. She asked about me.

"I don't work out with weights and stuff or ski. But I like hikes," I said.

"I really want to go on one," she said.

I recommended Cadillac Mountain.

"Would you like to go sometime?" she asked.

"Uh, sure. I guess. Yeah, I'd like that. Haven't been in a while."

Jerry punched through the door, not even turning to acknowledge me. "Hey, Jerry," I said. No answer. Just shot back to the bar. I heard some bickering, which led into the kitchen. As swiftly as Jerry arrived, he departed.

"Hold on. I'll be right back," I told Juliette.

"No problem. I've got it covered."

I found James in the kitchen and asked what was going on. He said he spent the night out, and Jerry went looking for him.

Couldn't find him anywhere. This morning, Jerry waited on his doorstep till he got home. And he told Jerry he was with me all night. Why me? James admitted he just needed a break. The guy was getting on his nerves.

"You seeing someone else?"

"I wouldn't call it exactly that," he said.

"Well, you're going to have to face Jerry sometime. Be upfront." James just nodded.

Mrs. Lyncoff stood at the desk, asking Juliette where I was. I heard Juliette say I'd stepped out for a quick minute. Riker had reclaimed his post. I slipped back into place and asserted a sheepish grin. Juliette got distracted by a phone call. Mrs. Lyncoff asked how the fish expedition progressed. I explained I had no discoveries yet but continued to work diligently. She just walked away.

Juliette hung up from the call and started giggling. "What's so funny?" I asked.

She pointed at Riker, leaned toward me and whispered, "Look. His zipper is wide open and no undies. Should we tell him?"

"Nah, let's leave that to Mrs. Lyncoff," I suggested. We cracked up, tears welling. Till my attention turned to Mindy, standing, waiting for the restaurant reservation book. A frown engulfed her face as she snatched the book from my hand and left.

Chef bolted out of the kitchen. "Where in the sam hell are the beets?"

"Huh?" I asked.

"My beets. They keep disappearing, and I'm trying to make beet puree for the lamb chops."

Juliette and I looked at each other, trying not to lose our composure. "You playing a joke?" Chef demanded.

154

"No. We have no idea what happened to them. Check with Tracy. She's the one always horsing around." He stomped off to find her.

"Hmm, sounds good. Beet puree. Blood bath on a plate." I shot a dirty look behind his back. Juliette's approving eyes lay on me.

Mr. Mac motioned to me and asked if I could bring him some of that good barbeque later this evening. Of course, I would, I told him. He seemed so lonely. I felt badly for him. He remained ever so nice, not a weird man after all.

The rabbi and his wife descended the stairs and into the bar lounge. The lounge had filled, but they managed to steal seats next to Kamal and his wife. All acknowledged one another.

"What can I get for you, Rabbi?" James asked.

"A Chablis for my wife and vodka tonic for myself, please."

"Absolutely. Coming up."

Kamal extended his hand and introduced himself.

"The pleasure is all mine," the rabbi insisted. He turned and admired the view out the window, said he'd love to plant a garden out there. Forever his and his wife's pastime, they not only planted beautiful, exotic flowers, but they had a vegetable garden, which they cooked from. Both he and his wife loved to create meals, but admittedly, his wife remained the better chef. No competition there.

Kamal shared they had a live-in cook and gardener, as well as driver, in Saudi. And they often ate out. So, no cooking for them. But they did enjoy a good meal.

Mr. Thompson and his lady friend grabbed the last two seats at the bar. "Well, howdy," he addressed the rabbi. "Let me buy these nice folks a welcome drink, James."

"Yes, sir."

The rabbi and his wife gratefully accepted. The group clinked glasses.

"Is everyone going to the barbeque tonight?" Mr. Thompson asked.

The response unanimous, Mr. Thompson suggested they all head to dinner after their round and grab a table together. All murmured in agreement.

The barbeque stood smoking with lobster tails, lamb, peppers, and onions. Chef donned a tall white hat, proudly flipping his delicacies with tongs. Mindy served drinks to Mr. Thompson and the gang's table and sneered at me as I passed. What'd I do?

I grabbed a plate for Mr. Mac, starting with the salad station. Kamal told the rabbi about the King Saad International Stadium his company just built. He boasted it has one of the largest stadium roofs in the world. Kamal insisted his new friend visit. He'd already had an acceptance from Mr. Thompson. Kamal assured them it would be his honor to host. I topped Mr. Mac's plate with some lobster and chops before serving, pleased to see Simon sitting with him. Mr. Mac's eyes lit up at the creativeness as he graciously accepted. I brought him a lemon infused water and offered to arrange a plate for Simon, but he said he'd be joining the other lot shortly.

Juliette called me over to relieve her for a break. "Gladly," I said.

"Thanks Stan," she said, ruffling my hair just as Mindy walked in. "I won't be long."

CHAPTER EIGHTEEN

Riker stood in my place next to Juliette at the desk, while I played sergeant of arms, watching the door. Mr. Mac struggled down the stairs hanging to the banister, so I leapt up to assist, holding his arm.

"You all right Mr. Mac?"

"The knees are a bit rusty."

I saw him to his lounge chair and brought him a coffee.

"How'd those photos of the statue turn out?" I asked.

"Superb. Just what I hoped for."

He suggested I join him, have a seat. I asked if he'd be staying the rest of the season to which he was unsure. He'd planned on only visiting a few days but decided to remain. He really didn't have anyone or anything to rush back to. The Maycliff, he said, started to feel like home.

"I hope you don't mind me asking, but have you ever been married?"

"Almost," he said.

"What happened?" I asked cautiously.

He looked at me intently.

"I had a very beautiful lady a long time ago," he said. "She was the love of my life. We were actually childhood friends. I had known her since I was five years old." His eyes began to well.

"She, my sister, and I did everything together. We were insepar-able. She lived right across the street from us. We were into all sorts of sports in those days. Hard to imagine now," he chuckled.

I continued to focus on his every word. "What happened?"

"Then, we grew up and went our separate ways to college. But we both knew we'd end up together in the end. It's just a knowing that you have, when you're with the right one."

"And?" I asked.

"When she returned from school, I was seeing someone else. More out of loneliness. And you know what I should have done?"

"No, what?" I anxiously asked.

"I should have broken it off with this other woman and been with the one I wanted to be with. But instead, this love of mine ended up leaving town. She thought I'd moved on. But I never did."

He cleared his throat. "After she left, I did end that relationship. But I made the mistake of not running after her until it was too late. She'd taken a job and her life had changed. I wrote her every week for over a year, trying to win her back. And in the end, I did."

"That's good," I said.

"Well, I lost a lot of time without her. She was about to quit her job and come back to me and…"

His glassy eyes reddened.

"Then she died. Suddenly. Tragically. She took a bad fall and broke her neck."

"Oh my god. I'm so sorry, Mr. Mac." He wiped the tears from his eyes and swallowed, taking in a deep breath.

"Lesson learned the hard way. Sometimes they're right in front of you. But it's so easy, so natural being with her, you don't notice until it's too late." He placed his hand gently on my arm and leaned toward me, whispering in my ear, "Find the right one and don't let go." He rested back and winked at me.

The warmth of his smile silenced us both for a moment. My mind raced to Mindy. And I thanked him for the advice. I wished I could talk to him more often.

"Now, let's change subjects," he suggested.

"Well, I do have a question for you," I said.

"Fire away."

"Do you hear a noise at night when you sleep?"

"Yes. Every night," he said. "It's the Midshipmen toad fish. Slimy litter buggers, who create a hell of a racket. I've studied them before."

"How come you haven't said anything, complained?"

"No point. It's an environmental issue. Nothing you can do about it. Just have to wait till mating season ends, sometime in October."

I told him Mrs. Lyncoff had me on a mission to rid these buggers. I'd never seen him laugh so much. He wished me good luck.

Juliette appeared with a morning dish of blueberry-topped oatmeal, setting it in front of Mr. Mac and excusing herself for the interruption.

"Why, what's this?" he asked.

"I thought I'd surprise you," Juliette said.

"That's so very kind. It's looks delicious. Thank you, Juliette."

"My pleasure, Mr. Mac. May I get you anything else?"

He said the dish was perfect, all he needed. Juliette said Chef requested my help in the kitchen. She could sit with Mr. Mac now, since she was on break. She touched my shoulder as I rose, as if to say, "good job." I excused myself to the kitchen.

Chef placed a bucket in front of me and asked me to de-shell the crabs. Simon suddenly barged through the door, wanted to see what went on behind the scenes. Intrigued, he asked if he could help pick out the crabmeat. Chef didn't mind, till he caught him nibbling as he worked and made a semi-snide remark. Simon paid no attention, just nudged me and kept munching. My mouth watered. I wanted to join in but knew that would be deadly.

From the kitchen window, I could see Mr. Thompson, Kamal, and the rabbi huddled behind the maple tree on the back lawn. Their spouses nowhere around. I figured the rabbi stood scouting out an imaginary vegetable garden.

"What are those musketeers up to?" Simon asked. He stuffed more crab in his mouth, leaving no meat for the bowl, before venturing out to the tree. Mr. Thompson peered around focusing on Simon, and the three dispersed from behind, coming in to view. The four walked back to the inn and went their separate ways.

When I'd finished with the crab, Chef asked me to chop some veggies. "Did you ask Tracy about the beets, Chef?"

"Said she had nothing to do with them."

"That's odd. She'd be the first one I'd suspect."

"Well, I'd blame it on that damn Pickering if he were still around," Chef blurted.

I choked up. "That one beet did him in pretty well."

"Not well enough," Chef said. "A few more bites and lethal toxins may have set in."

I asked Chef about the country club he worked at in Palm Springs. Said he'd been working winters there for fourteen years. A few more and he may retire. He'd like to spend more time hitting golf balls around and reading. Cook for fun, not for work. I told him I'd love to go there sometime; heard great things about California. He encouraged it but said his particular club's staff had worked there for ages. Impossible to get a job there now. I told him I wanted to go to New York this year. Although a big city, like I found Boston to be, it's somewhere I've always wanted to experience. Not sure I could afford it though. Chef said he lived in New Jersey before California. That's always an option to commute to the city. Good idea, I thought.

My attention turned to Juliette as she strolled carefully by the open kitchen door, her arm wrapped around Mr. Mac's. She was making him laugh. I wondered where she was going with him. From the kitchen window, I could see her still holding on to him standing on the terrace. She was pointing out to the water and talking. She looked at him momentarily then patted his arm gently. They appeared to be watching something. Chef distracted me, talking about New Jersey. When I peered out again, they were gone. As Chef and I hit a lull in our conversation, my attention shifted to Juliette as she swept through the door. She unraveled her ponytail, letting her silky waves fall just over her shoulders.

"Hey guys." Her hips swiveled to the coffee machine. "I'm getting Mr. Mac a coffee. Anyone care for a cup?"

"Sure, I'll have one." I joined her, studying her almond shaped eyes as she passed me a mug.

Chef asked how many reservations we had so far for this evening. She thought about twenty people.

Juliette asked if I had off tomorrow, did I want to go on a hike? I'd the daytime free and thought that a great idea. I needed the exercise. Riker appeared from behind, announcing he'd like to go too but had to work. What about the next day, he asked.

She admitted tomorrow was better. Norma would be covering her shift, she said as she slipped halfway out the door.

"Are there extra vases around, Chef? Mrs. Lyncoff's favorite ones got knocked over and broken." He pointed to the closet and said they were all in there. I grabbed a vase that looked most like the ones the cat and I shattered and switched the flowers at the front desk. I could see Mr. Thompson, Kamal, and the rabbi chatting their way up the drive. Simon was not around.

James twirled a penny on the fountain's rim and when it almost stopped to fall, he flicked it in. He reached in for someone else's lucky coin and did it again. He kept going, deep in concentration till he bored of it or just had to get to work. He pushed through the door, carrying a small case. I followed to the bar.

"How's it going?" I asked.

"Oh, it's going. Downhill fast."

I asked if he'd had the talk with Jerry, and he did. He told Jerry he needed time and space. But Jerry wasn't taking it well. Blamed me.

"He thinks something's going on between us," James said.

"Well, of course, since you told him you spent the night with me. Frig. He'll never speak to me again." James just shrugged.

I looked at the bag. "You going somewhere?"

"Oh, no. That's Fancy," he said.

"Huh?"

He unzipped the bag and pulled out a little Maltese, modeling a pink studded collar, hair-bow, and freshly painted nails to match. "Meet Fancy." He shoved the dog in my arms. Fancy's little rough tongue licked my cheek. Jerry's new dog, he said. Jerry had bought her as a surprise for the both of them. But Jerry's so mad, he's making him take the dog for now. James claimed only to babysit till Jerry calmed down.

Mindy rounded the corner, reservation book in hand. Asked if we could hang out tomorrow, maybe go to lunch.

"Uh, well. Um. Actually…I can't. I have plans."

"What kind of plans?"

"Well, I have to babysit Fancy, this here dog of James's. Well, actually Jerry's. Yep, James just asked me." James's silence cut the air. He knew he played the cover up.

"Okay," she said. "That's too bad, because I had a fun idea." I suggested perhaps we could do it over the weekend. She said, we'll see, leaving a trail of coolness behind. I explained to Jerry that I felt sorry for Juliette. She didn't know too many people in town, so I agreed to go on a hike. I couldn't back out now. Course I couldn't, he said slyly. His mind remained in the gutter.

"Stanley!" Mrs. Lyncoff shouted down the hall. I threw the dog in James's arms and hurried to the desk. "This is not the vase I mean. Please get the proper one, now."

Pushed to talk, I explained that a cat knocked it over. I didn't know whose cat it was. It just appeared. She told me not to be ridiculous. She'd never seen a cat around, and to fess up when I'd made a mistake, admit I'd broken it. She warned the replacement would come out of my wages. On this unfair battleground, I was about to surrender.

"No, Mrs. Lyncoff," Juliette stepped in. "It wasn't Stan's fault. I did it, accidentally knocked it over. I'm really very sorry. I should have told you earlier, but I didn't realize how important it was to you. It can come out of my wages."

I couldn't believe what I was hearing. I wanted to stop Juliette from taking the fall, but I couldn't make her look like she was lying to Mrs. Lyncoff.

"Very well, Juliette. Thank you for telling me the truth. I'll let this one pass," Mrs. Lyncoff said.

When Mrs. Lyncoff disappeared from view, I thanked Juliette.

"Why did you do that for me?" I asked.

"I just wanted to help you out," she said. "I feel like Mrs. Lyncoff is on your case a lot."

"She is. Thanks a ton. I owe you one."

"No, it's fine," she said, resting her hand briefly on my chest.

"I have to go walk James's dog. I'll see you in a bit," I said.

I liked Juliette's modest smile she always flashed at me. I snuck Fancy outside for a walk, as James had asked. We hid behind a bush in case Mrs. Lyncoff looked out. I'd had enough trouble for the day. I could faintly hear Mr. Thompson, Kamal, and the rabbi quietly talking. They mentioned a golf game and shared a pat on the back before heading in.

I crept behind them, peering around for Mrs. Lyncoff. Mr. Thompson stood at the desk, accompanied by his lady friend. Said he suggested to the girls, which included Kamal's and the rabbi's wives, they have a spa day. Asked Juliette to book something for the ladies, while he and his two new companions enjoyed a day of golf tomorrow. He stood by while she made the call.

"The ladies are all set, Mr. Thompson. Their full package starts at nine. And your tee time is eight o'clock."

"Super. We need a caddy, too."

Mrs. Lyncoff overheard as she plowed by, suggesting I'd be delighted to be their caddy. Just one more friggin' hat.

***

The rabbi carried his own bag, and I lugged the other two, along with a cooler pouch. Another caddy would have been good. After each shot, they handed me their club as I handed them their beer. I replenished Coors as rapidly as they slipped down. One six pack already toast. The golf cart selling drinks arrived in perfect timing. They bought another six pack for me to carry and offered me one. I wanted to accept but had no hands left. I also wanted to hitch a ride on that cart.

I could only hear tidbits of conversation. Kamal told them his development company was coming to the US, starting with a chain of restaurants. He asked Mr. Thompson if he was looking for investments.

"I might be interested," Mr. Thompson said. "Tell me more."

"It's about opening up restaurants all around the United States that serve fresh Maine lobster. We start one main restaurant and franchise the rest in Oregon, Nebraska, Alabama, everywhere. We buy the lobsters wholesale and ship them overnight. They keep beautifully. This will make lobster affordable to everyone. Lower costs, more profit," Kamal explained. "We can sit down later, and I'll show you the plans."

Kamal suggested to the rabbi it might be a good opportunity for him to invest, too, with his love of food and cooking. The rabbi agreed it sounded like an interesting concept. He'd like to hear more about it.

Guess it proved true that business was conducted on golf courses. Mr. Thompson and Kamal grabbed their bags from me and asked me to run to the clubhouse for another six pack, threw me some dollars. I had some money of my own and bought myself a beer to swig down before heading back out. The heat had revved up since morning, and I was thirsty. I had to fight for position though, trampled by other parched golfers. The eighteen holes progressed slowly on the hundred-year-old greens.

I dropped the three back at the inn and insisted James join me at Aussie's for a drink later. We stuffed Fancy under the table. I told him about my day as a caddy and Kamal's restaurant plans. I couldn't quite explain it all. Sometimes things get distorted when eavesdropping. I wished I had money to invest; so did James. He asked if I looked forward to my hike with Juliette tomorrow.

"I am. I like Juliette. She's nice."

"Not to mention attractive," James coaxed. "And sweet."

I let his comment dissolve, as I gazed around the room.

"Jeez, something going on there?" he asked.

"No. I just like her to talk to. She's good company."

"Good company?" James provoked.

"I guess, maybe if I weren't dating Mindy, she might be the kind of girl I'd go out with. But don't repeat that to anyone, not even Jerry. Especially not Jerry since he's mad at me."

"I won't. I promise," he said.

"You know, Juliette's the one that saved you from getting fired," James said.

"Huh? What are you talking about?"

"I know all, as you've probably figured out by now," James said. "When Mrs. Lyncoff was about to throw the hatchet down on you, because of something Chuckie told her, some lie, Juliette told Mrs. Lyncoff that Chuckie and Joan were in the bush. So you should be grateful to her for protecting your hide."

I was stunned into silence. I had no idea.

"Why would she do that?" I asked.

"Jeez. Why do you think?"

"She took the blame for the breakage of Mrs. Lyncoff's favorite vase for me, too."

"That's a catch," he said.

James let me simmer awhile then started on another subject.

"Mo told me the guy who bought Coconut Joe's Ice creamery is that ex-cop that caused a scene at the inn. Apparently, he's bad news. Into all sorts of illegal stuff. He sold a whole bunch of illegal explosive devices over the Fourth of July weekend. One kid nearly blew his hand off," James said.

"I thought I saw him in town."

"Yep, he's here, all right. Apparently, he stayed in town 'cause he had nothing to go home to," he said.

"Hmm. Well, I've gotta get back to the inn to fight fish." We both got up and headed our separate ways.

I grabbed my warrior equipment, trudging down the ridge to the slimy rock, my control central. I blasted the sound and frequency to their highest levels, the hydrophone resonating the consistent hum to my eardrums. It felt like it fried my brain. And all I wanted to do was fry fish. I sat in darkness, pondering how these fish even had sex.

Another night of research accounted for, I gave up. I remained no better off. Lying awake with the constant noise, my mind repeatedly raced over my conversation with James. I woke tired from another sleep deprived night but looked forward to the hike. I wished I'd been more relaxed with Juliette but acted a bit like a bumbling fool, not really paying attention to our talk. I tried to make it a casual friend thing, but in a weird way, it felt like a date.

Mindy seemed more than pissed off when she hunted me down. She said Riker told her I'd gone on a hike and with whom. Her veins protruded from her temples, and her voice deepened. Her squinting eyes dug into mine.

"Why'd you lie to me, Stan?" she demanded.

"I'm sorry. I just...I didn't want to hurt your feelings or get you upset. You're often too busy for me, with your new job and all. I didn't expect you to make plans with me. And I'd already committed to her. I felt sorry for the girl. She's new in town and asked me to go on a simple hike. That's all."

"You could have asked me to join," Mindy belted out.

"I know. I'm sorry. But I think she's shy. And I want to spend time with you, alone, not with anyone else. And I didn't want to make a big deal out of it. Just a short hike. You know we all kind of hang around each other here."

I reached out my hand to grab hers, but she slapped it away.

"Don't touch me!" She shouted. "You lied to me. I don't know how I can ever trust you again. If you want to date her, go ahead."

She studied my face. "I don't. That's ridiculous. I'm dating you. I don't want to date anybody else."

I tried to grab her hand again, but she backed off, retracting her arms to her chest.

"I can't talk to you anymore right now. You're a huge disappointment," she said as she stomped off.

"Mindy?" I called. "Mindy, please?" She kept walking away. "I'm sorry."

CHAPTER NINETEEN

I shot down the creepy back stairway and out the door. The day looked gloomy, overcast with sprinkles. I zipped my windbreaker and raised the hood. I wanted to pick up flowers for Mindy and thought I should stop by the five and dime on the way. I needed to face Jerry at some point.

I grabbed a coffee to go, bumping into Chuckie at the desk on the way out. "Oh. What are you doing here?" I asked.

"Came to get my last pay check."

I asked him how it was going, not that I cared. He said he'd found a job at a new ice cream shop in town, Coconut Joe's. I said I'd heard of it. He claimed to love it, because he could nibble all day. Looked like he had been. Joan worked there too, doing the books. He gloated the two of them pretty much ran the show, didn't have to answer to anyone, except Joe. Chuckie handed Juliette a free ice cream card and told her to stop by sometime. Said she needed to taste the new peanut butter and jam swirl. Where's my ice cream card? I waited for him to pass me one, but he didn't. Juliette smiled and teased she'd share. Norma descended the stairs and handed Chuckie an envelope. He cackled and shot out the door.

I swung by the five and dime. Fancy sat atop the counter and barked when I walked in. The little muffin stood and wagged her fluffy tail, pink nails pawing at me. Jerry focused on a magazine, not veering off course.

"Hey Jerry."

He grunted, still focused on his read.

"I like your dog."

"Cut the crap, Stan."

"I don't know what you think has being going on, but you're dead wrong."

"I understand you have a new girlfriend. Is her name, Juliette?" he provoked.

That stumped me. I turned and left. My stomach tumbled upside down. A darkness overwhelmed me. I felt suddenly alone. How could James do that to me, tell him anything? I stumbled aimlessly to the flower shop and picked out the first bouquet I saw. My mind lay blank on the walk to Mindy's. I knocked on the door several times but no answer. I left the flowers leaning at the front.

I decided to head to the ice cream shop. Chuckie manned the counter. I asked to speak with Joe. He wanted to know why, but I told him it was personal. Joe reluctantly allowed me in his back office. I explained the fish situation and asked for suggestions. He said he had just the thing I needed. He scrounged around in a box and handed me a bag.

"Here. On the house, this time. Just be careful lighting the fuse," he said.

"Are these like firecrackers?" I asked.

"No," he laughed. "They're stronger than that. They're called squibs. Just be sensible. Don't blow your finger off."

Oh god. What had I gotten myself in to? I needed my sanity, though. These fish had to go. And Mrs. Lyncoff would be pleased. I thanked him and grabbed the bag. I asked

Chuckie for a peanut butter swirl. Of course, he charged me. I started to get excited. A new plan of attack. I scarfed down my cone vindictively.

Smoke penetrated the door of the linen closet. Tracy, Sam, and all the maids engulfed in fumes. Tracy became one smiling face I longed to see. She seemed more of a friend than James now. She insisted I sit for a while and catch up. Said the girls were just talking about the sale of the inn, still worried about it. But she distracted herself gossiping about this morning's episode. A guest got her hair caught in the sink drain while washing it. The clump was too big to yank and she'd been leaning there for quite some time when Tracy found her. She had to call Riker to dismantle the pipe and plunge the woman's hair out from below. Tracy was grossed out at the thought of that plunger ever touching her hair. I agreed. And left them chomping on chocolates. I just wanted to stop by briefly to see what they were up to.

I waved to Mr. Mac in the lounge, and he gestured me over. He said he'd be delighted if I joined him a minute. I was always welcome to sit down when I had the time. I grasped the opportunity. I wanted to know more about him. He seemed such an interesting man. I asked what line of work he'd been in.

"I was a lawyer for years, defense attorney. I retired years ago from the big stuff, but I've been doing a little paperwork here and there for young colleagues. Kept my mind fresh. But I'm done with that now. It's getting too much for me."

That's why he had so much time on his hands. He admitted he missed the old days sometimes, the action, but not the hours or headaches. He used to stay up all night studying cases.

"What are you going to do when you go home?" I asked.

"Not really sure yet."

Now I understood why he stayed so long at The Maycliff. He had no plans. I excused myself to change into uniform. I spotted Simon getting out of a Mount Desert Realty car, holding a slew of papers. I'd seen him in that car a few times. Riker pulled up the minivan and helped Mrs. Butterfield and Pickering out for her unusual return visit. I wondered if Mr. Mac felt excited.

Once dressed, I stood behind the desk to help Juliette, when Mindy walked in, threw her arms around me, and thanked me for the flowers. She'd brought them with her. She knew they had to be from me. I tried to brush it off as no big deal with Juliette looking on. But Mindy kept insisting it a huge thought and how happy I'd made her. She grabbed my hand, and I pulled her outside. She apologized for her behavior earlier. She wanted to do something fun together as soon as we both had time off. I concurred. She kissed me and left. I subtly slipped back behind the desk.

"Can you hold down the fort a minute?" Juliette asked.

"Sure."

Juliette grabbed a clear plastic box out of her purse. It held a white corsage. She carried it carefully over to Mr. Mac's table and stood chatting with him. He beamed when Juliette handed him the flower. She bent over and gave him an endearing hug.

"What was that for?" I asked.

"You'll see," she said.

"Oh, okay. Well, what did you get up to today?" I asked.

"I went on a hike with my roommate. It was fantastic," she said. "You want to go again sometime? I'm always up for going."

I didn't want to hurt her feelings, so I accepted but knew I probably shouldn't.

My body heated with emotion at the sight of James. I pulled him aside and confronted him, asked how he could share my thoughts about Juliette with Jerry, when I'd specifically asked him not to. And he promised he wouldn't. He said he didn't mean to; it's just that Jerry was throwing a fit. So James looked for a distraction. He said it backfired on him, because Jerry really didn't think it was a big deal, having a crush.

"I don't have a crush!" I shouted. "I never said anything about a crush."

"Okay. Quiet. Calm down. I'm sorry. I thought you'd understand. You know I'm trying to work things out with Jerry."

"James, you don't do that to a friend. When someone tells you something in confidence, you keep it to yourself. It's that simple. And I'm not your decoy."

"I know. I said I'm sorry. It was a mistake. I won't do it again," he said.

While James apologized, I stayed ticked. I thought I could trust the guy. What else had he let slip? I wished Steve was here.

Simon strutted in, asking if Mrs. Lyncoff was around.

"Probably in her office," I said.

"By the way, Mary must have given up. My shoes haven't moved in two days. Maybe she knows I'm checking out tomorrow."

"Must be," I said, "or she's finally accepted you."

"Doubt that," he said.

"You going back home?"

He said he was. His work was done. I wondered what that work could be. He never seemed to do anything but play.

Mrs. Butterfield had come down from her room and was sitting with Mr. Mac. It was nice to see him with company. She signaled me over. The first thing I noticed was the corsage pinned to her dress. I peered back at Juliette for a brief moment. I had to ask Mrs. Butterfield to repeat herself. She requested

I look for Pickering. He's getting so cheeky, she said. Ran off again. I covered the inn, calling him. Nothing until a whimper came from the closet that housed the payphone. The white cat stood guarding the door. I brushed him aside and found Pickering on his hind legs, jumping. Mrs. Lyncoff trekked by, demanding I remove Pickering at once, repulsed I put the dog in a closet. But I didn't, I tried to tell her. That damn cat must have done it. Surprisingly, Mrs. Butterfield did not fuss when I returned Pickering to her.

"Well done, Riker." Mrs. Lyncoff found him vacuuming up a spill. Honestly, that guy runs and finds something productive to do when he sees she's around. Otherwise, he's a lazy ass.

I parked myself near Juliette, and we talked through the evening till our shift nearly ended. Mindy had gone home. Juliette asked if I'd like to go for a drink, and I reluctantly thought I'd better not. Another time. Riker had left the vacuum out, so I asked if she didn't mind covering till I got back from returning it. No problem, she said.

I opened the linen closet quietly, hoping I might find Tracy and scare her. She usually finished turndown around now. I twisted the knob as slowly as I could and was just about to shout, boo. But instead, I found Riker and Mindy. They shot back when I entered, said I frightened them. I didn't catch them embraced but suspected they were.

"We were just looking for some kitchen towels," Mindy said. Her voice high in pitch. She acted overly enthusiastic to see me.

"I didn't ask," I said.

I walked out of the closet, and they followed. Riker sped in front.

"Hey, will you walk me home?" Mindy asked.

"I'm kind of tired. And it looks like Riker can do that," I said.

"I'd like you to come," she said.

"Not tonight."

I left them in the hallway and returned to the desk, telling Juliette I actually would love to go for a drink. Instead of Aussie's, we found a quiet little bar off the main strip. Juliette's movements were quiet and precise. She focused on our conversation with an infectious smile.

"Hey, I've been meaning to ask. Did you tell Mrs. Lyncoff that Chuckie and Joan were in the bush?"

"Yep," she snickered.

"Wow. Well, thanks for saving me. I would have gotten fired if it weren't for you," I said.

"I know. And I didn't like the way Chuckie treated you," Juliette said.

I was taken back by her kindness. I told her I'd make it up to her sometime, but she insisted I didn't need to.

"Did you ever hear about the bellman from last year that I worked with?" I asked.

"No. Tell me," she said.

"His name was Steve. And I became really tight with him during the summer. We used to go to Aussie's a lot and just mess around the inn." I went on to tell her the whole story about his death.

She placed her hand on my arm momentarily, while her crystal eyes sunk into mine.

"I am so very sorry, Stan. That had to be a horrific time for you. He sounds like a great guy. I would have liked to have met him."

"He would have loved you," I said.

I told her Mindy and I might go to New York this summer. I'd look for work, while she attended school. She asked why

I didn't hang out with Mindy more. I explained she's really busy with her new maître d' job. An inquisitive look embraced her delicate features.

"What about you? What happened with your boyfriend?"

"I just trusted the wrong guy. That's all. I had to end it," she said.

"Ouch. I'm really sorry, Juliette." I wanted to hug her to make her feel better. But that would be awkward. It was different with the cop scene, her being new and everyone around, but here in this serene bar might send the wrong message.

"How long did you date him?"

"Just a year. It's for the best. Really. I'm happy it's over."

"Well, he's an idiot if you ask me. His loss," I said. "You'll find someone better. You deserve it."

"Thanks Stan." Her hand briefly touched mine gently.

I walked her home and we set a time for an early morning hike.

Before bed, I carried my new weapon to base camp. My hands felt a little shaky. I carefully attempted to light the fuse a number of times before it took and quickly tossed it in. Staring down, it appeared to have died when it hit the water. I tried several more. Goddamnit. I needed something water proof. I'd have to pay Coconut Joe another visit. There must be something more lethal.

***

I rose to the most spectacular autumn day, crisp air with a slight change in the leaves' colors. The morning hike with Juliette was an awesome way to start the day. I got some exercise, and it felt great shooting the breeze, with no strings. I sometimes talked to Juliette about Mindy, trying to figure her out. It was helpful to have a sounding board.

I threw a sweater over my uniform and drove Simon to the airport late morning. He'd dined with Mr. Thompson, Kamal, and the rabbi last night. They'd all been in the oil business at one time or another, he said. Smart businessmen. And with Kamal's knowledge in development and Simon's expertise in architecture, he enjoyed talking to them. Perhaps he could help Kamal with commercial designs in Saudi or the US sometime.

"Watch out for those blueys," I said as he stepped out of the van.

"No worries, mate. Pay heed to Mary. By the way, I left her a pair of old thongs. See if she gets confused and moves them."

I thought I'd just steer clear. That would freak me out. I bid him farewell and took advantage of the wheels, swinging by the hardware store for a net and fishing pole. I had an idea.

Norma embraced the door as I entered, her ears protruding from her head. She stared at my fishing gear inquisitively.

"You still working on the noise issue?" she asked.

I assured her I kept on it but nothing new to report. She looked back at my equipment.

"I'm not even going to ask," she said.

Her beveled look remained for an extended period before she unleashed her next item. She wanted my help covering up any rumors going around about the inn being sold. She insisted they simply weren't true. The Davies would continue to own the inn. They were traveling in Europe all summer, so wouldn't make it up this season. But they had no intention of selling. I told her I hadn't thought twice about it, although I had. She said Mrs. Lyncoff overheard some of the staff talking to guests about it and intended to put a stop to it immediately. If anyone would spread rumors, it would be Norma. Maybe that's how they got started.

Purse in hand, she stated she had to run some errands in town. She'd be back shortly if anyone needed her. I noticed her sideswipe the fountain and discreetly drop a penny in.

Kamal descended the stairs, his diamonds glistening from afar. They seemed bigger to me now, shinier, more magnificent against his body. Kamal, Mr. Thompson, and the rabbi continued to spend time together and discuss possible business plans for the remainder of their stay. Their check-outs were scheduled within days of one another. They seemed so different yet got along so well. I wondered what their lives entailed and if they'd be back next year.

The once vibrant colors of the large withering bouquet caught my eye on the kitchen counter. Mindy had forgotten her flowers a second day in a row. They just lay flat, with petals scattered about.

CHAPTER TWENTY

I woke in darkness, water spitting at my face. Where was I? In a fog, I raised my head slightly and peered around. I'd fallen asleep on a couch on the back patio. It must be night. The sprinkles picked up speed and belted at me, hurting my face. It was hail. I rolled off the couch and shuffled to the back door, but it was locked. I couldn't remember where I'd been the night before. I made my way to the kitchen door, but it wouldn't budge. I never had a key. It remained my job to lock the doors and windows at night, so how could I have locked myself out? I racked my brain to remember something, anything. Snippets started to arise as I tried to piece them together. I remembered being at Aussie's Pub, but with whom? I think James was there and I may have cursed him out. I did. My head throbbed. I felt sick. Shots of B-52's surfaced in my mind. I sat under cover on the kitchen step, letting my head fall in my hands. Blood grazed my palms. I vaguely remembered climbing down the back rocks, trying to scoop fish in the net. I don't recall catching any. Feeling a light brush against my body, I looked to find the white cat stroking his side against mine, tail raised to its limit. What do you want? The hail subsided, turning back to rain droplets as dawn's light emerged. For a moment, I imagined I saw Steve.

My job also entailed unlocking the doors in the morning, so I had to get inside somehow. On the side of the building hung a trellis, housing chrysanthemums. I began to crawl up the rickety wooden structure, placing every step precisely. I made it to the top, holding one hand on the trellis and pushing the window up with the other. It wouldn't budge. Appeared sealed shut or firmly locked. I'd try to make my way over to another window. I released my hand from the frame, detecting Mrs. Lyncoff's face. She appeared on the other side of the glass. Startled, I lost my balance, and the wooden structure peeled off and snapped, tumbling me to the ground, petals and stems slapping my face. The front door swung open. Mrs. Lyncoff's grimaced expression did not need words attached.

"I'll fix it," I offered before she had time to speak. She hastily turned her back to me and stomped off. I retrieved the big ladder and materials and got to work before my shift began.

Expecting breakfast would be heavy with a full house, Mindy arrived early, passing me on the way. She didn't say a word, even when I greeted her. Was she at Aussie's last night? I struggled to remember.

"Hi, Stan," Juliette said. "I had fun last night."

"At Aussie's?"

"Yes, silly. I hope you didn't get in too much trouble with Mindy, though."

"Uh. About what?"

"You know. The kiss. I hope she didn't take too much offense that you kissed me in the bar in front of her. I would have stopped it, but I didn't know it was coming."

Oh crap. "Uh. No. Hmm. I'm sure she didn't." How do I get out of this one?

"You mentioned having dinner tonight. Are we still on for that?" she asked.

"Um. Dinner? I guess so."

"Great. I've got to get to the desk. See you in there."

The Opossums strolled by the ladder. Beer Gut shook it and laughed. They sometimes came in for continental breakfast, to fill up on the bottomless bread and muffins. Beer Gut could really sock it away. Only one would order and all eat. No one ever said anything, I guess because they were local. They always managed to afford a Bloody Mary, though. James must have given them freebees.

The ladder wobbled side to side as I hung tight. Tracy on one side, Sam on the other, amusing themselves at my expense. Once stabilized, I climbed down, gazing at a rather shoddy job against the house, hoping the surviving flowers masked my work.

The familiar peeling of the motor raced around the circle before parking by the staff entrance. I carried the ladder back toward the woodpile, greeted by Riker's vindictive smirk.

"You must be in some hellhole," he sniggered. "Man. You've got some balls."

Oh my god. He was there, too. I vaguely recalled. Think I told him off as well. I ignored him and found another path indoors, avoiding Mindy. Thankfully, she left after breakfast, taking a break before her dinner shift. I wondered if I should cancel on Juliette tonight.

Mr. Mac waved as I passed the lounge, Mrs. Butterfield and her mutt by his side. She rarely found it too early for a cocktail, but it looked as if she sipped on tea. Mrs. Lyncoff stood talking to them, her hand resting on his chair-back.

My buzzer found me escorting new guests to their room, loaded bags in hand and around shoulders. I wobbled up the stairs carefully, not to experience another terrible mishap like the inspector's last year. Mr. Dunlop shunned me after that.

The young couple visited from Singapore, taking a month to travel New England, New Brunswick, and Quebec. I liked that we shared the same height.

"What's our room number?" The Singaporean man asked.

"Room eight."

"Very well. I requested a lucky number. That's good," he said.

He introduced himself and his wife as Tai and Mai Wong. He shared snippets of home. Said they ride bikes all over Singapore, including to shop for groceries, the wet market for veggies and fruit, and the cold market for other stuff, except fish. He went into a long story how he's been a fisherman for years. Spends all day, straw hat repelling the heat, spearing the devils for their dinner. Mai fillets them. I placed their bags down and stood while he finished talking. I told him that sounded like a lot of work for a meal. That triggered the thought of my fish. I was just about to ask if he could help.

"I'm just kidding," he chuckled. "Everyone has this misconception all we Chinese do is pick rice and fish. I'm in the shipping business, containers. Send and receive shipments all over the world. We're getting lots of gweilos moving to Singapore. That means Westerners, white people." He laughed in a funny manner, deep in his belly. "Gweilos help our economy, so no complaints there."

"What do you ship, if you don't mind me asking?"

"Not at all. Along with expats' personal belongings being shipped when they move, we also transport supplies and natural resources. We have one of the business ports in the world, I'll have you know."

"Tai, stop bragging," Mai said, rubbing his back adoringly.

He insisted he was only sharing relevant information. "It's good for the boy to learn these things."

"Interesting," I agreed.

"Anywhere we can get Laksa?" Tai Wong asked.

"What's that?" I asked.

"Oh, stop it, Tai," his wife insisted. "There's no Chinese around here. It's his favorite noodle dish. You'll just have to go without it for a while, Tai. We're here to try the native cuisine."

"Mai does make the best Laksa ever. Speaking of, I'm starving. Where can we get a bite to eat?" I offered a cheese platter or sandwich to tide them over till dinner opened, but that didn't appeal. They'd go into town to find something. Tai reached in his pocket and counted out pieces of unrecognizable change. Must have been Singaporean money. He tipped me and on route to his car, dropped eight coins into the lucky pool, one by one.

They whipped to town, returning with a bag of fish balls. "Mind if we fry some up?" Tai asked.

"No. It's fine by me. Chef's not in yet."

Tai grabbed a shallow pan from under the serving counter and poured oil three quarters up the iron skillet. He cranked the gas to its highest point to get it nice and hot. He insisted I watch how it's done and learn.

"We try one. Check out temperature. Then throw rest in," he said.

When the oil bubbled, he tossed a fish ball into the pan with a splash. I imagined a Midshipmen going in. The oil instantly spilled over the lip and into the flame. In a millisecond, the fire ignited the whole pan of oil, dangerously blasting it to the ceiling. Panicked, my life numbed before the inferno. Would the whole inn catch fire? I shot to the other end of the kitchen and grabbed the fire extinguisher. Fiddling, trying to figure out how the damn thing worked.

"Oh my," Tai said, sounding bewildered. "This isn't normal. Bad oil."

I finally released the safety gauge on the extinguisher and pushed down. White substance sprayed fiercely over the pan, into the air, and backfiring all over the kitchen. Specks of white powder floated in slow motion everywhere, even out the kitchen door, covering every conceivable space.

"Not good," Tai said, shaking his head. "America."

He snatched his packet of fish balls and left just before Mrs. Lyncoff and Chef barged in, having smelled the burning. She looked up at the blaze-charred ceiling then at me. I stood holding the empty extinguisher, scoping the snow-covered room and brushing some powder from my hair to my face.

"What in the hell?" Mrs. Lyncoff shouted.

"I can explain," I said.

Chef demanded I clean up every fleck. "Do you know how toxic this stuff is? I have to cook here tonight. You'd better make it, so I can serve dinner off the floor. That damn clean."

I swept then mopped, because I realized, once I started, the white powder turned to a glue-like substance when mixed with water. Then it would never come clean. I replayed the incident in my mind, trying to convince myself this had nothing to do with me. Just a coincidence. Either way, I was swimming against a current. Hours into it and body deflated, I put the cleaning supplies away, hoping it was a satisfactory job.

In the lobby, I ran into the last person I expected to see. Chuckie. He met me head on, pushing through the front door with a load of ice cream. He started delivering a variety of tubs to the inn weekly, per Mrs. Lyncoff's request. His eyes squinted, forehead frowned, as he trekked past me.

He turned briskly for a second. "You played the fool last night." And off he went.

My mind wandered to that psychic, Petra. Her words of warning resonated through me—I could bring the inn down. Did I have a girlfriend? A black shadow hovering over my future, challenges I must overcome. That I should live a long life if I chose the right path. I felt shattered.

I sought Juliette on the front desk and suggested we have an early morning breakfast, rather than dinner tonight. Explained I wasn't feeling that well. She looked a little disappointed but agreed to meet then.

On my trudge across the drive, I spotted Pickering on top of Fancy, having a go at her in the bush. I didn't even care if she was in heat. She seemed to be enjoying the moment. Damn lucky. It really was a dog's life.

CHAPTER TWENTY-ONE

I shoved down my pancakes and eggs at Nick's coffee shop, Juliette across from me. I still felt a little down, how the previous day unfolded. Juliette seemed to be one of my few allies. I told her it's probably best we don't hang out for a while, at least till I sorted things with Mindy. Mindy was somewhat emotional and reactive, I explained. Maybe once she calmed down, we could meet again. Juliette played as though she was cool with it.

Yesterday's rains transformed into a reasonable temperature with blue speckled skies. Mr. Mac and Mrs. Butterfield sat on the patio. It felt good to see him out of his chair. We had our first cruise ship lunch of the season arranged, which included a tour of the inn, Mindy handling one group, James and I our own. In turn, the new ship had offered a luncheon on board for our Maycliff guests. They wanted exposure, a marketing ploy. Mr. Mac and Mrs. Butterfield would be attending, already smartly dressed and prepared for their outing. Mrs. B asked me to keep Pickering in my room for the afternoon. I dropped the lovebirds at the pier and waited as a few cruise ship passengers climbed in the van. Mr. Mac's arm lay wrapped through Mrs. Butterfield's as they descended the ramp to the dingy.

Mindy remained frosty toward me. No words spoken. James was fine.

"I'm sorry again about breaking my word and mentioning anything to Jerry about Juliette. I deserved the telling off," James said.

"I agree. You did," I said. "But truce." We shook hands, and he pulled me in for a hug.

"I don't know how you're ever going to mend it with Mindy, though. But maybe that's a good thing."

I didn't want to think about it.

Fifty-eight passengers descended upon us, including the ones I'd picked up. The big buses pulled out front with the rest of the guests. Most appeared in their seventies and couldn't walk the full premises. But those who did enjoyed the tour. And they raved about the meal from soup to dessert, wine and atmosphere. Old people seemed so gentle and appreciative. I took a few back to the ship, while scooping up Mr. Mac and Mrs. B. They looked like a longtime married couple getting in the van. They'd had such a wonderful time, discussed going on a cruise together sometime. They'd been served a four-course meal, which they could only nibble at. Too much food but delicious. And the boat had live entertainment during lunch. Simply magnificent, Mr. Mac said. Mrs. Butterfield delighted they'd had the opportunity to shop in the variety of stores. Already having conjured up their evening dinner plans, the two would separate for a late afternoon nap back at the inn. Mrs. Butterfield waited in the lobby, while I grabbed Pickering from my room. Luckily, Fancy was nowhere around. Mrs. B would flip if she saw her baby involved in illicit acts, I'm sure.

Chef appeared madder than hell. He claimed he had a delivery of beets this morning sitting on the counter.

Demanded to know where they went. He'd run out of beets for the luncheon and had to substitute cauliflower. I assured him I had no idea, but I could help look. He needed the beets for dinner and grumbled I search for them. Riker stepped out of a guest room, having fixed a clogged tub. I asked if he'd seen the beets. He just made a dirty gesture with his hand near his pants. Tracy admitted she'd seen the beets on the counter this morning but hadn't touched them. And Juliette never went in the kitchen. I searched everywhere I could think of, even back in my room where Pickering had been. Nothing. On my way to tell Chef, I passed the woodpile where the big garbage bin sat, an empty box of beets by its side.

The Wongs lounged on the patio, gazing at the sailboats slipping by. I offered them a drink, but they'd wait till four. They nibbled on some pumpkin tarts they'd bought in town.

"It's a little early for Halloween treats, isn't it? It's not till next month," Tai Wong said.

I told him every holiday seemed to start earlier each year.

"You know we have something similar in Singapore in July, called Ghost Month. It's a festival, where the souls of the dead roam the earth." Chills crawled up my spine at the thought of Mary lurking around. "We burn incense, make food and material offerings, and set a place at the table with elaborate meals for our lost loved ones."

I hoped he didn't do the cooking.

"It doesn't sound like Halloween is about the deceased. Seems more like a gimmick for fun. Is that so?"

I agreed.

"Well, if I were here for that tradition, I'd dress in drag as a blonde gweilo," Tai said.

"Oh, stop it, Tai." Mai slapped his arm gently.

Well that would be interesting. "I think I'm going to skip Halloween this year. But I like the idea of Ghost Month. That sounds eerie."

"We'll take that drink now, Stan. A whisky for me and Chablis for the missus. Three-thirty is close enough."

James stood polishing glasses.

"Oh, by the way. This is from Jerry. I told him the truth that I wasn't with you that night." He handed me a bag of candy and a comic book. "He said to say sorry." That made me feel better.

"Hey sexy." Tracy slapped my butt as she approached the bar for a coke. I felt behind to make sure she hadn't stuck anything there. "Gotta do turn-down. Sam's sick. Couldn't make it in. Wanna help?"

"No thanks, not after the last time. You're on your own."

"So mistrusting," she said, as she strolled off, arms floating in air.

"There's a reason for that."

I asked James for a couple of good shots of vodka. Thought I'd slip it in her coke. Vodka seemed to be the most disguisable alcohol.

Mrs. Butterfield emerged in the lounge, telling Mr. Mac how dashing he looked. He returned the compliment and took her arm. I'd never seen him look so happy.

"Stan," he said, "this is for you."

It was a cool chalk drawing of the worn stature of the lady. "You did this?" I asked.

"Indeed. And I'd like you to have it."

"Thank you. I'm honored. It's so detailed. It looks like a photo."

His face lit before he turned to escort his lady to dinner.

Norma mentioned she and Mrs. Lyncoff would be attending the town council meeting this evening in regard to the inn and other businesses in town and asked I hold down the fort. But she had told me the inn wasn't up for sale and to stop the rumors. So, what was this about? Renovations?

I managed to slip the booze in Tracy's drink and give it a good stir with my finger. She'd left her coke in the linen closet while attending to the rooms. I slid out just in time to meet her in the hallway. "Hey," I blurted, as I hurried down the stairs.

I took Pickering outside for another jaunt, while Mrs. B enjoyed dinner. Dopehead stood next to Juliette at the desk, acting productive as Mrs. Lyncoff swept by. Pickering hauled me to a slight tree on the side of the circular drive, barking profusely and jumping against the bark. What'd gotten into him, a squirrel? He started running around the tree and me, wrapping his leash around my legs, making such a ruckus. I looked up to find the white cat peering down. Mrs. Lyncoff stepped outside and asked me to get a grip on the dog. The guests could hear all the fuss from the restaurant. Pickering's entwined leash pulled tighter as he tried to do another circle. Till I smacked the ground. Mrs. Lyncoff nodded and left. Damn cat. And dog. I lay there, imagining Steve teasing me.

James let Fancy out for a whiz. In Pickering's excitement, he hauled me to her, and the pair pranced to the watering hole for a drink. I hoped Mrs. Butterfield still dined. A stray penny lay on the bench of the fountain. Pickering's paw slapped it in like a hockey puck, and I wondered if he'd made a wish, too. Probably so, to get in Fancy's pants again.

Tonight would be a perfect opportunity to talk with Mindy. I had to resolve this. I waited by the staff entrance in the afternoon till she brushed by me. I pleaded she give me a chance to explain. But she ignored me. At the end of dinner, I knew I had to face her again. I just didn't know what to say, other than sorry. Riker kept interrupting. And Mindy repeatedly walked away. I told her I was drunk, so I got confused who I was kissing. It wouldn't happen again. Just a meaningless mistake. I quieted for a moment. She didn't warm. She actually seemed chillier, as she repeated the "confused who I was kissing" phrase, turning it into a question. This wasn't going well. At least I gave it a shot. I'd have to think of a special way to make it up to her, win her back. I never liked seeing her and Riker walk home together. That always burned, even worse now that she snubbed me.

Tracy staggered down the hallway, slurring her words and pointing at me. She wasn't much of a drinker.

"You'd better sober up before you drive," I said. She plonked herself down on a chair. I yanked her up. "Come on. I'll take you home." She cursed me out the whole way, said she had things to do tonight. I suggested she put her complaints in writing and get in line for vengeance toward me. There were people before her.

Mr. Mac and Mrs. B remained inseparable over the past few days. They shared all their meals together outside Mr. Mac's chair. They even ventured into town twice. The two submersed each other in gaze. I felt certain they'd get together when they left the inn, maybe even marry. Seemed like a family, with a dog and partial cat. Today, I drove them to Jordon Pond House for popovers and tea and waited in the van. I could tell at the end of lunch, Mrs. Butterfield had substituted her tea for gin, all giddy and chatty. He held her hand tightly and pressed lightly on her back to help her into the van. Mr. Mac said they'd gone on a little stroll by the pond after lunch. Absolutely magnificent. Tonight, they'd be dining in his room. He asked me to arrange two lobster thermidors, a bottle of Moët, and a double Tanqueray martini.

"We'd like a six o'clock delivery, please. But if you can come earlier to get the fire going, that would be terrific."

"Of course," I said.

Mrs. B asked me to take Pickering for the evening. Their dinner obviously played out well. They only asked me to drop their tray, not pick it up. All went quiet the rest of the evening. I never saw Mrs. B leave his room all night. God, even Mr. Mac was getting some. Good for him. Guess you're never too old.

The following morning, I brought them to play mini-golf in town, and in the afternoon they hit croquet on the lawn, over cocktails. Mingling at the bar early evening with Mai and Tai Wong, the couple chuckled at Tai's jokes, while James kept their drinks filled. Mrs. Butterfield didn't like her cocktail going below the halfway mark without another one in the works.

The two moved to a table near the crackling fire and cozied up. I heard Mr. Mac planning a trip to visit Mrs. Butterfield in New York this winter. She said they'd go to the Metropolitan museum, Carnegie Hall, Petrossian's for caviar and foie gras. They'd have so much fun.

While they became intimate, I slipped out the back with my fishing rod and net. I climbed down the embankment, my flashlight guiding way to the rocks. I found my spot and firmly positioned myself not to fall in. I'd checked the tide chart to make sure the tide lay low enough to reach the bottom, where the slimy pests hid under rocks, according to Mr. Mac. I still had some explosives left in the bag. I thought, if I could catch one of these toadfish, I'd plant a squib in its mouth and toss him back in. Whammo! He'd blow them all up. I scrambled with the net, while my pole stayed imbedded between rocks, fishing on its own. I repositioned myself to lie face down, closer to the action, digging and scraping on the ocean floor only to catch small rocks and other fragments. I knew those fish were in there. I just had to go deeper. I rolled over for a breather. More stars had entered the stratosphere, and they felt a temporary relief. I flipped back around, attacking lower, really edging my net into the gritty bottom. Still no success. I bounced up and this time straddled two rocks, digging deeper and harder, each time feeling success until I raised the net to find seaweed, pebbles, and clams. My fishing pole was equally ineffective. That's it. I'd have to get some fishing pants and boots and jump in the frigid water next time. I'd plan to move the rocks about with my feet. I refused to give up on the mission from hell. The thought escalated until I heard Mindy's voice on the back terrace. I could swear she was talking with Riker. But I'd seen them leave earlier or at least standing on the front drive. I called Mindy's name, but the voices went silent. Clammy fingers in ears, I struggled to sleep, conjuring up ways to win Mindy back.

As the lovers spent one last night together, darkness fizzled into day. Mrs. Butterfield snuck out of his room early morning to pack. She had to get back for her great-niece's wedding. She'd arranged a late checkout, so at least they had part of the day to enjoy. They lunched and even managed a walk up the long drive, hand in hand. Mr. Mac's eyes welled as he embraced her. A lingering hug. Mrs. Butterfield looked so glum. Riker opened the van door, and Pickering hopped out, tearing up the drive to greet James and Fancy, the two balls of fur dancing about. I retrieved Pickering and popped him back in the minivan. As they started up the drive, a pining Fancy raced behind the van, trying to keep up. Soon, her heartthrob turned onto the main road and vanished. A wincing Fancy laid down and closed her eyes. Mr. Mac had retreated back to his lounge chair. I placed Fancy by him, hoping they'd console each other. Both appeared lost. I talked to Mr. Mac periodically, trying to cheer him up. But his somber demeanor didn't waiver. I thanked him again for the great drawing. Said I'd keep it in a special place. I could tell he appreciated the compliment. He inquired about the soup of the day, so I checked with Chef. He'd be serving his traditional clam chowder with a shot of sherry. That reminded him to delegate a job to me. He asked me to take the clams out of the fridge and soak them for twenty minutes in fresh water. Then rinse and put them back in the cooler. Mr. Mac wasn't interested in the soup. Felt it was too heavy for him tonight. I tried to convince him into something else, but nothing sounded good. I returned to the kitchen to prepare the clams, as requested, letting them bathe while I ran some errands. I tried to surprise Mr. Mac with a complimentary cup of tea and cookies before his nightly retreat to his room. But he'd already left the lounge.

CHAPTER TWENTY-TWO

Dark clouds loomed at the start of day. Torrential rains and hurling winds attacked, while lightening belted the skies. The storm struck abruptly, as it always did in Bar Harbor.

Juliette grabbed me on the way past the desk. Said she'd been inundated with guest calls all morning, complaining they're sick—vomiting, diarrhea, horrific stomach cramps, nausea, fever—asking for a doctor. But she can't get a hold of one because of the storm. No one's going out. The roads are completely flooded. Mrs. Lyncoff didn't plan to be in till this afternoon. And she couldn't reach her either.

Just then the power went out, as routine in this weather. And it always sets off the fire alarm. I grabbed the flashlight and raced to the pay phone, thankfully catching the fire department in time. Last year, when the alarm triggered, they'd rolled up the engine before we could call it in false. All the guests shot down from their rooms in pajamas. Sounded like this time, the guests lay too sick to care.

"We have to do something," she said. "These guys are really ill. But why so many of them?"

"It could be a flu. But why aren't we sick then?"

"Or food poisoning," she said. "Most of them ate here last night, and it was a set menu, so they all had the same. And we didn't. Chef wouldn't allow us any steak or clam chowder."

The clams. Had I left them to steep too long? I can't remember the time it took to run errands around the inn. Oh my god, I hoped this wasn't my fault. I felt queasy at the thought. I agreed we had to help these sick guests. And Chef and Norma weren't in. They might be stranded, as well. I prayed it was the flu or some rare disease. But either way, we were on lockdown.

No one could call anymore, as the phones were out. Juliette and I each held a flashlight and scrounged through the blackened kitchen for some broth and clear drinks. Thunder consistently crushed through the walls as we scrambled.

I steered away from last night's dinner and grabbed some chicken. I lit the gas stove and boiled the meat, throwing in pinches of salt till it flavored. We scooped out the poultry and filled bowls of broth. Juliette and I agreed we had to get this to all the guest rooms. They couldn't come down or call. Tracy, Sam, and the other maids found their way down the gloomy stairs. They'd arrived early before the downpour. We loaded thirty-six trays with broth and warm ginger-ale, my mother's antidote when I fell sick. And one by one, we delivered them.

Mr. Mac lay in bed looking a little pale but insisted he felt fine. He said he went to sleep early, without dinner. Juliette ran and got him extra towels and a cold washcloth for his forehead anyway.

Mai curled up under the linens belching, while Tai remained trapped in the bathroom. "Should stick with fish balls," he strained to say through the door.

We found most guests in the same condition. With trays delivered and fresh towels dispersed, we started stripping beds.

Guests were sick every which way and sweating profusely, so they desperately needed fresh linens. We washed everything by hand since the electric stayed out. Pretty ghastly job. Then we did another round, checking on guests. I boiled more pots of broth, and we toasted mounds of bread, no butter, seeing who could stomach seconds. We needed to keep these guys hydrated.

Juliette kept trying to reach a doctor from the pay phone.

"Still, no one's answering," she said. "I'm worried."

"We'll just have to keep a careful eye out," I said. "If anyone seems deathly ill, we'll have to call an ambulance. Surely, they'd come, no matter what."

"I hope so," Juliette said.

In between breaks from running around, the maids, Juliette, and I huddled in the bar around the fireplace. We made that our base camp. I gathered wood from other areas of the inn to keep the fire going, as the outside supply would be drenched. We quickly grabbed food out of the fridge to salvage its coolness and feasted on lobster and crab, because that might go bad if the electric didn't come back on soon. We also nibbled on Chuckie's melting ice cream. We lit candles around the room. And Tracy told creepy ghost stories. The worst being the "I believe in Mary Worth" one, where you stand in the bathroom with a candle and repeat her name three times, then the bloody woman reveals herself. I kept waiting for our Mary to appear and get angry. The dark spooked me enough, without horrifying images placed in my head. Juliette squished up against me. Sam on the other side, but not so close.

The rains picked up speed, and thunder would not give up the fight. We could hear the wind scream through the windows, causing a noisy vibration. Light flashed intermittently, illuminating our faces for only an instance. Juliette looked content. I felt scared, although I wasn't going to show it. And Tracy just kept at it, trying to frighten me around corners. I wondered how long this would go on for. A day or week. A silhouette cast itself from the side of my eye, as we sat gathered around. My adrenaline shot up in panic. A real shadow stood by the lounge entrance. It looked like Mr. Mac standing by the doorway. Another arrow of lightening hit the room, followed by deep thunder. The candles extinguished.

"Mr. Mac?" I asked, struggling to see.

Only silence embraced the room. I repeated myself. The others looked around inquisitively. They didn't see anyone. Told me I imagined it, or maybe it was Mary. Tracy made a ghostly sound and wiggled her fingers in my face. I remained adamant it looked just like Mr. Mac before the candles went out.

Tracy and the others assured me they saw no one. I didn't know how they could have missed him in plain sight. He'd left the room. Maybe he'd fainted. We shot up and crept around the shadows, calling him, but no answer. A stream of lightning ripped through the hallway and the front door swung open with such force it dented the wall behind it. I ran to shut it, greeted by rain showering me. The downpour strong and carried by the wind. Juliette and I agreed we best check on Mr. Mac, while the others visited the Wongs and other guests.

Exit signs barely lit the stairs. We knocked on the door several times and only entered when he didn't answer.

"Mr. Mac?" I called. He lay back in bed, asleep.

"Maybe we'd better get him more soup?" Juliette suggested.

I thought that was a good idea, although he hadn't touched the first bowl. But a warm one would be better, and he'd be hungry when he woke, not having had dinner last night. She suggested we put an extra blanket on him. He might be cold. I grabbed the blanket at the foot-bed and pulled it up past his shoulders. A chill swallowed me. I felt Mary's presence. And Steve's. The white cat lay still by Mr. Mac's side, his eyes closed. I stared at Mr. Mac, the color extracted from his face. The rawness surrounded me as all came into focus.

"Mr. Mac?" I gently called. "Mr. Mac?" Silence.

My efforts of CPR weren't working. Juliette tore downstairs to call 911 on the payphone, while I continued CPR.

It took some time for the paramedics to show, but we knew it was already too late. While they worked on him, we rang Mrs. Lyncoff's number to let her know what happened. Only her machine picked up. Juliette finally tracked her down at Norma's. The two couldn't get out of her drive; the water had become so deep. She said she'd been ringing the pay phone, but we weren't picking up. We couldn't hear it.

Mrs. Lyncoff managed to hitch a ride with lobsterman Bert and his lifted truck. She arrived drenched and in a distressed state. She marched directly to Mr. Mac's room. The gang huddled in disbelief as reality swept through the place. I hoped for a miracle. The medical team seemed to take forever.

"I pray he's going to be okay," Juliette said, clinging to my arm as we waited.

"Me too," I said.

As he lay on the stretcher, blanket over his body and head, they carried him down the flight of stairs and stopped for a moment. Mrs. Lyncoff leaned over and lay her head on his chest, arms wrapped around him, tears cascading down her face.

"Goodbye, my dear Mac," she said.

The moment cemented itself in silence until Mrs. Lyncoff raised her head.

"How can we inform the family?" one of the paramedics asked.

"I am his family," Janet Lyncoff said. "He was my brother."

Only time had a heartbeat. I couldn't believe what Mrs. Lyncoff just said. They were related? There was no movement after the paramedics removed his lifeless body from the premises. The day remained dreary. I glared as if watching a movie but saw nothing. The last twenty-four hours seemed a wash. Nothing played in my head. It just lay blank.

Mrs. Lyncoff did not show the next day for work, yet the gossip continued without her, how no one knew Mr. Mac was her brother. We didn't understand why she kept it a secret. And how come, when he finally found happiness, it perished? I felt as though I'd lost a grandfather and friend. I revered his drawing even more now, grateful he'd given it to me.

They determined his cause of death, natural. It didn't appear to be food poisoning or flu. The funeral took place days later at the local cemetery, succeeded by a gathering at the inn's lounge, surrounding his chair. Mrs. Lyncoff's features had softened, and she appeared childlike. The photo of the three kids sat at the forefront of his table. Mindy approached me with a hug and said how sorry she was. She knew how I felt about him. The staff paid their condolences to Mrs. Lyncoff during the course of the afternoon. But she appeared distant, motionless. Vacant.

Days following, when I walked in the lounge, I looked at that empty chair. The room seemed sterile to me now. No one sat in his spot. Only the photo remained. The sick guests stayed in bed for days following. The illness turned out to be food poisoning, but not because of me, mercifully. The purveyor delivered bad clams. A number of their customers had fallen ill.

Mr. Mac thankfully hadn't eaten the shellfish. That would have made matters far worse, his suffering, then lawsuits. At least he went peacefully. I questioned if I really saw him that night in the doorway of the lounge or if the shadow cast was his spirit. I guessed the latter.

Norma tried to get a hold of Mrs. Butterfield for days but only reached her answering machine. She stood by the desk, asking about any return calls.

"Mrs. Butterfield just called in. She's on hold now," Juliette said.

"Oh good. I'll take the call here," Norma said.

I could tell by Norma's reaction how devastated Mrs. Butterfield must be over Mr. Mac's death. Two lonely people who find comfort in each other at the end of life, just to lose it all. A few tears spilled from the creases of Norma's eyes as she tried to console Mrs. Butterfield. I don't know whether Mrs. Butterfield felt Mr. Mac was her soul mate, but I knew Mr. Mac had only one. At least he found love and happiness again.

"I'll take the call in the office now." Norma placed the phone on hold and trotted up the stairs. Clearly, it would take some time for Mrs. Butterfield to absorb the news.

Juliette stood crying, hiding her face in her hands. The emotion of it all had gotten to her. Empathic, I joined her behind the desk and held her for a short while before turning into Riker. He stood like a bodyguard. I knew this would not be good, traveling back to Mindy. But I didn't care. I loved Mindy, and if she couldn't understand that, I didn't know what to do.

The mood of the inn needed to lighten. It lay somber and not good for guests, who had already been through hell. James refilled drinks for Mai and Tai Wong who clung to their favorite bar stools. Tai had bounced back to his normal self.

"Psst." James gestured to me, slipping to the side. "I found out from Mo what happened at the town council meeting last week." My interest peaked. "Jeez. It turns out the inn has been looking at a private sale. And you know who was going to buy it?"

"Mr. Thompson?" I asked.

"No. Simon. That's why he came here. He was scouting us out and checking out the operation, also looking for investors. Maybe that's why he hung out with Mr. Thompson, Kamal, and the rabbi."

"And?" I asked curiously. "Is he going to buy it?"

"No, thankfully. He decided not to, which explains the realtor he went around town with. He perused other opportunities, as well. Not sure he's bought anything but certainly not The Maycliff. And, the town council shot down any plans to make this a spa. So..." He flung his hand back, then slapped it into mine. "...looks like we're still employed here."

I didn't plan on returning next year but felt relief from the good news. At least I didn't bring the inn down. And Tracy would be thrilled.

James also found out the reason Mrs. Lyncoff never introduced Mr. Mac as her brother. They'd been estranged for years. This trip mended their quarrel and reunited them, whatever that fight might have been about.

Tai and Mai spoke Chinese amongst themselves, cackling in the corner. "Stan, I teach you Mandarin while I'm here. Say, 'Tishi ging' and hold out your hand."

"Tishi ging," I repeated.

"That's so rude. Means, 'tip please.' You shouldn't ask for a tip!" Tai's head bobbed in self-humor, while his wife quietly snickered, hand over mouth. I just politely acknowledged his wit.

Seeking Mindy in the kitchen, I thanked her for the sympathy at Mr. Mac's memorial. I asked if we could go for a drink tonight after work. She accepted, her mannerisms cushioned. Chef stood on the phone, his voice raised talking to the purveyor from whom he'd bought the clams. He yelled that the contaminated clams hurt his reputation and threatened never to purchase through them again. He'd find another supplier. Then hung up.

That evening at Aussie's, Mindy and I talked endlessly about Mr. Mac and all that had gone on in the inn this summer. She apologized for being so sensitive. And I did, for being such a jerk. She forgave me. Said she'd thought about New York and would like to give it a try when the season here closed. I anxiously agreed to look into it. We kissed and held hands the whole way to her house, but she felt too tired to have me stay. So I went back to fight fish.

I'd borrowed fishing clothes and gear from Jerry, an avid fisherman. He'd take his row boat out on days off and find a spot to jump in. Wouldn't leave till he caught something. Or hitch a ride on Bert's lobster boat. I climbed down the embankment with a heavy load. At my headquarters, I planted myself in perfect position to jump in the icy water. Freezing even with the proper waders and boots, I grabbed the pool light, attached to several extension cords, along with my new spear toy. I stabbed hard and shuffled the rocks with my feet, poking again and again. I let the pool light hit bottom and reached for the net. Spear in one hand, net in other, ferociously jabbing and scooping at the same time, like a mad man, constantly shifting rocks. I would get those slippery toads, if it killed me. I schemed, decided to stop and stay still for a few minutes, so they'd think I'd gone. I hoped I was disrupting their little party. They thought they could have all the fun. On a count of five, I went on another rampage, saltwater splashing fiercely against my face and into my eyes.

I didn't care. I kept at it relentlessly, heavily ramming the spear down over and over again, my breathing fast and strenuous. I pounded the ocean floor with as much force as I could muster until I became chilled and worn. I examined the spear head for any particle of toadfish. Even a smidgen would please me. But it remained unblemished. I threw the paraphernalia on the rocks and pushed myself up and out, trudging back up the hill. Although this felt like a major setback, I'd formulate a new plan. I was inching closer to success. Time was of the essence for these slime balls.

It usually spooked me entering the servant quarters, especially so late at night, everything gloomy and quiet. And the back stairs where Mary was supposedly pushed down always carried a chill. My door creaked when I pushed through it. Bam, I felt something smack me in the face hard. A huge furry spider. Frig, that hurt. Flashing orange and green lights beamed around the room. A ghostly sound crackled from a corner tape deck. A hideous witch hung from the ceiling, and a bloody arm protruded from my bed sheets. Dammit. I calmed when I realized Tracy paid me a visit. I climbed out of my wet gear, letting it drop to the floor. My sticky hands ripped down the flying goblins and disposed all to the hallway. I needed to sleep peacefully. I anxiously shimmied into bed until the droning circulated through my entire system. Not until I was mentally worn out, with Mindy on my mind, did I finally fall asleep.

CHAPTER TWENTY-THREE

A couple of days passed before Mrs. Lyncoff's solemn body returned to work. She struggled to boost her spirits, focusing on her to-do list. Fall, although designated off-season, proved just as busy as summer. It had come in to full order, with its array of oranges, reds, and yellow leaves, and a briskness to the air.

Octoberfest prepared to round the corner. The biggest deal in town. Each year, a different venue hosted and this year landed on The Maycliff. Mrs. Lyncoff had ordered traditional dress for the staff to wear, deliveries already arriving. I dreaded stepping into lederhosen, even for Halloween. Chef accepted masses of food and beer deliveries, luring my help. Various tents popped up on the back garden's expansive lawn, while I assisted in table set ups.

Mr. Mac would have enjoyed the ruckus of preparations and entertainment of the event. I'll bet he'd have left his spot and walked the festivities. Mrs. Lyncoff asked me to pack her brother's belongings, as they'd sat idle for days. I delivered all to her office, even their photo in the lounge. I pondered the drawing he'd given me, his fascination with the stone lady statuette.

The Wongs stood on the patio, Tai snapping multiple photos before prowling the grounds capturing more images.

His wife, a facial hair away. Don't know what the intrigue of an empty place could be. Days turned to hours then minutes. The crowds inundated us, as the German festival uncorked itself. Men, women, children, baby-strollers, and dogs graced the event. Even a pet pig and ferret.

Norma covered the front desk for the day. Juliette and James erected themselves authoritatively, assigned to one of the more popular stands, beer, while Mindy and Riker covered a bratwurst station, complete with sauerkraut and all the fixings. Mindy slightly waved. Riker just leaned his elbows on the counter, palms squishing his face, waiting for his first customer. Tracy and Sam trailed the marching brass band, twirling their dirndls as they danced. Mrs. Lyncoff designated me what I would call the event coordinator, assuring all things ran smoothly. My job entailed strolling the premises, giving direction, and cleaning messes, including those of dog, pig and ferret.

Bert's Lobster Stall remained a favorite. He kept the crowd circulating with hundreds of prepped meaty rolls. A line skirted Coconut Joe's. Its obtrusive sign hung crookedly over an awning, advertising glazed fruit, cotton candy, ice cream, and toasted coconut. I looked for Joe to ask inconspicuously if he had anything else for me, a bigger, more dangerous, waterproof explosive. But the impatient crowd obstructed my view. Jumping to see, I caught glimpse of Chuckie manning the concession. I jumped higher this time. The wind of my landing brushed against Mrs. Lyncoff. She peered down on me. Enough to get me moving, until I tread in dog poop. Crap. I pulled out the roll of bags Mrs. Lyncoff had given me and began cleaning it up, when someone knocked into me, sending me head first to the ground. No one acknowledged I'd been shoved. The crowd simply stepped over me and kept going, except Tai Wong, who snickered as he rapidly shot photos of me. I lifted myself and finished the job, dumping the soft, warm substance into the local trash.

The intensity of the folk music and its vocals increased as the day progressed, so did screams of laughter, crying children, and various pitches of barking hounds. A yellow lab yapped incessantly in anticipation of a continuous flying Frisbee. Food flew and beer spilt, as I dodged my way toward Mindy's stand. Riker clung to her, squeezing the back of her neck, as he pulled her closer and implanted a noogie. She laughed and slapped him gently. Distracted, I almost tread on Fancy.

"Hey, what the hell?" Jerry barked.

"Sorry. I didn't see her."

The Opossums strutted over, reeking of pot. Beer Gut scarfed a brat down his throat and spewed beer all over Jerry's sneakers. Jerry acted offended and annoyed. Beer Gut apologized but accidentally repeated it. The trio, plastered, staggered arm in arm, trailing beer along the way.

I tagged beside Jerry and thanked him for the "sorry" gifts. We apologized to each other for the misunderstanding over James as we walked to his and Juliette's station. I needed to check on them, make sure all lay in order. Mrs. Lyncoff would want a report from me, I felt sure. My lederhosen strangled my crotch all day, so I kept pulling on it. James handed Jerry a Munich brew, Spaten, and he offered me the first sip. Lips to rim and hand on balls, my eyes peered up as Mrs. Lyncoff's plunged down. She swept her finger left to right and shook her head before marching behind the band.

James pulled me aside. "Did you see that ex-cop at his stand?"

"No. I haven't yet," I said. I didn't share that I'd paid Coconut Joe a visit. After all, I wasn't sure James could keep quiet. And I didn't want to end up in jail.

As the marching band passed, Sam took a spill at her turn. For fear she'd get trampled on, I rushed to help. Her eyes softened as she gave way to my arms.

"You okay?" I asked.

"Yes, I think so. Thanks for saving me."

"No problem. This is a rough crowd. They'll stomp on anyone. You'd better catch up with the others," I said.

"I will. See you later," she beamed.

Juliette appeared as Sam vanished. She was on break. Both of us starved, we needed a bite to eat. At Mindy's stand, Riker leaned in whispering in her ear. She giggled till her eyes hit mine and pulled away from him.

"What can I get you, Stan?" she asked in a flirtatious manner.

"A couple of bratwurst and some potato salad, please?"

"For you?" she asked.

"One for me and one for Juliette."

Mindy looked at Riker. "You can get it." Her attention turned to the next customer.

"Hey Mindy," I interrupted. "We still on for tonight?"

She shook her head. No explanation. Girls seemed so weird.

Juliette and I found a rock in the slightly wooded area next to the grounds, hidden from the crowd. Juliette snuck a couple of beers from James. I told her Mindy and I were supposed to go to the movies but seemed to get mad every time she saw us together. Juliette agreed she acted a little cold. She also felt Riker and Mindy often flirted with each other. I suggested he needed to get a life of his own, including a girlfriend. Juliette admitted she found him kind of cute.

"You've got to be kidding," I said.

"No. He's kind of attractive in a bad-boy sort of way," she said.

Suddenly, I felt like hell and full.

"Hey. I'm going to the movies tonight if you'd like to come. I try and take a group of seniors out whenever I have free time. And tonight, it's the movies," Juliette said.

"Sure. I'll come."

"Great. Eight o'clock. *Dirty Dancing* is playing. It's supposed to be pretty cool. It's been out for a while. I hear movies are always released late in this town," she said.

"Sounds perfect," I said.

The Opossums and a group of strangers swung beer mugs side to side as the intensified band pumped out a few German drinking songs. Munich brew splashed from every angle as glasses and people swayed together. Mixed aromas— pork, veal, chicken, and fish, along with warm pretzels, vanilla honey dumplings, and stale beer—penetrated the air. The three marsupials staggered 'round front, egging me to follow. Beer Gut grabbed a wad of change from his droopy pants, exposing his unappealing crack. He threw a coin in the air, attempting to boot it in with his butt. Several attempts later, he squeezed it between his cheeks and dropped it in. Disgusting. That penny would need a deep cleanse after touching that tissue. I should throw in a little soap. He gave me a thumbs up. I shook my head and retreated to the party.

Before the stations dismantled, I dashed to collect trash covering the grounds. Dirty napkins, fish sticks, meat chunks, bread bits, plastic beer mugs, and more dog crap. At five o'clock closing, I looked for Mindy, but she'd gone. Mrs. Lyncoff asked me to break down the tables, as well. The event rental company would handle the awnings tomorrow. Time dragged out. Finally given clearance and released, the clock read seven thirty. Juliette had waited and helped out.

"We still going?" I asked.

"Of course," she insisted. "The group will already be there. They arrive early."

"Okay. We'll have to run." I grabbed Juliette's hand and pulled her up the drive.

CHAPTER TWENTY-FOUR

The movie house played the romantic comedy, the only one we could see, because the small, old theatre ran the same movie all week, day and night. We sat upstairs in one of the private balconies behind a red velvet curtain, with the group of seniors behind us. Juliette slid her hand subtly next to mine. I slipped mine next to hers. We sat the whole movie with our hands touching. I tried to pay attention to the film, but kept stealing glances at her. The walk home seemed endless after leaving Juliette at her doorstep. I tried to rationalize the evening and process all the information swirling in my head.

Two envelopes lay on my bed. I sliced the first open and read, "I know what you did." Panic struck me, as I fiddled to rip open the second. "Just kidding! Your friend, Tracy."

What the hell!

Juliette and I had agreed to meet early for pancakes at Nick's. At least she seemed a girl I could talk to. She rarely mentioned her old boyfriend. I'm sure she wanted to get over him after whatever he did to her. On my way to meet her, I swung by the hardware store. Arsenic, I thought. Maybe something like weed killer. I looked around, contemplating the best kill job. A sales clerk startled me, asking what kind of pest I wanted to rid. I hesitated, fumbling on my words, not knowing what to say. I desperately wanted to ask what poison suited water best but couldn't reveal my fish killing objective and have the environmentalists after me. I eyed boxes of moth balls in the household section, but they might float. Drain cleaner looked interesting, but the liquid form would wash away. I wandered back to the toxic aisle, perusing my choices again. Hmm. I zeroed in on the rat poison. Seemed my best bet. The pellets should dissolve in the water once they hit bottom, right where the fish lie. I grabbed a half-dozen boxes.

After breakfast, we walked back to the inn together.

"What do you have in your bag?" Juliette asked.

"Oh, just some stuff for Mrs. Lyncoff," I said. I didn't want to reveal my plans and have Juliette be an accomplice.

"I wish we didn't have work today," she said. "We could have done breakfast and a hike."

"Me too. I'm desperate for a day off," I said.

We talked about the long winding drives we passed on our way. We couldn't see the mansions at the end but knew they were there and wondered what it would be like to live in one.

When Juliette settled in behind the desk, I needed a diversion. I waited by the sprinkler, hoping to catch Tracy as she passed. She sometimes went outside for a smoke, rather than the linen closet. I hid so she wouldn't see it coming and patiently waited until I heard her voice, timing it just right. Then I full throttled it, anxiously waiting for a curse word. No sound led me to peer over the embankment. My elation quickly turned to fear. Mrs. Lyncoff stood drenched, hair matted to her head. I urgently turned off the sprinkler. I think the only reason she didn't kill me was she still mourned Mr. Mac. Her finger raised left to right before she disappeared. Tracy pointed at me, laughing and calling me a numbskull. She told me she'd lured

Mrs. Lyncoff out there because she'd seen me. I didn't share her humor. And I don't know how I messed up that one. I should have looked.

Norma fiddled with papers at the desk, arranging the Teamster's visit. They, alongside the Solomon Transportation Company would be meeting for negotiations. A couple of brawny guys carried through an oversized TV to the bar lounge. Norma rented it so guests could watch the World Series. From the desk, I could hear pans clanging in the kitchen. I walked in to find Chef bent down, digging around the area. I asked what he was doing, but he just thrust me a dirty look.

"Goddamn beets," he mumbled.

I slipped safely out the door, initiating a scavenger hunt for the root vegetable. Sidetracked intermittently by early check-ins of the two opposing groups. The head of the Teamsters introduced himself as Paul Hustler, and the CEO of Solomons, Roy, shook hands. They appeared remotely polite, as they spoke. I overheard Mr. Hustler mention job security, pensions, and salary. They needed to find a long-term solution to these issues. Roy nodded. The conference commenced immediately after all had checked in, negotiating for hours behind closed doors. The meeting finally adjourned in time for game one of the World Series, the Los Angeles Dodgers versus the Oakland Athletics. Every seat in the lounge filled, leaving only standing room. James pumped out drinks, while Mindy and I served. Mindy pulled me aside and apologized for missing the movie last night. She was really tired and went home to bed. She asked if we could go tonight instead. Although I liked the movie, twice in a row was too much. But I didn't want her to know I'd already seen it and I ached to be with her any way I could, so I agreed.

The bar's exhilarated hum led to shouts and applause with each hit and home plate clearance. There lay a defined line between the crowd. Mai and Tai Wong occupied a space at the bar, Tai sneaking a few snapshots of the anxious spectators. I slipped out of the room occasionally to channel my efforts toward the missing red plant, including a search at the front desk. Juliette seemed bored since everyone crowded in the bar

"Guess who asked me out for tomorrow night?" Juliette provoked.

"Who?" I asked.

"Riker."

"What the hell? You're not going to go out with that delinquent, are you?"

"I might as well. I'm not seeing anyone. We're just going to grab a bite." I could sense her studying my face.

"Whatever," I said. I walked away annoyed. And anyway, I had a mission to carry out on a vegetable.

I persevered to the delivery area, the linen closet, and various other spots around the inn. I highly suspected the maids' linen closet but found nothing. Chef's mood had altered to a calmer level, although he sulked over missing the accompaniment to his dinner special.

Day two of prolonged meetings. The stagnant air strained as the two groups recessed for the game, the lounge a pressure cooker inside and out. The sports fans appeared to have assigned seats. Riker pushed in and delivered Roy a paper, the transportation man slipping him a tip. Mindy pursed her lips at me from afar, her dimples creasing further, emitting flurries through me. We had a nice time at the movies the night before. Held hands and kissed in the theatre, upstairs in one of the booths. The ticket taker looked at me when we arrived and said, "You're back," but thankfully Mindy didn't hear.

"What's up, man?" Riker blurted, as he brushed by me. I ignored him.

Mr. Hustler stepped outside the room, murmuring with another Teamster member about the changes that needed to take place. A strong stance must take place, he said. They could not give any slack. He insisted they stand firm.

Roy appeared to conspire with a neighboring colleague, while half-heartedly watching the game.

Drinks filled, I slid near James. "Can you believe Juliette's going out with Riker tomorrow night?"

"What do you care if you're not dating her?" he asked.

"I don't. He's just not good enough for her."

"Let it go. You have enough problems of your own. At least he'll leave Mindy alone now."

That's true. The thought made me feel slightly better. I asked how things were going with Jerry, and he admitted they'd improved. Said he'd backed off a bit, not so needy. James shared he talked to Chuckie after Octoberfest, and his boss, Coconut Joe, is dating his friend Moroccan Mo from the town counsel. James felt hurt because Mo didn't even tell him, and he didn't like the age difference, the ex-cop being so much older. At least he's moved on, I thought.

At closing, Mindy stayed for a drink. We sat in the hidden area on the back patio, where I found that husband kissing his wife's best friend. We sipped beers and discussed New York. Mindy had already looked into schools and sounded excited. She'd take winter courses at NYU and get credits. She'd also looked in the paper for apartments in New Jersey, a wide variety from which to choose. We decided to leave on Halloween, after the inn closed. Another beer in, we kissed over and over again. I wanted to be nowhere else but by her side.

Two nights I'd climbed over the wall and thrown rat pellets into the toadfish infested waters. I'd spill into bed, cozy up, and wait for the arsenic to settle into their little bellies. I relished in the image. A slow, painful death. Then poof. Gone. I imagined a trail of them, floating away on the chilly waters of Frenchman Bay. But instead, their obtrusive motorized vocals grinded me to sleep yet another night.

Day three of the talks dragged on. Breaks throughout the day led to icy exposure. It did not appear the negotiations were going well. I heard Mr. Hustler threatening to walk. Riker stood nearby him, looking like a doormat, till called to fix a leaky sink in Roy's room. I did not want to get on the bad side of Mr. Hustler. With the Teamsters' mafia connection, I envisioned someone ending up with broken bones or even worse, dead. And I didn't want it to be me. Tai Wong approached Mr. Hustler, and the two engaged in conversation, I suppose over baseball. My ears had moved out of range, with the increased commotion. Another day of meeting's recessed, everyone merged back into the turbulent lounge. The Dodgers were ahead two games, a side the Teamsters seemed to be on.

Riker left early to go on his date with Juliette. Norma covered the desk. Mrs. Lyncoff stayed in her office most of the time since Mr. Mac's death, and Norma had become her eyes and ears. She asked how the groups' were doing, but I denied knowing anything. I said they pretty much vacuum sealed the doors each morning. I'd heard she'd spread word in town that the two groups negotiations carried on beautifully and they'd almost reached an agreement. I knew that not to be true.

Tai Wong sat in the closet booth on the payphone, talking container ships, while feeding the slot to keep the call going. Mr. Hustler stood by the lounge entrance and disappeared into it as Tai passed, the two exchanging a word or two. Tai joined Mai at the bar, no camera in hand. I became pleasantly surprised to find Riker back in the lounge. Mindy iced him with her glare. He stood by the fireplace, perusing the room and occasionally looking at the game. I thought he had a date. When I asked him, he said he had to postpone it. I wondered if Juliette stayed home, feeling upset. Roy and his team appeared energized with the close of this night, shouts bellowing from their side of the fence. The Athletics won a game.

***

Juliette bubbled over the desk.

"Sorry about your date last night. I heard."

"No biggie," she said. "We should do breakfast again."

"Uh, sure," I blurted as Tracy yanked on my sleeve and pulled me down the hall. She'd found a document on the ground marked "Confidential" and it wasn't clear who it belonged to. It had numbers and graphs but no names. She didn't want to disturb Mrs. Lyncoff in her office or share this with snoopy, Norma. She asked I take care of it. I decided to drop it in my room and ask Mr. Hustler if it was his when he wasn't so distracted.

Day four turned more silent. Only bathroom breaks seemed to be taken. I wasn't allowed in the room to refresh anything. This, I thought, could be a very good sign of progress or an extremely bad one. Volcanic. Game four of the World Series about to start, the lounge sat partially empty. I could feel the tenseness leaking through the conference door. I waited, trying to focus on the game. Finally, at the second inning, the doors barged open, and the two groups flooded into thick space. No one talked as they walked to the lounge. The bar area remained quiet, not even shouts at the plays. Mr. Hustler called me over for a scotch order. Every time I brought him a cocktail, he'd slip me a five, even though he signed the check to his room. After another win for the Dodgers, Roy and his gang abruptly left, snubbing me on the way out as if I were to blame for their team's loss. The Teamsters stayed on and drank. Mai went to bed, but Tai joined in. Mindy asked me to stay on to serve them, so she could close out the till. The remaining chits would all be signed to their rooms, no cash transactions. Mr. Hustler griped about being fed up, there being no point in continuing with negotiations. They should head out in the morning. I thought I best go get that paper if he might leave tomorrow, check if it was his.

"Mr. Hustler?"

"Yes, Stan."

"Excuse me, but we found this document in the hallway, and I thought it might be yours."

He grabbed it from my hand and studied it, his frown rapidly decreased and transformed into an elated expression. "Good work, Stan," he said. "I'll take over from here." He ordered a Dewar's and pulled his troops in tightly, placing the paper down within the circle of men. I hoped I didn't do anything wrong. They stayed huddled for an extended period, whispers rotating through the group. Finally, they broke back.

"The bottom line is, the Solomon group's been lying to us this whole time," Mr. Hustler said. "This is our ticket. We're all set for tomorrow to bring them down."

Mr. Hustler's whole demeanor had changed. He sounded eager since I gave him that paper. It must have been really important.

I'd paid another visit to Coconut Joe, when last in town. He gave me a stronger explosive to massacre the fish and stressed I be super careful. I arranged to meet Jerry and James at the town pier, but I didn't tell them exactly why. Just said I needed access to Jerry's boat to take care of the toadfish that bothered the guests. The bar to the island covered by the tide, we paddled through in twilight, saltwater misting our pores. I spotted the old storm drain pipe engulfed in the high waters and told the guys to halt.

"We have to stay back about fifty feet," I warned. "Is this about fifty feet?"

"Why so far?" Jerry asked.

"Safety reasons," I said.

I carefully struck a match to the fuse, trying to tune out the petrified muttering going on between James and Jerry. It ignited and sizzled. I quickly belted that sucker as far as I could across the water. And boom! Fire, lights, chips of rock, and massive water shot out in all directions. An explosion surely heard by the guests of the inn. A small disruption for the favor I'd done them.

"Yes!" I yelled in victory, thrusting my arms in the air.

"Are you goddamn insane?" Jerry screamed.

"You had dynamite on this boat?" James shouted. "You're a crackpot!" He shook my neck like he was going to strangle me, then settled back down. "Don't worry? You could have blown us all up. Jeez."

"He's right," Jerry said. "You're nuts!"

I just shrugged my shoulders, pleased with myself. Triumphant, the battle was over.

They urgently paddled out of the area, seemingly furious with me. But they didn't understand what I'd been through.

***

The morning wind wailed outside my window. I had not slept well. The indestructible, slimy, bottom-feeding, sex-sucking toadfish survived. And I was out of ideas for now.

Orange, yellow, red, and purple leaves drifted and swirled. Piles of magnificent foliage seized the grounds. Hummingbirds had turned the wishing well into a bath. Mrs. Lyncoff ran at them, shooing them away. She then checked both shoulders before launching her own rocket of desire. The parlor doors closed as I made my way downstairs. The groups started their meeting earlier than planned. Luckily, Chef had put the coffee on for them. Sweat trickled past my eyebrow as I anxiously waited for a sound or a click of the door knob. Tai and Mai sat on the patio sipping tea. He asked for water, so I brought a couple of glasses over, but he declined them.

"No, silly boy. Hot water for the tea. And more bags please," he said. "Tea bags, not shopping. Aye yai yai," he said, shaking his head on his way to the pay phone. "And we'll both have scrambled eggs with a side of guacamole."

He didn't have to be so sarcastic. I liked him till this point.

Chef slumped over, chopping beets in the kitchen. I gave him the order, and he asked I get the guacamole out of the walk-in fridge.

"Oh, I see you found the beets."

"No. I ordered more. And keep your stinking hands off them."

Whoa. Everyone needs to chill a little around here. I grabbed the small bucket of guacamole and peered out the kitchen window as I scooped it into a bowl, adding a slice of lemon and some chips on the side. I noticed Riker in the bush talking to Roy. I didn't know the meeting had broken. Roy appeared mad and Riker defenseless. I stayed and stared.

"What are you doing?" Chef asked.

I insisted I was looking at the foliage, but I stayed a few minutes after they dispersed, wondering what they talked about. Mrs. Lyncoff popped in magically and told me to get my rear in gear. Guess she'd bounced back to normal.

I delivered the eggs and Mexican dish to the Wongs, becoming distracted with a lobster boat powering by until Tai's gagging caught my attention. He held his throat, making all sorts of funny noises. His face suddenly looked like a tomato. I figured he was joking around, so I just watched until Mai shouted for water. Oh, now you want water, I thought. Tai fell to one side of his chair. Looked like his head would blow. I floored it to the water pitcher and poured a couple of glasses. He grabbed one from my hand and chugged the whole thing down. Then the other glass. Should have taken the water when I offered it. When he was able to speak, I asked him if he choked on a chip.

His voice sounded raspy, and he struggled to breathe. "You trying to kill me?" He said I'd served him wasabi, not guacamole.

Uh oh. I apologized profusely and offered to get the right dish, but he waved his hand no. Just asked for more water. He must have taken a huge bite of the green stuff. Guess it burnt his throat pretty badly. At least he didn't seem mad. I didn't know we served wasabi. I asked Chef. He said it was a special for tonight, lightly seared tuna with a wasabi soy sauce.

The meeting broke before game five began. Mr. Hustler looked quite chuffed. He pulled me aside and slapped me a hundred, expressing what a good job I'd done. Roy and his guys appeared distraught. But all gathered in tradition to watch a little baseball. The one thing they shared in common, the number of cocktails that dissolved before them. Half the room roared with excitement, while the other sulked into their drinks. The focused Teamsters suddenly jumped to their feet, propelling their arms high, belting out cheers as the Dodgers finished off the Athletics. The Solomon group disappeared from the room, while the Teamsters stayed for another drink. They watched the sports channel highlights of all the games and opened a few bags of chips they'd brought in. Mr. Hustler asked me to give the group a lift into town. They planned to do a little bar hopping and celebrating.

After dropping them, I met up with the gang at Aussie's pub. The Opossums sat on a park rock across the street from Aussie's, smoking a joint and drinking beer. Coconut Joe and Mo curled up on a nearby picnic bench, his arm tightly wrapped around her. Entering the saloon doors, The Grateful Dead's "Touch of Grey" blasted amongst the semi-crowded pub. Riker stood by the mangled bar, being his usual self and picking on James. He always had to pick on someone. Chuckie just sat there, clinging to his beer and watching Riker. I warned Riker to stop. But he appeared in a foul mood, and his shot consumption heated him further. He grinded his head into James and shoved him back against the wall. As James came at him, Riker punched him in the face.

A rush of fury ignited me, fueled by my anger. My fear stepped aside, I pulled James up off the wooden floor and left him weaving. Jerry ran to his side. Riker's attention turned toward me. He lunged at my chest, ramming his head straight into the ball of my gut. I couldn't breathe as the air stripped from my lungs. I had no choice but to fight Riker now; fear turned to adrenaline. I gasped and wheezed as I frantically punched and kicked. It hardly made a difference. I swung at air. He moved with such speed it was hard to hit the target. I wasn't going to give up, though, and let the bully get away with tormenting James like that. His sniggering infuriated me, and I had to stick up for my friend. I hit him hard in the chest, then the face. He yanked the neck of my sweatshirt and pulled me toward him, lifted his knee intensely, and booted me in the stomach. The blow left me breathless and dizzy. I blocked his next shot. Without warning, Riker pounced on top of me like a raged animal and twisted my body flat on my back, his knees pressed tightly against my aching hips. I swung one arm, then the other, trying to hit him anywhere. But his arms were like iron rods and had my shoulders pinned to the ground. I felt his nails dig into my face as he swiped them across it. He pressed his forearm down on my throat, and I struggled once again to breathe. He released me, and I swung into his gut. I glanced at the bouncer, arms folded, just watching, and could faintly hear the chants of the gathered bar crowd, "Fight, fight, fight," before two more blows to the face, which knocked me a bit unsteady. I wound my arm back, putting all my weight into it, planting my steely fist like a torpedo into his right cheek, hammering him to the ground. He went down hard, with the crowd's awed shouts. Didn't look like he'd get up. They yelled I was the victor, and all the chants began. I turned back toward the bar.

Juliette yelled, "Watch out!"

I pivoted to find Riker's arm in mid-stream, throwing me a dirty hit from behind, when Mr. Hustler caught him. He then grabbed Riker by the front of his shirt and lifted him in the air.

"That's it for you, bud. No more fricking around. Got that?" Mr. Hustler said.

Riker sheepishly nodded.

"Good. Now let's go have a little chat." He yanked Riker by the ear, pulling him outside, a few brawly Teamsters following. I envisioned a body bag, again. As much as I disliked the guy,

I worried for his fate. Juliette grabbed me a wet cloth from the bartender and started patting my wounds.

"Are you okay, Stan?" I read the look of concern all over her face.

Chuckie's beer was implanted in his face as he shook his head at me.

"Yeah, I'm good. Thanks Juliette."

She asked the bartender to get me a cold beer. "You did great," she said and kept gently tapping my face until Mindy appeared and snatched the cloth out of her hand.

"He's mine to worry about," Mindy angrily stated.

"Hey," I said. "You don't have to be so rough. She's trying to help."

"It's okay," Juliette said.

She backed away out of sight. I don't know where she went. I looked all around the room.

Mr. Hustler and his gang reentered the pub, what seemed an eternity later, strutting toward me. "Let's get out of here," he said. "There's a car waiting."

CHAPTER TWENTY-FIVE

Riker showed for work, legs and all. But he walked funny and remained unusually quiet all day. I could see no visible bruises but knew something must have taken place. Too bad the Teamsters planned to check out. I liked having them as bodyguards. Maybe they had an idea how to annihilate these mud-loving toadfish. But I didn't dare ask. Mr. Hustler might think I suspect them as murderers. Could jeopardize my own safety. He pointed at my battle scars and called them minor. The Solomon group had left first thing, not really speaking to one another or anyone else. Tai Wong and the Teamsters would check out after having lunch in town. They arranged to eat at Shutters Inn. Don't know where Mai went. They jammed into The Maycliff minivan illegally, with the shortage of seats. When I pulled up to the front entrance of Shutters, the tall, lean lady with the red feathered top and elevated heels appeared. She'd been the one who visited Ms. Malone, the toy lady, and always left with a big box. This time, she wore pink. She slid the van door open and greeted everyone to her inn. Said their masseuses awaited their arrival. This inn had a spa? I thought they had lunch reservations. What kind of inn had that many masseuses? Oh my god, even these guys were blessed.

Juliette and I sat for lunch in the private husband-cheating area, while Riker covered the desk. I grabbed us both a ham sandwich before Chef arrived. Juliette said her ex-boyfriend wrote her, begging for them to get back together, but she wanted nothing of the sort. She'd moved on. She wanted someone like me, whom she could talk to and trust, who liked to do the same things like hiking and movies. I admitted I liked spending time with her. She seemed so calm compared to Mindy. What a relief.

"I know you're heading to New York, and I'm sure things will work out for you well there. But if you ever get a chance, you should come to Stowe. I'll teach you to ski. And if you stay, my parents are good friends with a chalet owner. It's really quaint, right on the tip of the mountain. Bet you could get a job there."

"That sounds really great," I said. "Maybe I will, sometime."

She gently touched my bruises and rested her head on my shoulder, thanking me for being such a good friend. Tingles ignited me. I lifted her head carefully. Her eyes gleamed into mine and, without warning, I kissed her. A more passionate kiss than I'd ever experienced with Mindy.

The thud of a door slammed inside the inn, awakening us. "I better go," she said.

Juliette squeezed my hand before rising. I sat contemplating New York. The squeal of the screen door opened. I turned expecting Juliette to come back through. But there stood Mindy. I froze thinking she'd seen something. The two had to have passed. That was close. But surprisingly, she cozied up, saying she'd found the perfect apartment for us in Hoboken. We could easily catch the train to the city. But we needed to act fast before the place disappeared. I agreed, hesitantly. Said I wanted to see what it looked like. Her enthusiasm turned to upset, assuming

I didn't trust her, but I assured her I did. The vision of that psychic resurfaced. It always brought me down.

"I have to get to work," she said.

"Okay. Well, let's talk later and figure something out."

"Figure what out? There's nothing to figure out, Stan. Why do you make everything so difficult?"

"I don't. Why are you always so angry with me? I still don't know what I did wrong in Boston 'cause you won't tell me."

"You want to know?"

"Yes. I would," I said.

"In Boston, when you said you'd like to be maître d', you never even considered me. I wanted the job. I've been going to school for this business. But you acted as if you were the only one who could handle it," she said.

"That's it? That's what I did? That's not how I remember it. I only mentioned it in passing. And you should have told me you were interested in it, too. Anyway, you got the job. So it doesn't matter. You deserved it."

"I've got to go. I have to get to work," she sighed. I shook my head.

I searched for James, but he wasn't in yet. I needed a sounding board, fast. Not sure I should tell Tracy, but I couldn't hold it in any longer. I hunted her down and held her captive while I explained what happened with Juliette and the kiss. Then Mindy.

"Sounds like you've got yourself in a heap of trouble."

"I know that. I'm just asking for advice," I said.

She recommended I decide which one I wanted to be with, make a choice. But I'd better work fast and stall Mindy on the apartment.

I picked up the Teamsters, along with Tai Wong, after their pleasure-filled afternoon. They melted into the van, snoozing on the way home. Their bags had been set aside in the parlor for them to grab and head out. I hoped for another hundred slapped in my palm, but all I got from Mr. Hustler was a slap on the back and another thank you before departing.

I waited for James in the empty lounge, so I could confide in him as well. I eyed the fake bookshelves, curious what might hide behind them. I shimmied a stool over and climbed on top. They looked like the old Britannicas. My chest beat faster, partially scared something might pop out or I'd get caught by Mrs. Lyncoff. She'd say I was snooping around and do her finger thing. It was hard to get a grip because there was no handle. I fiddled my fingers into a crease and pulled it toward me. There stood a variety of buttons. Looked like a radio of some sort but not a normal one. A secret one, with a walkie-talkie. I turned a knob, and the electric came on, but nothing happened. I wondered if this had something to do with the original owner's bootlegging days. My buddy Steve had shown me the hidden door to the basement and all the trunks whiskey had been transported in. I felt a little nervous, like I'd discovered something covert, and quickly shut the books.

James arrived with Jerry in tow. I shared with them my findings. They took a peek and agreed. This was some sort of underground communication system. Our minds raced for an answer until I refocused back on the Juliette story. They suggested I spend a little more time with Juliette over the next few days and see how I felt. I liked that idea if I could do so without Mindy finding out.

I asked Juliette to breakfast the next morning. It ended up a comfortable, easy conversation, and we laughed a lot about silly stuff, making a little fun of Riker along the way. She touched my scratches on my face, saying they looked better. Juliette said she'd be taking the seniors to the movies again tonight and asked if I wanted to come. That sounded perfect.

Mindy pulled me into the restaurant and shoved the newspaper ad into my hands. I acknowledged the apartment sounded good. She said she'd spoken to the landlord, and we needed to send a check right away to hold it.

"Uh, okay. Well, I can do that maybe over the next couple of days," I said.

"No. That's not soon enough," she squealed. "I'll just do it myself tomorrow."

"No!"

"What?" she asked.

"I mean. Let me do it."

"Well then, it needs to be tomorrow," she demanded.

I nodded.

I grabbed a coffee and walked the stretch of the back lawn, my headquarters. Coconut Joe would be coming by next week with more ammo. It took time to get. I stared out, hypnotized by all that had taken place this summer. A tour boat motored by, and I could faintly hear The Maycliff mentioned. I tried to decipher the guide's muffled words, describing the inn, but I couldn't. A sharp tap on my shoulder jolted my head, but no one stood behind me. I envisioned Mary.

Sauntering aimlessly back, I stopped short at the marble lady statue, gazing at the photo of Mrs. Lyncoff, Mr. Mac, and another child all on horseback. I looked around before picking it up and staring at the faces, trying to recognize the adults as children. Mrs. Lyncoff looked to be much younger than the other two. The face of the unknown child had a strong resemblance to that of the stone statue, the one Mr. Mac was obsessed with. Mrs. Lyncoff must have moved the photo here.

The edges of the paper lay torn, browned with time. I flipped to the back. I could barely make out the faint pencil script, "Mac, Janet, Mary. 1933." I carefully returned the photo to its origin and steadily backed away. At my slightest movement, the photo fell forward. I acknowledged the moment and kept going.

Near the inn's closing, Mrs. Lyncoff became very ill with the flu. Riker's face turned to fury when she asked me to hold down the fort and relieved him of all duties. As more guests had vanished and the inn rested at quarter occupancy, there became no need for both of us to stick around. Riker stomped off, and I went to clean all the fireplaces. One down and many to go, a hurling scream resonated through the inn from Juliette's direction. I sprinted to the desk, hands dressed in soot. Water gushed from under the mechanical room's door, a heavy stream soaking every carpet fiber. The inn stood drowning, fast. This was it, the prediction. The final annihilation. And I caused it. The psychic was right. This happened under my watch.

Riker had already left. And Chef just stood there, watching. Tracy yelled to call a plumber, her sidekick paralyzed with hands over mouth. James grabbed the phone book to help Juliette find a company. Mindy had just come on scene. Time critical, I bolted to the mechanical door to find it locked.

"Where's the key?" I shouted.

Juliette scrounged around, all nervous and jumpy.

"I can't find it! It's not where it's supposed to be," she cried. "Riker had it last."

I ran behind the desk, throwing things off the counter. And found it. The water level had risen. I sprinted to the flooding door, fiddling to unlock it. Finally. I shot to the water line and desperately rotated the main shut-off valve. The rip tide ceased. We stood in the floating inn, feet drenched, wondering what happened.

Tracy volunteered to run to town for the special vacuum, while we waited for the water company to answer our emergency call. When they finally arrived, they quickly assessed the pressure had been set so high, the main pipe ruptured. Mrs. Lyncoff sniffled in just after Norma, as I water-vacced the place. Juliette relayed what transpired. Mrs. Lyncoff questioned the gauge setting, how it got so high. Juliette explained Riker fiddled with something earlier. Maybe he adjusted it. He'd told her a guest complained they had little water pressure in their shower.

That jerk did this on purpose, I thought. He didn't even put the key back in its place. Mrs. Lyncoff's brows closed tight as she turned into me.

"Thank god you were here and knew what to do," she said. "This could have been disastrous."

Thankfully I'd watched the water company open the main valve in the beginning of summer, so I knew which knob to turn. Although back in the library of good, Mrs. Lyncoff still handed me the dreaded to-do list to close up shop.

Juliette embraced me for fleeing to her call and saving the day. Mindy pushed her aside and did the same. Tracy followed suit, which didn't seem to bother Mindy. Sam just stood back. James teased I'd become a hero, squeezing the back of my neck. Even Chef and Norma shook my hand.

Within a week, we sat at closing. As much as I thought about it, I just couldn't pull away from Mindy. I stood on the terrace observing a circle of seagulls dive-bombing for fish. Their pursuit too late. I had experienced the best sleep ever for two consecutive nights. Coconut Joe hadn't made it by yet, but I didn't need him anymore. The humming had replaced itself with the hoot of an owl, which pacified me. No more drilling in my brain and torturing of my soul. Just peace. The fish had mated themselves to extinction, temporarily taking up new housing in the deep waters of the Atlantic till next May, same time the patrons would return. The last of the guests checked out. It was time to go.

I grabbed my bag and set it by the front desk, placing the drawing Mr. Mac had given me on the countertop. Tracy choked up as she and Sam stood ready to depart. She declared how much she'd miss me. She'd be all right shortly, I thought. I'd planted a stink bomb in her car beneath her seat cushion. It would blow as soon as she sat.

When all dispersed, Juliette grabbed my hands. "Well, I guess this is it. My job is done here. I hope to see you again." Her lids batted and head tilted down. "Let me know if you ever make it to Vermont."

I opened the door for her and walked behind her. The air felt brisk and refreshing; some vibrant colors endured. I pulled her in and held on longer than intended. Reluctantly, I released her and brushed her hair to one side, ending with a gentle kiss. We squeezed hands and shared a moment of knowing before she turned. My eyes followed her past the fountain. She twisted back and sat on its edge. Her lips moved but I couldn't read her words. She effortlessly opened her hand and gently rotated it. The shiny object dropped almost in slow motion. She looked happy.

When Juliette dissolved from view, I wrapped the cord around the water vac and carried it toward the van. I stopped abruptly, thwarted by three little beavers crossing my path, each with a big red beet in its mouth. I followed them to a ditch on one side of the drive. Several beets lay near their dam. One rodent posed in the stream, chomping on the sweet vegetable. Well, at least, the beets hadn't gone to waste. Some guests were enjoying them.

The white cat suddenly appeared before me as if to get my attention. I followed his trail as he shot off to the dumpster, where Mrs. Lyncoff stood emptying a box of beets and breaking down the carton. I walked toward her.

"Mrs. Lyncoff?" She looked surprised and placed her finger over her mouth. I could now see the piles of beet boxes hidden behind the trash bin.

"You're the one who's been taking the beets?" I asked.

"I had to, for everyone's sake. Chef's become obsessed with them. He'd put them in everything if I let him—soups, sauces, salads, eggs, lobster, every conceivable dish. He's ultimately responsible for the food he serves, so I couldn't argue with him. Something had to be done. I saved us all from a beet diet."

"Wow. I won't say anything." Although I wanted to swipe my finger at her.

I thought about Steve, how he would have reacted. If he would have exposed her.

I took a last look at Mr. Mac's chair, envisioning him in it. We had a lot of great conversations, especially one that stuck out in my mind. James startled me when he grabbed me from behind, planting a noogie on my head. We promised to keep in touch. He got way too emotional on me. I walked him to the fountain and hugged him only briefly, not to drag out the departure.

Mindy and I had arranged to meet after work and catch the train to New York. That time had come. She strolled up to the fountain.

"I have to go back in and get my bag," I said.

"Hey Stan?"

"Yeah?"

"I received a letter this afternoon from the school," she said hesitantly. "I didn't get into NYU."

"Oh no, Mindy. I'm sorry to hear that. You must be crushed." I started to hug her, but she pulled back.

"Well, we didn't exactly get the apartment either," I said. "The check never went out. It's still in the outgoing mail. I just noticed it. It's okay, though. We'll figure something out when we get to New York. I'll just go get my stuff. Be right out."

I could see Riker pull down the drive on his Yamaha. Guess the thug came to say goodbye. He and Mindy were goofing around, poking at each other and laughing. Sickened me, but he'd soon be out of the way. I watched as their playfulness quickly turned sour. I could hear their shouts from inside. What the hell?

I pushed through the door. "Hey, what's going on?"

"Stay out of it," Riker yelled at me and turned back to Mindy.

"You said you were coming with me," he shouted.

"I never said that!" she screamed. "You're a fool."

"I can't believe it," Riker said. "You're going to stay with that weasel?"

"Oh, stop it, Riker!" She shoved him hard. "Just leave me alone and go."

I walked toward them to break it up.

"I said stay out of it. It's none of your business," he hollered at me.

"It is my business because she's my girl," I yelled.

I walked closer, ready to punch him.

"Just go inside," Mindy said, pushing her hand out to stop me from coming closer.

I could not believe what I was witnessing. I went back inside and could still hear them screaming at each other. The last thing I caught was Riker shouting that if she didn't come out alone, he'd be gone forever.

I picked up Mr. Mac's drawing, admiring it. Reminded of his words of wisdom. I gazed at the woman's face with unbroken silence, oblivious if the ruckus continued outside. "Mary," I said out loud. I felt flutters. It was the best gift I'd ever received. I knew what I needed to do.

Mindy broke through the door. "Sorry about that. There's been a misunderstanding with Riker. It's all good now. Ready to go?"

"Are you kidding me?" I asked.

"No. Why?"

"I can't do this anymore. Enough," I said.

"You're breaking up with me just like that?"

"Yes, Mindy. I am. Why the hell did I even do this for so long? Hang onto you."

"What?" She looked stunned.

"This isn't what I want. And I'm sorry, but you're not what I want."

"I don't understand, Stan. What are you talking about? That meant nothing to me outside. Riker's too much of a wild card. He doesn't support my career like you do. He cares too much about his own things. He's difficult. You make my life so easy. I chose you."

"You know you and I don't belong together. You never wanted to be with me. You just kept me tagging along to console you, so you'd have someone to push around. I can't do this anymore. I'm going my own way now."

"I can't believe you're saying this, Stan."

"I know. Because you didn't think I had it in me."

"That's not true. I just can't believe you're ending it. And like this."

"I don't mean to be cruel, Mindy. But admit it, you never really wanted me anyway. Otherwise, you wouldn't have treated me the way you did. And look at you now; you don't even seem that upset. Not one tear. I deserve better."

Her mouth opened slightly, but no words formed. She looked at Riker outside then back at me. We stared. She tried to read my expression, but it lay dead-pan. There was nothing left to say.

"Can't we..." she started to ask.

"No," I said. "It's over. Goodbye, Mindy."

She scrutinized my eyes one last time before walking out the door.

I reflected on how all this time I'd been chasing Mindy, when whom I really wanted to be with was Juliette. I couldn't let her go. I had somewhere to get to. Vermont.

Riker tracked his shuffling feet and scratched his shark-infested arm before throwing on his jacket and backpack. He straddled his Yamaha and Mindy climbed on. The two shot up the drive.

Both hands hid in my pockets, twirling the loose change as if it were my thoughts. My eyes cast to the pool of dreams. Copper painted its floor. My turn to get lucky. I held my arm stiff, grasping at my wish. On the count of three, I released it. Tiny ripples glistened, gradually dissolving to stillness. My focus now on the inn's entryway, the trellis spread a shadow upon its barren gray slate. And so did the stately stance of the white cat. I recognized those eyes. They clung to mine without waiver until I withdrew.

I needed to catch the soonest train to Vermont. I hitch-hiked to the station, thinking solely of Juliette. It didn't matter that I had no plans. And I didn't care about consequences. It lay in my gut. I had to go.

The motion of the trains' pulls lulled me deeper in thought as I stared out the window at the last of the foliage. The conductor took my ticket.

"What are you doing in these parts?" he asked.

"I was a bellman at an inn."

"Oh," he said slyly. "The bellmen know all the secrets."

I grinned, knowing there was only one secret that mattered.

He examined my ticket and studied my face.

"Where are you from?"

The vision of my parochial town smothered me. Every chug of the train fueled me, driving a deeper wedge between my past and the ensuing unknown.

"Nowhere special," I mumbled.

The conductor punched my ticket and handed it back.

"Okay, where are you going?" He winked.

Before I could answer, I looked up to an astonishing sight, Juliette walking down the aisle toward me. Her angelic features illuminated as our eyes collided. And I realized it doesn't matter where you're from. It only matters where you're going.

"Home."

ACKNOWLEDGMENTS

Thank you to my extraordinary parents, John Alvin Davis Jr. and Agnes Dollar Barr Davis, for the great opportunity to run the family inn, which inspired *The Bellman* and *The Bellman's Secret*, and for always believing in me. And to my dynamic, beautiful children—Nicholas Barnes, Austin Barnes, and Catherine Barnes—whom I am immensely proud of and for whom my love is indefinable. Let go of the ropes, be yourself, and fly toward your dreams.

To my sister, Doreen Davis Owen, for her relentless compassion toward others and endless support of me. My brother, John Davis, who always encouraged my writing and anything else I wanted to do. My brother, Arthur Davis, who showed me life's balance. And to my in-laws—Heather Davis, who is pure joy, my neat nephews Luke and Hunter Davis, steadfast Phil Owen, and Diane Doe Davis. With gratitude to my best old friend, Monique Lung, for her innovative ideas and championing me on. And to my great friend, Barbara Milne.

To my publisher, Tyson Cornell of Rare Bird, for this tremendous opportunity and whose professionalism has been an absolute pleasure. And to his outstanding team—Julia Callahan, Guy Intoci, Hailie Johnson, and Jessica Szuszka. I am grateful to all for their expertise, passion, and delightfulness.

To my editor, Pat Walsh, for his incredible talent and vision, and Richard Thornton, who opened the door for me.

To the following family and friends, who have also supported me:

Ian Hayward, Christianne Hayward, Jamil Kabani, the team at Christianne's Lyceum of Literature and Art, Jeremy Sheppard, Josephine Wong, Julia Hibbard, Cristal Niza, Annie Hui, Juli Bennett, Fariba Kolahi, Chrissy Carpenter, Damian Sage, Tim Neame, Molly Wolter, Marilyn Goettee, Michelle Mosher, The Hanna Family—George, Lena, Michael, Andrew, & Tiffany, Zeila & Arthur Barr, Wilhelmina & John Davis, Billy & Arlene Barr, The Barr Cousins—Jeffrey, Bill, Kevin, Linda, Billy, Amy, Bobby, MaryAnne, Tom & Jenny, Kim Haney, Chris Bettini, Mark Bettini, Judy & Milt Hagedorn, Vilma Andres, Jay Jay Sahin, Judy Levin, Jo-Anne & Colin McIver, Gayle & Phil Patton, Ray Lung, Ken (Mucker) Smith, Michelle Souza, Webb & Renee Farrer, Jeff Martin, Kevin Brenner, Layla Nowain, Celeste Bragg, Jihan David, Mimi Hahm, Dave Fournier, Rosy Wolfe, Alfred Sevilla, Denise Moreno, Gordon MacGeachy, Aren Afsharian, Karen Kadlec, Barb Lunter, Dan & Tere Hall, Paul & Evelin Brinich, and many other friends I'd like to acknowledge. Last, to my sweet dogs and cats past, a huge part of my life and always uplifting—Moët, Chandon, Tequila, Schnaaps, and the exceptional Tigger, to name a few.

In fond memory of the inn's maids—Nancy, Pam, and all the girls—who often played tricks on me. And to the bellmen, whom I enjoyed running around. No job, off limits.

With special thoughts to all the children and animals in the world who need a little love.